There Are No Children Here

Leanda Wood

PublishAmerica
Baltimore

First printing

ISBN: 1-4137-4932-1
PUBLISHED BY
PUBLISHAMERICA, LLLP.
www.publishamerica.com
Baltimore

Printed in the United States of America

To Steve, without your guidance and encouragement, I would never have written this book. Thank you.

To Mum and Dad for putting up with me all these years, and being there for me.

To Colin Boys, for rescuing my data after I stupidly deleted it.
Thank you; it would never have been published if not for your hard work.

There Are No Children Here

Chapter 1

1938

I SAT THERE LOOKING OUT OF the window, my hands resting on my chin. My long legs swinging backwards and forwards with excitement. It was dark and I could see my reflection through the large bay windows of my parents' sitting room.

"Ayala," my mother called from the kitchen. "Come away from that window, they will be here soon enough. Come and help me set the table."

I jumped down from the chair from which I had been sitting and ran into the kitchen, bumping into my mother on the way through.

"For heaven's sake, child, calm down. It's not as if you haven't seen them in months; you see them every week. And it's not proper for a young lady to be running around like that. Remember you are fourteen now, so stop running around like a bull in a china shop."

I loved some of my mother's sayings; they always got me thinking and imagining things like "A bull in a china shop." How funny. I always pictured a bull running loose in a china shop terrifying everybody. And another one was "People in glass houses shouldn't throw stones." I mean why would anybody want to live in a house made of glass?

But my mother was right as usual. I was excited, as I always was on a

Friday evening when all my cousins, aunts and uncles would come over to celebrate the Sabbath. Sometimes our neighbours would also come over to celebrate with us, even though they were not Jewish but Polish themselves, they always understood and enjoyed our way of life. I loved being so close to all my family. It gave me a sense of security and protection. They would turn up with their food and wine, and it would be kisses all round. We would all sit down to our lovely prepared table and what feast we would have. I particularly liked it as I was always allowed the ceremonial sip of wine. I would always be allowed to stay up late and join in with the merriment of my happy family. Oh, how I loved those Friday nights of ours.

My eight-year-old brother Marek would always fall asleep around ten thirty and would have to be carried up to bed by my father. Each week he would say how big he was getting, and that this would be the last time he would be carrying him up. But every week the sight of my little brother's adoring baby face asleep on my mother's lap would bring out the "Ahs" and "Oh bless him. Don't wake him. He looks so angelic the little love," and my father would be forced to carry him once more.

During the evening I would go upstairs to my bedroom with my favourite cousin, Bluma, who was a year older than me and we would talk about girly things like boys and our favourite Hollywood stars. We would listen to music such as Glenn Miller and Gracie Fields on radio. As the evening drew to a close everybody would get up and slowly make their way home. I would help Mama to tidy up; and yawning, I would say my good nights and head off to bed. Just as I would be nodding off into my slumber, my father would pop his head around the door and say, "Good night, my sweet child, and may your head be filled with wonderful dreams."

My father, my beautiful handsome father, he always reminded me of a film star; tall and well built with thick dark hair that was slightly parted at one side and a slight fridge that would fall adoringly over is big brown eyes. I could see perfectly why my mother had fallen in love with him. I would imagine that when I fell in love with someone, it would be with someone just like my father; handsome, gentle and kind. My father was a hardworking man, a well-known local shoe-mender in a small suburban area of Warsaw where we lived.

We was by no means rich, but the steady flow of local people wanting their shoes re-heeled or re-soled proved a profitable business, one which gave us a comfortable if not modest three bed roomed roof over our heads, and always plenty of food on the table. Life for us was good. We were a happy close-knit family, with lots of friends in our neighbourhood, and there was always someone willing to lend a hand or help out in any way, if ever the need arose. There was always a sense of community within our little suburb.

That's the way life was for us all, easygoing and secure.

School for me was the greatest time; I loved every minute of it. I had lots of friends of all races and religions. But for me, my most favourite of persons was my best friend Kamila, a Polish girl from my neighbourhood and who was also in my class at school. She was a very outspoken girl who said what was on her mind. I liked that about her, as I was quite timid and shy, but when I was with her, she brought out the boldness in me. And from the first day we met, I knew that we would become good friends. I would go over to her house after school and sometimes she would come over to mine. We would have dinner, play records and do our homework together. We were inseparable. We shared many secrets together, things that we wouldn't tell anybody else. There was a great amount of trust between us. Her father was a doctor and her mother was a secretary for the local council. They were always friendly and welcoming towards me. Sometimes on a Sunday we would all go to the park for a picnic and we would sit and eat our sandwiches as we watched the ducks and geese on the lakes, and we would sing Polish songs. These were my most favourite of times.

I came home from school one day to hear my mother and father quarrelling. This surprised me because my parents never argued. There were no spiteful words as such, more like a heated discussion, but still it was something that my parents just didn't do.

I walked through the door to find my little brother Marek sitting on the stairs looking sombre.

"Marek, what's wrong?" I asked with concern.

"Mama and Papa, they say the Germans are coming, and that they are going to take us away. Mama says this is stupid, that it's just rumours, but Papa says it's true because one of his customers has just come back from Germany and he said that all the Jews are being beaten and sent to prison; not for doing anything, just because they are Jewish. Papa says that there is talk that soon they will come to Poland and do the same to us."

"Oh, don't be so silly," I said, trying to sound convincing. "Like Mama says, it's just silly rumours. Of course no one is going to come and take us away; they wouldn't dare," I said with a nervous laugh. Of course I *had* heard all the talk and the rumours about the Germans, about how Hitler hated the Jews and how the Nazis were taking over the homes and businesses of Jewish families. I had heard his wild ranting and ravings on the radio, but had never really taken any real notice of it. Up until recently it had been just talk; wild gossip, but just lately I had been hearing things a lot more frequently.

Just the other day a girl in my class at school was saying how her grandfather, who lives in Germany, had his grocery shop taken away from him by two German soldiers; they just came in off the street, and without any

11

warning beat him up and kicked him out on to the street. Now the German soldier's family runs the shop. And a Jewish boy from my school just disappeared and nobody knew where he had gone, then a couple of weeks later we learned that he had emigrated to America; apparently his family knew about the Jewish problems in Germany and left before anything had happened here. I had seen things too. Only last week on my way home from school I had seen an old Jewish lady being attacked by a local gang of youths, they were throwing stones and calling her a "dirty Jew." I had told Mama of these things I had seen and heard, but she told me it was just silly rumours and that the Nazis were just bullies and no way would they dare to do the things that people were saying. I didn't let my young brother see how concerned I was, I mean if my parents are worrying about it then it must be true.

I gave my brother a reassuring hug. "Go on, silly," I said. "Go to your room, play with your train set and I will talk with Mama and Papa, see what all this nonsense is about."

I went through to the front room; I was annoyed that my parents could talk about such things in earshot of my younger brother, being only eight and on the sensitive side. I was angry that they couldn't keep such worrying things from his young ears.

My mother was standing in front of our open fire, with a worried looked on her face. Her long dark hair swept to one side over her right shoulder; her eyes looking tired with anxiety. My mother was a beautiful woman; tall and slim with long black luscious hair that stopped just beneath her shoulders and big brown eyes. It's strange but I always thought my mother looked more beautiful when she was upset, when she had a serious look about her.

My father was pacing about the room puffing frantically on a cigarette, leaving the room full of smoke and smelling stale.

"Mama, Papa," I said cautiously. "What is all this talk of Germans?"

"Ayala, I didn't hear you come in. Have you been eavesdropping?"

"No, Papa. I came in and found Marek on the stairs; he tells me that he heard you and Mama saying that the Germans were coming and that they are going to put us all in prison, for no reason apart from being Jewish."

"Oh, Jakob," Mama said despairingly. "Go to him and see if he is all right."

Papa went upstairs to Marek and I was left alone with Mama.

"Mama, tell me the truth, is it true what Marek says about the Jews in Germany?"

"No, darling, it's just wild rumours, like I keep telling you."

"Then why is Papa saying these things?"

"He was just telling me what one of his customers had told him." She rolled her eyes and took a deep sigh. "Yes, there was a case in Germany, with some Jews who were arrested and sent to prison, but they must have done something wrong for them to be arrested. I mean nobody gets put into prison for nothing, do they?"

She said this as if asking me to convince her. She averted her eyes away from me, I could see she was just trying to pacify me, and not let me see how worried she really was. But I knew. I could tell.

"But I've heard things, Mama, and I have seen things myself, like the old lady I told you about last week. I have also heard Hitler on the radio, going on about how much he hates the Jews, and what he is going to do to us all." I had said too much. My parents didn't know that I was still listening to him on the radio. I was told once before by my father not to listen to such rubbish, and that I was far too young to be listening to such talk at my age. My mother looked at me angrily.

"Ayala, I thought Papa had told you not to listen to that rubbish. I'm very disappointed in you, Ayala. We will have to take that radio off you, if you keep on listening to that nasty little man. Now I told you, Ayala, there is nothing to worry about. *Nobody* is going to come to Poland and take anybody away especially *my* children. These Germans or Nazis or whatever they call themselves are just bullies with big boots and silly helmets, and as for old ladies being attacked with stones, well I'm afraid that sort of thing happens in every city. It's the sign of the times, I'm afraid. It has nothing to do with Hitler or Germans or anything else."

"I'm sorry, Mama," I said. "I didn't mean to make you cross, and I won't listen to that man anymore, OK?" I went over and gave her a kiss. "I love you, Mama."

"I love you too. Now stop worrying. Like I say, nothing is going to happen to us, OK?"

"OK, Mama."

I left the room and went upstairs. I stood by my brother's door and could hear my father reassuring my brother, just like Mama had done with me. I should have felt relieved, but somehow I felt even more concerned. I could tell my mother was just trying to protect us. I felt sure of it. She knew more than she was letting on. It wasn't like my mother to become so agitated with me; this was a sure sign that she herself was worried.

I spent the rest of the afternoon and evening in my room reading *Gone with the Wind*. Kamila had lent it to me after she had read it. It was a wonderful romantic novel about a woman, Scarlett O'Hara, struggling to find love during the Civil War. The strong personalities of the characters and descriptive way the author writes completely mesmerised and captivated me. Before I knew it, I had been sitting on my bed for nearly three hours. I was completely unaware of the time. It also took my mind off the earlier evening worries. My father was calling up the stairs, telling me it was time to turn out my light and go to sleep.

I went downstairs and kissed them both good night. My father was listening to the radio and my mother was reading a book. One of the many traits my mother had handed down to me, for she too was an avid reader. A real bookworm as the saying goes.

My mother looked more relaxed than earlier in the afternoon, when we had our little quarrel. I was pleased and somewhat relieved. *Maybe I am overreacting upon things*, I thought as I climbed into bed. I decided not to worry myself about it any longer. I closed my eyes and fell into a deep sleep, dreaming that I was Scarlett O'Hara being swept off my feet by a handsome stranger.

Over the next few weeks I spent a lot of time with Kamila. We were nearing the end of our school term and we were studying quite hard. It was the late summer of 1938 and one in which I shall never forget. The weather was beautiful and there were lots of people in the parks and down by the rivers. Families with their children out for a stroll, old people walking with their dogs and couples holding hands and strolling along without a care in the world. I remember the summer well; it was a lazy, hazy sort of time and Kamila and I would wander about together, to the parks or the open-air swimming pool and talk about school, the theatre and, of course, boys. She would swoon over Daniel, a boy in our school, but a year above us. Although Kamila would change her mind every week, and next week it would most probably be someone else. She was ever changing was Kamila. I would swoon over Isaac who was in our class. I was fast becoming a young woman. I had started wearing a little make-up and had started taking a little more pride in myself. My hair had to be perfect before I went out of the door in the mornings. Papa would tell me that I was quite pretty enough and that I didn't need make-up, especially at my age. Mama would always stick up for me by saying that as a young lady it was perfectly natural to experiment with such things.

"But, Helena, she looks older than fourteen and it might create the wrong impression," my father would say.

"Boys you mean, Jakob," my mother would reply. "Ayala is a sensible girl, and you must have more faith in her, and besides she *is* nearly fifteen, so stop fussing, Jakob."

My father would roll his eyes and sigh, knowing full well that he would never win an argument with two women.

14

I liked it when people told me that I looked older than fourteen, especially my father, because parents always told the truth. It made me feel so grown-up. I could see for myself the difference it made in me. It gave me confidence, which was something I greatly needed, as I was quite a shy teenager.

The week went by with no more mention of Germans or Hitler. I had kept my promise to Mama and had not listened to the radio anymore. Besides, it was rather depressing with all this talk of war, and it would only make me worry more anyway. Mama seemed more relaxed too, and this in turn made me feel more confident that things would be OK. There were still stories going around about the Nazis or Brown Shirts, as they were known, and what they were doing to the Jews. I mean it was common knowledge of how they were still arresting people and putting them into forced labour camps. But even though this was happening just over the border, so to speak, we still felt no real threat. I mean it seemed unimaginable that these things would happen to us.

Chapter 2

IT WAS LATE SEPTEMBER, JUST AFTER my fifteenth birthday. I was on my way home from school one afternoon when I heard someone calling my name. I turned round to find Isaac running up behind me.

"Hello, Isaac," I said surprised.

"Hi, Ayala. Do you mind if I walk with you?"

"Of course not," I replied.

My heart skipped a beat. We had known each other for about three years, being at the same school, but this year we were in the same class. His little brother Emmanuel was in the same class as Marek. I had started to look at him differently in the last year. His face was maturing with a more rugged, chiselled look about him. He had a dark mob of thick curly hair that matched his dark eyes. He was a big boy for his age, at least five foot seven or eight, and looked older than the fifteen years that he was. When we were younger he was just a spotty faced kid with glasses; and I would not have looked at him twice, although he did have a great personality and a good sense of humour with the most infectious laugh, but apart from that he was just another boy at school. Just lately, however, I had found myself staring at him and thinking how attractive he had started to become. He had caught me on occasions, and smiled across the classroom, only for me to turn away nervously, flushed with embarrassment. Now he was asking to walk the same way as me. This was a first; he had never done this before now. Maybe he was starting to look at me the same way, I mean I had started to wear my hair differently and taking more care of myself personally.

"How are you, Isaac?" I asked.

"Fine, just thought I would keep you company on the way home."

"Thanks."

"Where's Kamila?" he asked. "Doesn't she normally walk home with you?"

That was it. He was interested in Kamila, that's why he'd stopped me. My heart hit my stomach.

"Yes, she does," I replied with disappointment. "She stayed behind tonight to help Mrs Aron with the arrangements for the end of term dance on Saturday. I was going to help but I stayed behind yesterday, and my parents don't like me to be home late from school too often, especially if I have homework to do."

"I know what you mean, my parents are the same. My father is a solicitor, and he wants me to follow in his footsteps, so I get a nagging too if they think I'm slacking."

"Is that what you want to do?" I asked. "Be a solicitor like your father?"

"I wouldn't mind; it's a good profession, but I would also like to be an actor or something more exciting; I wouldn't want to disappoint my father though."

"You could always do it as a hobby, like at the local theatre, or schools," I suggested.

"I suppose so." He nodded.

We were walking so fast as we talked; before I knew it we were almost at my front gate. I wanted to slow down, to keep the conversation going, but Isaac's long legs were walking so fast I had to trot to keep up. "Well, this is me," I said as we approached my house. "Thanks for keeping me company."

"No problem." He looked at me nervously, as if wanting to say something.

"Are you OK?" I asked.

"Yes, err, Ayala; are you going to the school dance this Saturday?"

"Yes, I am. I have been really looking forward to it."

"I suppose you've got a date to go with, or are you going with Kamila?"

I stopped breathing for a second. *Oh my God*, I thought. *Is he going to ask me out?*

My heart was pounding and my mouth was going dry.

"Err, no," I said breathlessly, "I mean, err, no I haven't got a date, but I am going with Kamila."

I watched the disappointment appear on his face. My heart sank. *Now, he thinks I'm not interested. Oh God why did I say I would go with Kamila, I mean it's not as if she didn't have lots of people to go with if I didn't, someone as popular as her.*

"Oh, OK," he said disappointed. "Never mind, it's just that I was rather hoping that you would come with me as my date."

I couldn't believe it. My heart was on fire. I had to find a way of turning this around.

"Well, like I say, I *am* going with Kamila, but you know what she's like; she's always got lots of people following around after her, so she most probably won't even notice if I'm not there," I lied. "I mean I couldn't let her down, it wouldn't be right, but I could meet you there if you like; like I say she won't notice if I'm not around that much."

"Are you sure?" he asked nervously.

"Yep, I'll look forward to it."

"OK, great, I will see you there then," he said excitedly.

"OK, see you there."

I watched him walk off. I was floating on air. I had just been asked out on my first date. I was so excited. I couldn't wait to tell Kamila.

The rest of the week dragged by. I couldn't stop thinking about Saturday, and the fact that Isaac had asked me to got to the dance with him. I was over the moon about it all. Kamila was completely flabbergasted as I told her how Isaac had walked me home and then out of the blue had had asked me to go to the dance with him. Kamila had known of my fondness of him. I had told her so on many occasions how I thought he was nice, and how it would be if we went on a date together. Many a night we had sat at home and giggled about such things. Of course I didn't tell her how at first I thought it was *her* he was interested in.

"So what are you going to wear?" Kamila whispered as we stood in the school library.

"Oh God, Kamila, I don't know. I don't seem to have much in the way of evening wear."

"You could always borrow something of mine."

"Oh, Kamila, could I really?"

"Of course you can. I mean I know you're quite a bit taller than me, but I know I have some things that Papa has bought for me, and being a typical man it has always been too big. Look, why don't you come over after school and we can go through my wardrobe and have a rehearsal, so to speak?" She giggled. "It will be great fun and we can even practice your hair and make-up, OK?"

18

"Oh, Kamila, you're such a good friend. I don't know what I would do without you." I kissed her on the cheek.

"That's OK. It will be fun, and anyway it would be a pretty poor show if I couldn't do something to help out my best friend, now wouldn't it?"

I was so lucky to have a friend like Kamila; she was always there for me. She was my best friend, and our friendship was one of the main things I valued in my life.

I was a little ashamed that I didn't have something of my own to wear for the dance, but I had never been to a dance before. The only socialising I had done up till now was our Friday nights on the Sabbath with all my family and the odd wedding here and there. Kamila, on the other hand, had been to a lot of functions with her father the doctor, so she was used to dressing up and going to dances. She was so much worldlier than me; she had been out with a couple of boys too, so she had lots of experience as well. It wasn't surprising though as Kamila did have quite a lot of admirers. She was a pretty girl with thick blonde shoulder length hair that she piled on top of her head, which showed off her high cheekbones and big deep blue eyes. She had big red heart-shaped lips that when she smiled showed the straightest teeth I had ever seen and was enough to get any man's pulses racing. She was beautiful. I envied my friend in a lot of ways, as I always felt a bit dull compared to her, and in truth I guess I was. I mean I wasn't exactly ugly, but I was a typical Jewish girl of my age. My hair was long; like my mother's and up until recently it had been as straight as a dye, until I had started curling it. I always thought I had dull eyes, small and brown, not very bright compared with Kalmia's. One thing I did enjoy about myself was that I was rather tall for my age. Almost five foot six and still growing. Kamila was quite a bit shorter than me. Sometimes when I was feeling especially dowdy, I would stand next to her and tower right over her. I know that sometimes this made her feel quite intimidated, but none of this was done in malice. I loved Kamila, and as my best friend she had come to my rescue once again.

Before I knew it Saturday was upon me. I couldn't wait, not only was this the first time I had been allowed out without my parents till late, it was the first dance I had ever been to; and on top of all that I was meeting a boy there.

I had seen Isaac at school following our conversation; nothing had been said about it since and I was starting to think he had changed his mind, until Friday at lunchtime when he came up to me and discreetly asked if I was still going. With a relieved sigh I said that I was. I hadn't told my parents about Isaac and our meeting. I mean what was there to tell, I *was* after all only meeting him there; besides, I was afraid that if I did mention it, my parents might change their mind about me going.

"Well, don't you look lovely," my mother said as she came into my room.

19

"Do you think so, Mama?"

"Ayala, you look like a princess. My baby girl is all grown-up," she said with tear-filled eyes.

"Thank you, Mama."

I had spent the best part of the afternoon getting myself ready. I had curled my hair into soft ringlets. My hair felt soft to touch and bounced comfortably around my shoulders as I walked. I had also managed to buy a lovely pair of sequined hair clips that went perfectly well with the curved sequined neckline of my green satin dress. I was so grateful to Kamila for allowing me to borrow this beautiful item. It fitted me like a glove; tight at the waist with a slightly lighter coloured green bow, which tied up around the back. The skirt part of the dress swung out slightly just before it stopped below my knees. And I particularly liked the way the elasticised long sleeves ruffled around the wrists. I was allowed to wear my best shoes, an open toed number with a slight heel to them. I had only worn them once for my cousin's wedding. Mama said I could only wear them for best. But tonight she had agreed that no way could I wear my school or strolling shoes with such beautiful attire.

At seven o'clock Kamila came to pick me up as arranged.

"Ayala, you look stunning, I have never seen that dress on before, it was always too big for me, but it looks absolutely fantastic on you."

"Thanks, Kamila," I replied, starting to feel a little embarrassed at all the compliments.

"You're welcome and you might as well keep it; because I know it will never fit me like that."

"Oh, no way, Kamila, I couldn't," I replied, shocked at such a generous offer.

"Oh yes you can, so that's the end of it. Anyway let's go; my father is waiting in the car."

"Thanks, Kamila. You're the greatest friend a girl could have."

"I know," she laughed.

I said goodbye to my parents and skipped out the door.

"Ayala," my father called as I was getting into the car.

"No later than ten thirty, OK?"

"OK, Papa."

"Ayala," he called again.

"Yes, Papa," I answered, getting impatient.

"You look like a real princess."

A lump rose in my throat and tears were welling up in my eyes. I didn't want to cry as not to ruin my make-up, but one tear managed to leak out and run down my nose. I was angry with myself for being so foolish.

"Thank you, Papa," I said.

The dance was held in the assembly hall, the main hall of the school. There were decorations and banners with good luck and congratulations to mark the end of school term. Although this dance was mainly for the students that were leaving for good to go into work or collage, everybody of all years was also invited to attend. I myself still had another year of schooling to do.

The dance floor was filled with people dancing frantically and doing some very strange dance moves to the sound of the eight-piece band playing on stage. It seemed strange that this was the hall of which we assembled into each morning and sang hymns and said our prayers. It looked so different, and it seemed so funny to see some of our teachers all dressed up and dancing these funny dances with each other, it just seemed so out of character of them. I was totally in awe of it all. I was on top of the world. *If this is what being grown-up is all about, then I can't wait.* I thought. All of a sudden I had a burst of excitement in my belly, and really could not wait for the night to unfold. I looked around to see if I could see Isaac anywhere, but I could not see him. My heart dipped slightly, automatically thinking that he had changed his mind.

"Oh, this is fantastic," said Kamila, pulling me from my thoughts. "I wonder if I'll get asked to dance."

"Of course you will," I said. "Looking as lovely as that in your little black number," I laughed. "I was just looking for Isaac; he doesn't seem to be here yet. Do you think he has changed his mind?"

"No, of course not, why would he go to all the bother of asking you to meet him, just to let you down?"

"Yes, I suppose you're right."

"Look it's only seven thirty, he probably won't even be here till about eight; he probably doesn't want to appear too keen. Come on let's go get a lemonade or something, OK?"

We stood around the edge of the hall as most of the girls seemed to be doing, chatting away watching everybody having a good time. Within minutes Kamila had shot off to the dance floor with a rather handsome boy, leaving me alone feeling rather like a wallflower and quite awkward. But as I suspected, Kamila would not be short of offers to dance, looking as lovely as she did with her hair pulled up into a pretty bun, with little silver pins to hold it in place that complimented her black and silver dress. She looked radiant. I was just starting to feel lonely standing there on my own when I saw Isaac walking across the dance floor. He smiled as he approached me. He looked so handsome in his black suit and white tuxedo. My heart started beating faster and my throat went dry. I drank the rest of my lemonade in just one gulp.

"Ayala."

21

"Hi, Isaac," I replied, trying to sound confident.

"Wow, you look lovely," he said, eying me affectionately.

"Thanks, and you don't look so bad yourself."

"How come you're on your own?" he asked, looking around him.

"Kalmia's been swept off her feet," I replied, pointing over to where she was.

"Well, it looks like I got here just in time then, doesn't it, before somebody stole you to the dance floor, and I would have lost my chance to dance with you."

I could feel myself blush and I had butterflies in my stomach. I could tell this was going to be a good night.

"Come on," I said. "Let's go and get a drink."

Chapter 3

THE NIGHT SEEMED TO GO BY so fast. It was wonderful. At first I was full of nerves waiting for Isaac to arrive, but after half an hour in his company I started to feel relaxed. We drank lemonade and sat by the stage talking or rather shouting over the music. We talked about school and what we wanted to do when we left, what our favourite films were, what music we liked and what our overall ambitions were. His were to become an actor, but would most probably end up a solicitor, like his father. I told him I wanted to become a photographer, not like my father, "Because he mends shoes," I said, and we both laughed. He told me about his family, his brother and sister "Talia." I knew he had a brother, because he was in Marek's class at school. But I did not know he had a sister. She was 18 years old and taking a nursing degree. I learned that he was from a traditional Jewish family, who took their faith very seriously. I too had been brought up on the traditions of the Jewish faith, but my parents were slightly easier going with it. Although they were proud to be Jewish and celebrated it regularly, my parents always said that most of all they wanted their children to have fun and enjoy life. All the serious things in life would come later, when we were grown-up. I think this came from my father's mother, who was strictly religious and spent every waking minute reciting the Torah to him. Isaac said that I was lucky to have such understanding parents. He was easy to talk to, with a gentle manner about him, which made me feel relaxed. He was funny with a great sense of humour. It wasn't what he said exactly, but more like how he said it that made me laugh. Yes, he certainly had a character about him, which didn't surprise me that he wanted to be an actor. He certainly had the wit and charm to become a successful one if he really wanted to. Not forgetting his good looks of course. Every now and then I would look up to find Kamila on the dance floor, dancing with yet another of her young admirers. What a wild card she was.

As we sat there chatting, people from our class would come over and say hello to us. I felt quite proud to be sitting there with him, especially when the odd girl or two would come over and ask him to dance. At this he would politely refuse and say jokingly, "I'm taken I'm afraid." Looking at me all the while. This made me feel like the Queen of Sheba. I wondered if he would ask me to dance. I know he mentioned something about dancing at the beginning of the night, but I wasn't sure if he was serious or joking. Being the comedian that he was. In a strange way I hoped that he wouldn't. I had never danced with a boy before, apart from my cousin at Chanukah last year, and that didn't really count. I mean I didn't want to step on his toes or trip up and make a complete fool of myself. But of course he did ask me, and I accepted. I just took a deep breath and went for it, and it wasn't as bad as I had thought. Not only did I *not* step on his toes, I was actually showing *him* some steps. I felt quite superior. He was just a little bit taller than me; which made a change because normally I would tower over people, so this put me even more at ease. *Oh what a wonderful time I'm having,* I thought as I was being swayed about the dance floor to the sounds of Glenn Miller being played by the big band on stage. It all seemed so magical. I wished the night would never end. Of course before I knew it the night had ended, well for me anyway.

Kamila whom I had not seen all night as I had suspected came running over to tell me that it was nearly half past ten and that we should be making our way outside to meet her father to take us home. I was disappointed that the night had ended so quickly.

"All right," I said unenthusiastically.

"By the way, you have met Isaac, haven't you, Kamila?"

"Of course I have silly," she giggled. "He's in our class at school. Hi Isaac, sorry I've not come over till now, but I've been having the most marvellous time."

"That's all right, I've been having a pretty good time myself," he replied, smiling at me.

"OK, Ayala, I'll wait outside for you two to say your goodbyes, if you know what I mean," she said as she winked in Isaac's direction.

"Try not to be too long, you know what Father is like."

I could have died right there on the spot. I felt so embarrassed. *I'll kill Kamila when I get outside*, I thought.

"I'm sorry about that," I said.

Isaac could see how embarrassed I was, and like a true gentleman, pretended he hadn't even noticed. "About what?" he asked with a smile.

"Well, Ayala, I've had a wonderful time, and it's all because of you."

I felt my cheeks flush purple as he bent down and kissed me on the cheek.

"And so have I," I replied. Visibly shaken form the unexpected kiss. "I've had a great time. Thank you, Isaac."

"You're most welcome, and maybe we could do it again sometime, on a proper date if that's all right?"

"I would love to, Isaac, that would be lovely."

"Great!"

"I better go. Kamila will be having kittens by now if I hang around any longer. Not to think what my parents will do to me if I'm late."

"OK, see you soon, Ayala."

I ran off waving goodbye as I went. I could still feel the warmth of his kiss on my cheek as my face hit the cold night air.

The months flew by since the night of the dance. It was now December and the New Year was fast approaching. I had been out with Isaac quite a few times and was by now seeing him regularly. Mainly we went to dances together or to the picture house. My parents by now knew that I had a boyfriend; at first they were not best pleased, but after a girly chat with my mother and her telling me how important it was for a girl "staying true to herself," as she so politely put it. I put her mind at rest and told her that we had barely even kissed. After that she seemed fine. My father, on the other hand, was harder to bring round. But after a while, and with my mother's constant nagging about how she was only 15 when she had met him, he seemed to come round to the idea. Although I don't think he was altogether happy about the situation. After all I was his little girl.

To say that we had hardly kissed was an understatement; I mean a peck on the cheek each night was all we could manage to pluck up the courage to do. Holding hands was about as affectionate as it got. Not that Isaac was unaffectionate, but I was rather shy and I think he was scared to do anything too bold just in case he scared me off. I mean I had no intentions of giving anything or myself to him, but I would have liked a cuddle now and again.

But we were getting there slowly but surely. Isaac was wonderful to be with, he was kind and considerate, and he could make me laugh at the most silliest of things. To me he was adorable. I was in love for the first time and it felt wonderful.

The only thing that did overshadow my great happiness at this time was the fact that my earlier worries about the Nazis and Hitler had resurfaced again, but this time it was all the more real. Since November 9th when the Nazis had destroyed all the synagogues and Jewish homes in Germany and Austria, it was not as safe for Jewish people to be walking the streets like it used to. I mean Jewish people always had to put up with harassment and anti Jewish behaviour for centuries, but no more than that. In general people got on fine with each other, but recently it had got much worse. There were stories of people being beaten up for no reason by the Polish people, and being humiliated publicly. There was talk of the old orthodox Jews having their beards cut off in the street. The Jewish people of Warsaw had lived alongside of the Polish and Germans and other groups of people for years; and had always got along fine and dandy. Now all of a sudden things had changed and it seemed that the Jews were not wanted here anymore. I myself had not experienced any kind of animosity and never had done, but I had heard a lot of stories from my school friends, of people they knew being harassed. My parents had started to worry about me going out on my own, but I was growing up and I could not stay indoors forever, and like I say I had not had any problems of yet. The moment I do, I told them, I would come straight home. Besides, the main problems were in Germany. Only a small proportion of the problems had over spilled into Poland, because of the Jewish refugees coming to escape the terror over the border. But unknown to my parents, I was quite worried about it.

As ashamed of myself as I was, I had started to listen to the radio again, against the wishes of my parents. I hated being so deceitful, but I was so full of worry about what was happening across the borders; and slowly but surely things were starting to happen here. People were fearful and full of stories about what was happening to people they knew. I know a lot of it was just glorified gossip, but I also knew that most of it was true. Children from my school were leaving all the time, to get away from whatever they thought was coming in our direction. This made me worry all the more. I mean why would people be taking such drastic measures if it were just idle gossip.

I tried to put it out of my mind as much as I could. I tried not to listen to the radio, but somehow this little curious monster inside me kept spurring me on to listen every night, which brought fresh nightmares every time I closed my eyes. Pictures of us being rounded up and taken to some camp or prison. These pictures dominated my thoughts every day.

26

Christmas and New Year came and went. It was wonderful. We celebrated Chanukah, and lit our candles and sang songs. All my family gathered together. For the first time in a long time I forgot all my worries and just had a good time. Nobody spoke of the impending doom that was clouding everybody's thoughts and just carried on as we had always done. Isaac and Kamila both came over and we exchanged our gifts. Kamila had bought me a lovely vanity case with a lipstick and powder puff inside. I had bought her a pick satin scarf that she had seen in the market square some weeks before. It had taken most of my savings to get it for her. But she was my best friend, so I didn't mind that I was now penniless. Isaac had bought me the most beautiful gift I had ever received. It was a silver chain of about sixteen inches with my initials on a heart-shaped pendent engraved on it. I was beside myself with happiness. I showed all my family and they all agreed that I must be very special to Isaac for him to buy me such a beautiful gift. After opening such an exquisite gift, I felt quite ashamed that I had only given him a book in return. He was pleased as punch as it was the same book he had wanted for some time. A book of *Drama and Acting Techniques*.

"It's not the price or the gift," he told me, "but the thought that goes into it."

This made me feel so much better, but I still couldn't compare it to the luscious gift he had just bestowed upon me. Isaac and I were much more relaxed with each other by now. We had progressed from holding hands and a kiss on the cheek, to a full-blown kiss on the mouth and a very sensual cuddle. I had fallen in love with Isaac and he had fallen in love with me. This confession was made to each other a week before Chanukah after going to see *Gone with the Wind* at the Cinema. Isaac knew how much I adored this film and bought the tickets as a pre-seasonal celebration. How wonderful he was. Apart from all the other daily worries on my mind, I was by all accounts very happy.

Chapter 4

1939

THE COLD HARSH JANUARY OF THE New Year brought in the relief of the somewhat warmer spring. There's something about spring that brings hope and meaning to one's life. With the daffodils and bluebells starting to rear their beautiful heads, and people coming out of their houses once more, everything comes alive again. The thing about winter is that people sort of hibernate, scared to face the unforgiving winds and the freezing confetti of snow. I myself love the winter. I love to be snuggled up in a chair next to a roaring open fire. But even though I am a winter person, I too welcome the relief and warmth that the spring can bring. This year, however, relief was not a word on many people's lips. Events regarding Hitler and his henchman had taken a turn for the worse in Poland. No longer did the persecution of Jews solely reside in Germany. Hitler now had his murdering eyes on Poland. The threat of invasion and terror on the Jewish population of Poland was becoming all the more real every day. The fear and anxiety was growing stronger within our community. Things were changing so fast. People were leaving Poland as fast as they could; some went to England and America or anywhere they could escape the terror that seemed to be awaiting us. These were such trying times for us all. I tried to keep my mind busy all the time by reading books and wrapping myself up in my school work, or going for walks with Isaac or Kamila and talking about the nice things in life; like the theatre or leaving school and such things. Isaac was such a great comfort to me, always consoling me and telling me what a worry guts I was, and that things we not as bad as they seemed. He always seemed so strong, but deep down I knew that he was just as scared as me. Kamila was also a great source of comfort to me, she would tell me to keep my chin up and before we all knew it, things would blow over.

"You always did have a wild imagination, didn't you, girl?" she said to me one day.

"Oh, Kamila, I so wished it was my imagination. Everywhere I look I see posters and signs for people telling them to support Hitler, and every time I see a newspaper or turn on the radio, he's there telling us what he's going to do to us all when he gets here."

"OK, girl," she said, putting her arm around me. "I know it's hard but you have to be positive, nothing is going to happen to you; you're my best friend, Ayala, and I would die for you and no Hitler or bloody Nazi bully is going to take you away from me. Just they bloody well dare."

We sat there for a while both wondering when and where all this was going to lead to.

The strange thing was that Kamila didn't have to worry about her fate; I mean she was Polish *and* Catholic; she was safe from the fear and harassment. She didn't have the worry of where her family would end up or the uncertainty of what the future held for her.

"Mama, are you OK?" I asked one evening whilst eating our dinner.

"Yes, dear, I'm fine, just tired that's all," she replied with a waning smile.

I could see the strain on her face and the dark circles under her eyes. I had become worried for my mother as late. The tension and worry was taking its toll on us all. *It must be hard for her* to *keep all her worries to herself and look after us as well*, I thought as I sat there looking at her from across the table.

"Mama, please don't worry. Isaac says that the Polish army will not be defeated, and if any German comes over here, they'll have their guts for garters."

"*Ayala*," my mother and father said simultaneously. "Don't talk like that; it's so common and not very ladylike."

"Sorry, I was just trying to make us all feel better that's all."

"I know, dear," said my father, patting my hand. "But let's not talk about it now, shall we," he said, eyeing Marek over the table.

"And like I keep telling everyone till I'm blue in the face; *nobody* is coming to take us anywhere, OK?" said my mother irritated. "Now let's just get on with eating our dinner."

I felt awful that I had said what I had in front of Marek. I should have known how easily scared he was. On many occasions since this all started I had to sit and talk with him and dispel his fears. On the last two occasions I had to lay with him till he fell asleep; he being afraid that people in Nazi uniforms were coming to take him away. What could one say to an eight-year-old boy, apart from reassure him and tell him that his fears were just his imagination? Oh my sweet wonderful brother. How I loved him and wanted so much to protect my sweet sensitive boy.

I lay there in bed later that night. I thought about how I had upset my mother. I hated to upset or trouble her in any way. I loved her so much. We were such good friends her and me. Ever since I was old enough to remember I don't ever remember her really telling me off. Apart from the time when I was five and I had wandered off at my auntie and uncle's house in the country. He had a great big garden and a large pond at the end next to an apple tree. I had decided to go and explore and take an apple for myself that was lying on the ground. When nobody was looking I slipped out back through the pantry and ran down the garden that seemed to go on forever. I sat there eating the apple and looking into the pond at the large fishes swimming around the bottom. I was fascinated by the slender and gracious way they moved. I don't recall ever seeing a fish before this time. I must have been there for some time when all of a sudden I heard a lot of commotion and hearing my mother's frightened voice scream, "Oh danken Got." Which means "thank God" in Yiddish. It seemed I had been there for about fifteen minutes before they had found me. They had looked everywhere they could think of inside the house, until my auntie said in a nervous voice, "The fish pond." My mother by now was beside herself, and nearly collapsing with anxiety. They all came rushing down the garden to find me without a care in the world and not a clue of all the trouble I had caused. My mother scolded me, telling me I must never run off like that where I could not be seen, and telling me how dangerous it had been for me to be so close to such deep water. Me in my innocence kept saying, "I'm sorry, Mama; I didn't mean to take the apple without asking." I cried when I heard my mother telling me off like that, but I know it was also out or fear and relief that she was so cross.

It was now the middle of June and things in Poland were rapidly changing all the time. There were new laws for everyone and the sight of political posters with Hitler's face seemed to dominate every wall or building. My parents had now decided that I was no longer allowed out after school.

"Isaac or Kamila would have to come here," they told me one afternoon.

I protested with all my might, but try as I could, they would not budge. If I was to be honest with myself I was quite happy not to have to see all the propaganda plastered everywhere I looked.

I think the turning point for me came one evening after I had spent a fun night with Kamila in my room playing dominos. I got up after going to bed to use the bathroom. As I came out I heard what sounded like my mother crying. Then I heard my father's voice trying to calm her down. I stood on the top of the stairs leaning over the staircase to listen a little closer.

"Helena, listen to me. This is important."

"Jacob, no, I won't here of it. This is ridiculous. There must be some other way through it."

"Helena, there is no other way. We have to leave as soon as we can."

"Jacob, I have spent my life here, my children were born in this house." My mother's voice was strained and desperate.

"How can you expect me to just get up and leave everything behind me, all that we have built here together?"

"Helena."

"No, Jacob, enough. I won't talk of it anymore. I won't. This has blown all out of proportion. Can you really see men coming in here and taking us all away? It's ridiculous; it will never be as bad as they say."

"Helena," my father's voice was above a whisper, "they are shooting Jews in Germany. They cannot walk on the sidewalk anymore. They can't ride the trams. The children are not allowed to attend school. They are putting innocent men and young boys into prison and camps for reasons the mind cannot imagine. Do you want that, Helena? DO YOU WANT THAT?"

I jumped as my father shouted. I had never heard my father raise his voice in this way before. He sounded so desperate and scared. I started to cry.

"Stop it, just stop it, Jacob," protested my mother desperately. "You are scaring me. Please, please, I beg you, I don't want to listen to this any more."

"You have to know this, Helena, we cannot hide from the truth anymore. We have to go, otherwise who knows what might happen to us all. I don't want to end up like those in Germany and we will if we stay here."

"I will not go. I will not be driven out of my own home."

"Helena, FOR GOD'S SAKE, WOMAN!"

"Jacob, stop shouting, you will wake the children."

"Helena," my father's voice was defiant, "I am going down to the emigration office tomorrow. We are leaving as soon as we can."

"And where are we supposed to go, Jacob?" replied my mother, sobbing now.

"I don't know England, America; anywhere we can get away quickly. We will tell the children when we know for sure that we are going."

"I won't do it, Jacob. You can go, but I will *not* leave my home."

"Very well then, Helena, but the children will come with me." With that he came out of the sitting room and closed the door.

I crawled back into bed. I couldn't believe the conversation I had just overheard. I was heartbroken. I wanted to go down to my mother and ask her to tell me this was just a sick joke. But I knew it wasn't. I knew just how serious the situation we were in now. And besides, she would tell me off if she had known I had been eavesdropping. I felt sick to my stomach at all the things I had heard. All sorts of scenarios were going through my head. My tummy was going over and I was confused. *This can't be happening,* I thought as I lay there trying to take it all in. I could not believe just how desperate my parents were and how angry my father had become with my mother. They never had argued like this before. I was in turmoil. I wished Isaac were there to comfort me, to hold my hand and tell me it was all right. I pictured his face in my mind, his dark hair and enchanting smile. The thought of never seeing him again brought a new fear to the fore. I couldn't go. Not to see my Isaac again. I would just die. And how would I ever find another friend like Kamila? It seemed all too hard to bear. I lay there for hours turning everything over in my head. My main concern was Marek. How on earth would he take all of this? Over and over it went until sleep finally took me, and I was a little girl again eating apples from my uncle's tree.

I told Isaac what I had overheard the next day at school.

"Isaac, what am I going to do?" I asked with tears rolling down my face.

"Ayala, I don't know. I really do not know," he replied weakly. "To be honest with you, my parents have been contemplating the same thing for a while now."

"No, Isaac," I said, putting my head in my hands. "You can't leave me. What will I do?"

"It's OK, Ayala. They have decided against it, for a while at least. My father thinks that being a solicitor, he will be needed here when all this is over; and the culprits are brought to justice. And they will, you know. This will be over before it's even begun. I promise you, Ayala. I'll not let anything happen to you. I would die for you. I love you."

"I love you too, Isaac. With all my heart."

He pulled me close and I buried my head in his chest and sobbed. "I'm so scared, Isaac."

"Ayala Bergman. Now you listen to me this minute. I will not have you scared. No Nazi thug or bloody Hitler is going to do that to my girl. You have to get a grip on yourself, my darling; you are going to drive yourself mad with worry otherwise. I know that things are hard; I won't pretend that they aren't, and if I have to be honest, I am scared too, but being scared and worrying myself over sleepless nights will not change that fact. So come on, girl, dry those tears. I promise you that things will be OK. I promise."

"OK," I said, taking reassurance in his words. "OK."

Late in July 1939 my parents called Marek and myself into our sitting room. I knew instinctively what this was about. I had heard quite a few conversations late at night since the first time I had heard them. Mama still protested that she was not going anywhere, but Father was going ahead anyway and had applied for immigration papers for all of us. I was ready to tell them that scared that I was; there was no way I was going to leave Isaac and my best friend Kamila. I had listened to Isaac that day, and he was right; worrying wasn't going to change anything. Since then I had become much stronger in my way of thinking.

We came in and sat down. Marek sat on the grey and pink floral chair by the fire. The size and shape of it made Marek looked even smaller than his nine years. My mother stood by the fire, looking drained and tired. All the worry of late had really taken its toll on her and she seemed distant and sad. It broke my heart to see my beautiful mother like this. There had been times in the last few weeks that I so much wanted go to her and tell her that I knew of Papa's plans, and that it was going to be all right. But I couldn't because she had no idea that I had known of this all along.

My father spoke first.

"As we all know, it looks like after a lot of uncertainty that this country that we were born and raised in is going to be overrun with Nazis and henchman wanting to scare us out of our country. I have heard and seen with my own eyes and ears what these nasty people are capable of. So after careful consideration, your mother and I have decided to leave Poland and start a new life in England."

I sat there with my head down. I knew I had to pretend that this was the first time I had heard this. "I don't want to go to England," I said, tears rolling down my cheeks. "I don't want to leave my school and my friends, and I don't want to leave Isaac either."

"I do," said my brother excitedly. "I don't want to stay here and get killed by the Nazis. I'm for it."

"*Well, I'M NOT!*" I shouted.

"Ayala, don't shout like that at your brother," my mother cried.

"Well, it's not fair, Mama," I sobbed. "Why should we leave our home

33

that we love so much?"

"I know, darling, I know."

My mother came over and put her arms around me. "I do not want to go either, but we cannot take the chance and stay here. God knows what will happen to us."

"But what about school, and Papa's work?" I cried desperately.

"Ayala, the shop has not been taking that much business of late, people are already starting to boycott it. So you see we have no choice but to leave and start somewhere else," my father responded.

"Well, I will not go," I protested. "I will not go." And with that I jumped up from the chair and ran from the room.

Chapter 5

TELLING ISAAC AND KAMILA THAT I was going to England was the hardest thing I had ever done. I hated it. Kamila cried and said that life was just "*nikczemny*" which means, "wicked" in Polish. We both promised to write to each other every day. So this made me feel a little better.

Isaac just sat there holding my hand and said, "As long as you are safe, Ayala, that's all that matters."

I told him that as soon as this was all over I would come back, and we would be together again. My father had told me this on the day I ran from the room in tears. Stroking my face and wiping away the tears, he said to me, "Ayala, my princess, as soon as this is over we will come back, I promise. It's not forever, and this will be over as soon as it begins. Everybody says so."

This made me feel better and gave me a little piece of hope. I was grateful to my father for that. I was angry at having to leave my home, but I knew that my parents were just doing what was best for their children. I could not blame them for that. I felt sorry for them in some ways, because they must have been as scared as I, and yet they had to put a brave face on it. My father spent more time down at the immigration office every day, trying to get us visas to leave. He had been refused the first and second time he applied, for reasons

I did not know. He was growing quite desperate. Maybe it was because so many people were leaving Poland every day. It was terrible. Quite a few of my friends had fled to one country or another by now. Although I still protested I did not want to go. Secretly I was hoping upon hope that we would get out as soon as possible. The situation in Poland was somewhat depressing now. Although I loved Isaac and Kamila very much, I didn't want to stay here and be dragged into the war that was so imminent. These were such frightening times.

It was now August and we still had not heard from the immigration office. The Germans were advancing towards Poland with rapid speed. The Polish army was doing there utmost to keep them at bay, but compared to the size and weaponry that the Germans possessed it looked quite likely that at some point Poland would have to retreat. But we all held our breaths and prayed.

My parents were becoming increasingly worried that we would not get out in time. We were all scared. Marek had started having his nightmares again, and my mother looked more nervous and tense every day. The worst part for me was not being able to see Isaac after school, as he had also been told to go straight home after. I was so heartbroken.

One day towards the end of August, I stopped on my way home to see Kamila. She had not been to school for two days and I was worried my friend might be sick. I strolled up the path as I usually did. I knocked on the door. Her father answered. He was unusually cold and offhand towards me, and didn't invite me in as he usually did. I thought nothing of this at the time; as I put it down to the fact that everybody was tense and angry these days, what with everything going on. I waited for Kamila to come to the door. I heard her shoes clip clopping along the cold wooden floor of their hallway.

"Hi there," I said, as she opened the door. "I thought I would just check on you, make sure you're OK. Why haven't you been to school?" She looked at me with a look that will remain with me for the rest of my days; cold and hard as if she hated the sight of me. My tummy went over. "What's wrong?" I asked. Somehow quite scared of what she might say.

"I'm sorry, Ayala, but we cannot be friends anymore."

I looked at her dumbfounded.

"What?" I replied in a shocked voice. "What have I done?"

"Nothing, it's just too risky, what with everything that is going on."

"What do you mean?" I started to cry.

"You're Jewish, Ayala. I am not. I'm sorry but my parents think it is best. Goodbye!"

With that she shut the door. I stood there utterly shocked. I couldn't quite take in what I had just heard. The way she had spoken to me like that. I was numb. I turned and headed down the path. With trembling legs, and tears stinging my eyes, I ran all the way home.

"Ayala, whatever is wrong?" my mother asked as I came through the door.

"Nothing, Mama," I answered, sobbing, unable to control my tears.

"Well, it certainly doesn't look like it to me," she replied with concern.

"I couldn't hold it in any longer. I sat down heavily on the stairs and poured my heart out. I told my mother everything that had happened. She held me close and rocked me back and forth, as if a child.

"Hush now, don't you worry about it anymore," she said tenderly. "Sometimes in life, Ayala, we have to learn who our true friends really are."

"But she *was* my true friend, Mama, my best friend."

"Ayala, these are trying times for everybody. She is probably just scared. And going on orders of her parents. What is she to do?"

"But it is the way she spoke to me, Mama, like she hated me."

"Oh, Ayala, how could anyone hate you? Don't be so silly. All this talk of war is getting to everybody. People are just scared, that's all. When all this is over, she will come round, you just wait and see."

"But we were going to write to each other. That's what made going to England easier for me. Now I don't even have her to write to."

"You'll have Isaac, and besides the way things are looking the prospect of going to England is fading day by day."

"Oh, Mama, don't say that. I can't stay here now, I just can't, and besides I'm scared, Mama. I don't want to go to prison or get beat up by the Nazis just because I'm Jewish."

"Oh, come now, Ayala, that will never happen. Nothing is going to happen to anyone of us; and if we do stay here it just means that things will be a little hard for us, that's all."

She held me tight as she said this. I could hear the fear in her voice. I knew that once again, she was trying to protect me.

"Well, I want to go more than ever now."

"Well, let's just hope and pray, darling. None of us wants to stay and get caught up in this terrible war. Now go upstairs and wash those tears away, and don't you worry yourself about it anymore."

"Thank you, Mama."

It took me weeks to accept that I was no longer wanted in Kalmia's life. No longer did I meet Kamila in the canteen at school or wait for her outside the school gates. She ignored me all through our classes, and what made it worse for me was that for the first time in my life, I was being taunted at school for being Jewish. All this was just too much to bear. Never in my life before had I ever been bullied because of my race. Although Kamila herself never made any comments to me, she certainly didn't try to stick up for me either. I was totally destroyed by her betrayal of me. I kept thinking of all the promises we had made to each other. All the secrets we shared. I kept opening my wardrobe to look at the dress she had given me for the dance. I could not believe that this was happening. Isaac was as supportive as ever, but he in turn was getting his fair share of harassment. We spent most of our time together in the library where it was quiet, and we could be left alone to talk.

"Isaac, will you promise me something?" I asked one day as we sat in the library eating our lunch.

"What's that?" he replied curiously.

"Will you promise me that no matter what happens, you will always be here for me?"

"Ayala, I don't need to promise you that, we will always be together you and I. I love you, don't you ever forget that."

"I won't, I promise. I love you too, Isaac."

We walked home together that afternoon. We held hands and kissed as we stopped just before my house.

"I will see you tomorrow, Ayala. Keep your chin up, girl; and remember I love you."

"I love you too, Isaac. See you tomorrow." I walked up my garden path, as I turned to go in, we waved goodbye to each other. That was the last time I ever saw him.

Chapter 6

AFTER TWO WEEKS OF FURIOUS FIGHTING and countless deaths, the Polish army surrendered. Within days there were German army tanks and Nazi storm troopers everywhere. These storm troopers were just common criminals that roamed the street searching for people to persecute, like a poacher searching for game. Warsaw was the main city of Poland and by the middle of September had fallen to the German killing machines. Being the capital meant that it was the first to take the brunt of the Nazis fury. There were large gapping holes where houses and buildings once stood. Bombs rained down morning, noon and night. It was terrifying. People were being thrown out on to the street and businesses were being looted and taken over by the Nazi thugs. It was absolute mayhem. We were all so scared of what would happen to us.

The Star of David had to be displayed above shops and Jewish businesses, including that of my dear father's. We were not allowed to have bank accounts anymore, and we were limited to the amount of money we were allowed to have in any one household. Anybody found disobeying any of these orders faced the risk of being shot or beaten to death. The German government had established a Jewish council "Judenrat," a place to go to issue complaints and find out information on new laws and stipulations. It consisted of twenty-four specially selected members of the Jewish council. These people were responsible for choosing certain members of the public for work or resettlement. In the first few weeks of occupation it seemed that we were down there all the time, but none of the complaints we put forward ever had any positive outcome. On the way back from the Judenrat one afternoon with my mother, my younger brother and I watched in horror as Nazi soldiers forced Jewish women to clean and scrub the streets with their underwear. The humiliation of watching these women, some of them I had known all my life being made to take off their underwear in front of these monsters was sickening. They were beating them, and passers-by were laughing at these poor creatures' misfortune. My mother managed to get us home safely by using the back streets before we had been made to do the same. Marek was absolutely inconsolable with fear. There was nothing we could say or do to pacify his fears.

My poor father was still trying to get us out of this mad town, but every time he tried; he was refused. He felt terribly ashamed that he could not get us out. After the incident in the market my mother now admitted defeat and said despairingly, "I'm sorry, Jacob. I should have listened to you. You were right. We need to get out of here. Maybe if I had not protested for so long, we would be gone by now."

"It's all right, Helena. Do not blame yourself. It is not your fault," replied my father. "It isn't any one's fault."

In those first few weeks of occupation, I do not know how we all survived without being attacked or dragged away to some camp or prison, as so many people were at the time, but life had to go on as normal as we could make it. We still had to go out and get shopping and Papa still had to go to work, even though his takings were down because people were boycotting all Jewish businesses now. I had also turned sixteen, a special birthday, a day when I officially became an adult. I should have been talking about my future and what I wanted to do with it, but our future was something that none of us wanted to think about. It also should have been a time for celebration and happiness, a time I would always remember. Yes I shall always remember it, not with happiness, but with sadness and fear. That's how I shall remember my sixteenth birthday. We still celebrated the Sabbath every week. Our nerves were on a knife-edge. Everywhere we went we had to look over our shoulders or sneak around and try not to draw attention to ourselves. Even a trip into town was a heart-stopping experience for us. It was on one of these trips that I persuaded my mother to let me go to Isaac's house. At first she said, "Absolutely not. We are not staying out for longer than need be. It is too dangerous." But after hours of protests she eventually gave in.

I had not seen Isaac for nearly three weeks. They had closed all the schools down in the first week of the occupation, since then there had been no sign of Isaac anywhere. All sorts of scenes and scenarios were going through my head. I hadn't even seen him on my sixteenth birthday, something I knew Isaac would never forget. He was far too thoughtful to forget something like that.

My heart was pounding as I turned the corner into his street. Just as I turned I heard my mother gasp as I looked around me. We both stopped dead in our tracks. The whole street had been taken over by Germans. Houses that had once belonged to Jewish families were now overrun with Nazis. There were trucks and motorcycles outside every house. Some houses were smashed to pieces and others had bullet holes through the windows. I stood there, unable to take in the scene before me, knowing full well what this would mean. I started to cry and my legs were shaking. I stood there for what seemed like forever. I felt my mother's arm round my shoulders gently telling me we must go. I just kept standing there looking and trying to fathom it all out.

"Ayala, let's go. Let's go."

"Mama," I cried. "Isaac."

"I know, darling, but we must go before we are seen. We are taking a great risk. If the Germans see us, God knows what they will do to us."

"But, Mama," I kept repeating over and over.

"Ayala, come on let's go. *Now* please."

The sternness of my mother's tone brought me back to my senses. We turned and ran all the way home, and didn't stop until we got to our house.

I ran upstairs to my room and threw myself on the bed. Face down with my head in my folded arms. I sobbed and sobbed so hard I thought my heart was going to come out of my chest. I wanted to die.

"Ayala, darling, can I come in?" my mother's gentle voice was soothing and kind.

"I have made you some coffee. Here drink this; it will make you feel better."

I sat up and shook my head. "Coffee won't bring Isaac back, Mama, will it?"

"No, darling, it will not."

"Mama, I can't believe I will never see him again. I loved him so much."

"How do you know you will never see him again?"

"Oh, Mama, you saw all those German trucks outside his house. And you know what those Nazis are capable of. They killed him, Mama. I just know it." I was sobbing so hard my eyes were swollen from crying. My chest was heaving in and out so hard; I had to concentrate to breathe.

41

She pulled me to her breast and held me so tight I could hear the beating of her heart. It was beating just as hard and fast as mine.

"Ayala, darling, what makes you think he is dead? Isaac is a sensible boy. He is most probably in hiding or has been taken elsewhere with his family. You must be positive, Ayala. You can not give up on hope that easily."

"Mama, if he were in hiding, he would have found some way to get to me. I know he would have."

I felt my mother sigh heavily while I lay my head on her chest. Once again, she was there to comfort me. What would I ever do without my wonderful mother? She kissed my forehead.

"Lie down and sleep. You have had a shock. You need to keep your strength up, Ayala. We all do."

I awoke to find my father sitting beside me on a chair he had brought up from the kitchen.

"Papa," I said, my voice weak.

"Hello, princess," he replied, leaning over and gently stroking my cheek.

"Papa, what time is it?"

"It is just after four." I was confused. It felt like I had been asleep for weeks. My head was hurting, and my mouth felt like sawdust. I pulled my arm up to rub my sore eyes, and noticed I was wearing my nightdress.

"Papa, how come I am in my nightdress? I do not remember putting it on."

"My darling, you have been asleep on and off for two days. Your mother and I have been so worried about you."

It all started coming came back to me. Isaac, the Germans. The whole full horror of it replayed itself in my mind. My father went on to tell me how I had been quite delirious after coming back from his house. How I had cried myself to sleep and how I had been in and out of consciousness, calling Isaac's name over and over. I lay there listening and not remembering any of it. It felt quite strange to think I had been here in this bed for two days, and I could not remember it. Like losing two whole days of my life. I started to cry again as I pictured my beautiful Isaac's face in my mind.

"Come now, Ayala. No more tears. Everything will be OK. I promise."

"I'm so scared, Papa. What if they come here next? It's just a matter of time, isn't it?"

Sighing, my father answered, "I don't know. I do not know. Let's just pray that this will be over soon."

It took me a few weeks to gain my strength back. I was still heartbroken over Isaac and grieving for my first and only love. But I knew I had to carry on. Giving up would mean that the enemy had won. And I would not let that happen. For Isaac's sake I would not let that happen.

Every day there were more German tanks and troops of soldiers coming into Warsaw.

It was now the middle of October and the war had been active for about six weeks. Things changed every day and new laws were passed every other. Things we were allowed to do on one day were against the law the next. We didn't know if we were doing right from wrong.

One thing we did have our blessing to count for was that we still had our home. Most people including my beloved Isaac had lost theirs to the Nazis. We knew it was just a matter of time before they would come bursting through our door too. We lived in total fear. Gunshots rang out constantly. Our nerves were shot. Our lives were not the same anymore. The situation was so depressing. Every night the tiniest noise or movement sent us scurrying to the window, shaking with fear to see who was there. Our concerns for Marek became more intense every day. He had become withdrawn and quiet. He had become my mother's shadow, following her around the house everywhere she went. We all felt so helpless towards my little brother. It was painful to watch this nine-year-old boy become so dependant on my mother. What made it more painful was that there was nothing any of us could do to help or ease his fears. It was tragic.

One afternoon my mother and I, and of course her little shadow Marek, were sitting down to lunch in the sitting room. All of a sudden the front door flew open and there stood my father. He was holding his side and was bleeding profusely from his head.

"Oh, Jacob," cried my mother. "What has happened? What have they done to you?" she asked frenziedly.

"It is OK, Helena. At least I am alive."

"But what happened?"

We were all hysterical. I helped him to the couch while my mother got the first aid box.

"Oh, Jacob, look at your wounds. You need a doctor."

"And who will give medical attention to a filthy Jew?" He laughed in his pain; trying to lighten up the situation.

"Jacob, that is not funny. Just tell me what happened."

"They came into the shop. I was just closing for lunch. I thought it was just going to be another case of verbal abuse, or some free boot polishing as they normally did. Getting the dirty Jew pig to polish the good officer's boots is their normal anti Jewish rubbish. But this was different. They told me to come around the counter. I did as I was told. They then proceeded to tell me that the shop was no longer mine. I was told to empty the till. When I told them that I had no money in there apart from a few coins, they started lashing

43

out, calling me all kinds of names. I told them I had no money because nobody came to the shop anymore. This seemed to stir them up further. They beat me to the ground and kicked me on every part of my body. I thought they were going to kill me, Helena. But they picked me up and threw me out. So that is it. They can just come in and take what is not theirs, and get away with it. And there is *NOTHING WE CAN DO ABOUT IT*!"

Seeing my father in such a state, and shouting like this was very upsetting. I started to cry. Marek was also crying and shaking.

"Ayala, go upstairs with Marek while I see to your father's wounds, OK?"

"It's OK, Marek," said my mother calmly just as he was about to protest. "I'm only down here, darling; go on with your sister."

I was so angry and frustrated. Seeing my father like this, my beautiful kind papa. How could anybody be so cruel? How I hated those beasts. Every night I prayed that this would end soon. I asked God why he would allow this to happen to us. Why the world seemed to hate us so much? Why were innocent people being treated so cruelly? What had we done?

It just seemed so unfair. I wondered how much more we could all take.

So now Papa no longer had a job. Money was scarce enough without the added pressure of nobody bringing in a wage. It was not his fault. He was just a man caught up in the spider's web of fury, like the rest of us. But of course no money meant no England. No England meant no escape. Papa kept saying things like, "It's all right, there is still time." And "I will not let my family down again." Of course referring to the matter of his shop, which was now a place for the Germans to idly sit and drink bottles of beer from, whilst harassing the poor Jews on the street. It wouldn't have been so bad if the shop were at least being used for its proper means. But to see it just being used as a drinking lounge for the ever drunken "Blonde Bullies," as my father called them, was too much for my poor father to bear. The prospect of escaping was becoming more unlikely every day. I knew this, my mother knew this and so did my father, but he never said it. I think he just tried to keep everyone's morale up. Oh how I loved my wonderful father.

The main concern now was food. It was hard enough before the shop had been taken, as most shopkeepers no longer served Jews, but there was some that still would, if not being watched. But now the money was running extremely low. We were only allowed so much cash per household, which by no means would feed a growing family of four. And it was fast running out. My uncle Otto, who lived in the country, was sending us regular supplies of vegetables, which was something to be grateful for, but with a family of his own to provide for we knew this would not last forever. Papa's wounds took weeks to heal, but when they did, he went out every day to find work, only to come home again disappointed and depressed. I offered to go out to work myself, but my parents would not hear of it. It seemed that no matter which way we turned, we hit a brick wall. It was as if the world had it in for us. We were treated like vermin. I was depressed. I had lost my best friend, my boyfriend, the only person I ever loved, not to mention my education, and to top it all we were now poor. It felt like life could not get any worse than this.

Chapter 7

1940

CHRISTMAS AND NEW YEAR WAS A very depressing affair. For me it was especially hard, as I could not stop thinking of Isaac and how only a year before he had been here with me. I thought of how happy I had been. I could not believe how quickly life could change. I still wore the beautiful chain and pendant that Isaac had given me. It never left my neck. I still lived in hope that somehow Isaac was alive, in some camp somewhere, but in a strange kind of way; it was easier to believe he was dead. That way I would not get my hopes up to be let down in a big way. I thought also of Kamila and wondered if at all she still thought of me. I wondered if she felt any guilt towards me. I still hurt deeply over that.

We had the usual family gathering for Chanukah, of aunties, uncles and cousins, but this year we went to my auntie's house, as we could not afford to feed such a large crowd of people. My auntie's financial situation wasn't much better, but we all brought the little amount of food that we had. Of course we tried not to let the ever-worsening situation in Warsaw spoil what little bit of holiday spirit we had. But after a few glasses of wine, the conversation always came back to the war. It was hard not to talk about something that was dominating your whole life.

The New Year brought with it new rules and regulations. Jews were no longer allowed to ride public transport. They were no longer allowed in the parks. All Jews had to register all family members. And as of November of the previous year all Jews over ten years and older must display the Star of David on the right arm of their clothing. This new stipulation was just another way of singling out Jews from the rest of society. It was also a good way of identifying the Jews from non-Jews and making it easier to persecute them. At first I was totally against wearing such a thing, claiming that it would just make me more of a target for punishment. "It's like I'm saying, here I am. I'm Jewish, come and beat me, shoot me. Come do whatever you want to me. It's OK, that is what I'm here for."

"Ayala, if you don't they will shoot you," came my mother's reply.

"Yes, and they will shoot me if I do wear it," I cried. "We can not win."

"Ayala, please be sensible. I know all these rules and regulations are getting you down, they are getting to all of us, but if you don't you will be risking your life. Please, darling."

"But, MAMA, I CANNOT TAKE ANYMORE OF THIS. OUR WHOLE LIVES ARE COMPLETELY AT THE MERCY OF THESE MONSTERS. IT'S JUST NOT FAIR!" I was shouting with anger.

"Ayala, look at this way, if you wear it you will be saying that you are proud of being Jewish. Why should you be ashamed of what you are?"

"I'm not ashamed, Mama, but being what we are at the moment isn't doing us much good is it."

My mother, who had been sitting at the kitchen table, buried her head in her hands and sighed deeply. "I know that, Ayala, but what can I do? If I could change things, don't you think I would?" she replied in a tired voice. I felt ashamed of myself for being so difficult. It was just as hard for my mother as it was for all of us. Being our mother meant that she, like our father, needed to protect us and keep up the morale. But who was keeping up her morale or my father's come to that?

"Mama, I'm sorry," I said as I came round the table and put my arms around her.

"Don't say sorry, Ayala. I do understand how you feel. I too feel depressed and fed up with the situation. I feel as your mother I should be protecting you from all this, but I can't. That makes me fell ashamed."

With that my mother cried. I stood there with my arms around her.

"Mama, please don't cry. It is not your fault. You shouldn't feel ashamed about anything; you have done your best. We are still in our house, and we are all still together. That stands for something, doesn't it? So you have protected us. Please, Mama; never think that you are letting any of us down in any way, because you're not. You are the best mother a girl could wish for." I kissed her gently on the head.

"My Ayala, how you have grown up in this last year. You are not my little girl anymore." She turned and put her hands gently round my face and held me there while gazing deeply into my eyes. As I stood there and looked back at her, I could see the lines of strain and worry that had etched into my mother's beautiful face. I wanted to cry as I stood there looking at my sweet mother with tears in her eyes. I felt powerless at the thought of not being able to do something about this life of fear and terror that we were all living in.

"I shall wear it, Mama. I shall wear it."

And so I sat there and sewed my new label onto my clothes. This new order stated that it had to be a white armband with a blue star painted in the middle. It had to be just above the elbow, so it could be clearly seen. I looked at my new identification. *This will be my saviour or my demise,* I thought as I sat looking at it. I would let fate decide which.

The thought of going out onto the street with this badge on my arm, made me feel utterly sick. It wasn't because I was ashamed, it was because as soon as I stepped one foot outside, then I knew that I was to be hunted. So far we had managed to save ourselves from the barbaric treatment being handed out every day; this was pure luck on our part; and the ability to kind of mingle in so to speak. And we never stayed out longer than necessary, but slowly and as time went on, I had stopped going anywhere unless I really had to. Every shopping trip or family visit brought fresh nightmares of what I had seen that day. So-called soldiers beating old women, kicking them to the ground and mercilessly attacking them with the butt of their rifles. The public humiliation, which these evil Nazis took so much pleasure in, seemed to get worse every day. Men having to ride on each other's backs, and old people being used as cart horses. It was disturbing and painful to watch. I always reminded myself every time I saw some atrocity happen: "This is someone's mother or father or child. Somebody loves them. Somebody will grieve for them when they are gone." To this day I still say that over in my head when I think of all the suffering that went on. And now we had the added worry of remembering to wear our badges. Death was the punishment if we didn't. And sometimes death was the punishment if we did. We all had different ways of remembering to wear it. Mine was on my mirror in big black writing "REMEMBER YOUR BADGE." My father's was by his mirror in the bathroom. My mother's was by the street door next to Marek's as she felt she needed to take responsibility for him in that way.

Marek was still quiet and withdrawn. We tried to be jolly and easygoing around him, and we tried not to let him know too much of what was really happing out on the street. He had seen quite a lot for his young years, and this was having a terrible affect on him.

Sometime in April, we had news that my Uncle Reuben had been executed in Lodz ghetto for smuggling in food. He had been taken to the market square and publicly shot. This was a warning to anyone else trying to do the same. When we heard this news, we hit an all-time low. It made us think of our own mortality. And that this was the way of life now. First it is Uncle Reuben and next who knows. This wasn't just someone from our town, or an acquaintance. This was our uncle, my father's younger brother. We had received a letter from his wife "Yente," telling us of this tragedy. She was totally undone with grief. My father cried and raised his hands to the heavens, asking why this should happen. It was terrible seeing my father in such a state. But sadly it was something we were all getting used to. It was becoming quite normal for one of us to let go and cry, at least once a week. We felt so helpless for our Auntie Yente and her children, as there was nothing we could do. The ghetto or "Jewish quarter," as they politely put it, was a large area of the Lodz city that had been sectioned off to accommodate the Jewish population, and to keep them altogether. Its conditions were said to be awful. As terrible as this was for us and especially for my father, we had to carry on and just try to survive ourselves. There was no funeral or memorial for Uncle Reuben. They would not even allow us to do that. We lit a candle in our home and said a prayer for him. And prayed for his family too. There was nothing else we could do. The persecution of the Jews was getting nearer to home all the time, and we were about to find out just how near it was about to get.

One Saturday late in May, we were all in the kitchen eating some soup, our food rations were getting less and less each week. We still had our vegetable supply coming in from our uncle in the country, but this was beginning to slow down now, so soup was starting to become the regular main meal of the evening. We wanted to keep our provisions for as long as we could, otherwise it would mean a trip down to the food line every day and I know, as the proud man that my father was, this would be the finish of him, but it was inevitable that this would soon be the case. We sat there talking about our holidays before the war. We spoke of our trips to France and Holland, and the good times we'd had. This was mainly for Marek's benefit, to try and bring him out of his self a little. He was as quiet as ever and we all so concerned for him. All of a sudden there was a loud banging on our street door and German voices shouting, "*Offen hoch.*"(Open up.) We sat there paralysed. Our hearts stopped at the same time.

"Mama, Mama!" Marek ran round to the head of the table to where my mother was sitting.

"It's all right, darling. It is all right." My litter brother held onto my mother's side, his eyes wide and fixed with fear. He was shaking and there were beads of sweat on his forehead.

I started to shake with fear and there were tears starting to run down my face. *This is it*, I thought. *We are going to die.*

"*Eile, Eile.*" (Hurry.)

My father ran to the door. Upon opening it, he was pushed back by one of the German soldiers as they came through the door, and he fell to the floor hard. The door almost came off it hinges as they came through. By this time my mother was screaming and crying, "Jacob, Jacob!"

I was now huddled up to my mother as well as Marek.

The Nazis were screaming and shouting. My father got to his feet. "Ver are your papers?" the Germans screamed at us. My father tried to tell them they were upstairs under the bed, but they were screaming so hard they did not hear him. "VER ARE YOUR PAPERS!" they screamed again. My father managed to tell them.

One of the Nazis officers went upstairs with him, while the other stood guard by us, pointing his rifle. I could feel Marek shaking; any moment I thought that his little legs would buckle underneath him. The German just stood there staring. He was tall, over six feet. His eyes were the brightest of blue I had ever seen. They would have been beautiful had it not been for his fixed evil glare. They just looked right through us, penetrating us. His uniform was immaculate, not a crease or fold to be seen. His black helmet was decorated with a sliver looking eagle on one side. His tunic was dressed with all sorts of medals and another eagle on the left side.

"Vot is ze matter wiv him?" He spoke at last as he looked at my brother who was crying and shaking. We all just stared at him like frightened rabbits, unable to speak.

"Vot. Have you all lost your tongues?" he asked, all the time not taking his eyes from us, and still pointing his rifle. I thought that any minute he was going to shoot right through us.

"He is very frightened." At last I found my voice. "He is just a little boy."

"Vot are you frightened of, little boy, hmm?"

He came closer and lifted my brother's chin up with his fingers. We froze as he came closer. I was terrified beyond words. My brother looked up at him, with pitiful eyes.

"Do ve not want to speak wiv zee good German officer, hmm?" he sniggered.

Just then my father came back downstairs with the other German in tow. The German turned from Marek and stood by his fellow officer and proceeded to read our papers. They went through our names one by one.

"Jacob Bergman, Helena Bergman." And so on. Their voices were slow and droll, as if lingering out the fear and apprehension for us even more. "OK," said one of the soldiers. "Ve are checking this area for any radios that have not been handed in."

"No," answered my father. "We handed the radio in when we the law was first issued. Please check." My father held out his hand in a gesture for them to look.

Staring at my father all the time; he answered, "You know vot zee punishment for you vill be if we find one here?" My father nodded.

They went up stairs and left us downstairs on our own. They must have known how afraid we were, knowing we were too scared to take flight. We heard the drawers being thrown across the room, the cupboards being ripped open. The beds were being tipped upside down, just to search for a radio that we did not have. *Thank God Papa did get rid of it*, I thought, as we stood there motionless. No one said a word to each other apart from my poor father whispering to us all, "It is all right. They will be gone as soon as they realise there is nothing to find."

It seemed as though they had been up there for hours. I just kept thinking. *Oh please hurry up. Get this over and done with so we know at least what will become of us.* The waiting was unbearable.

At last they came down. Again we froze with fear at the sheer sight of them.

"Zar is nussing here, but be varned, any breaking of any rules vill mean death. Do you understand zis?"

We nodded our heads frantically. The sheer relief we felt was like nothing on this earth when they finally turned and headed off down the path. We waited till they were out of sight till we could breathe once more. We ran to each other and held each other and cried. Marek was almost on his knees; he had become weak with fear. My poor mother was inconsolable. She was shaking uncontrollably. My father spent the rest of the night trying to calm us all down. I myself have never felt fear like it. This was our first encounter with these beasts, and I prayed to God Almighty that it would be the last.

It took us quite a while to get over the shock and realisation of what had happened to us that day. Each one of us was quite different after that. It made us so aware that our lives could be snuffed out just like that. It was an awful realisation.

We were growing more concerned for Marek every day. Since our encounter with the Nazi thugs, he had deteriorated rapidly. He was acting strange and saying odd things to us that didn't make sense. And he had started wetting the bed. What made this awful situation even worse was that we couldn't even get any medical treatment for him. Nobody would want to treat an innocent child with problems, because he was Jewish. They wouldn't dirty their guilt hands. How disgusting of the human race. It was heartbreaking to see my brother in this state. It made me want to scream with anger. How could men get such pleasure from scaring an innocent child? I just couldn't understand it.

My father's quest to get us out of Poland had become more urgent than ever before. Since our visit from the Nazis, it brought it back to us how desperately we needed to get out, but most of all we needed to get Marek out before he completely lost his mind.

Again my father tried to get some help, but now it was even more risky than before. Again he became frustrated and ashamed that he could not protect his children. We kept telling him that it would be all right and that something would come up soon, but in our hearts we knew that we were here for the duration, or as long as fate allowed.

Chapter 8

IT TOOK QUITE A WHILE FOR things to calm down after the events in May, when we had our first visit from the enemy. Things in our family had changed after that day. My mother's nerves were completely shot to pieces, and my poor father was beside himself with worry over trying to get us out of Poland. I spent as much time as I could with Marek, playing with him in his room and reading him stories, and just generally trying to get him to open up a little. I had not been outside of the house since the afternoon in May. A trip down the bottom of the garden was my main source of fresh air. The problem that we had was that we did need to go out for things. The food shortage was so low now that a trip down to the food line was inevitable. But it was a case of we all go together or we all stay. My parents didn't want us left alone in the house, but they didn't want us to go out on to the street either. And my father didn't want my mother to go out all by herself. It was a complete catch-22 situation. In the end it was decided that my father must be the one who goes out for food. Nobody liked the idea of any one of us going on to the street, for it was such a dangerous place to be now. The Nazis' barbaric treatment of the Jews was getting worse. More and more people were being rounded up and sent to labour camps each day. People were being shot for not wearing their star or for riding on public transport, or for any reasons they could find. It was madness.

One morning in June we woke up to find that we were out of milk and bread. We had hardly any money left, but we managed to scrape some up. My father left for the town and on his way out, told us to be alert and not to open the door without checking who was there. My mother kissed him on the cheek and told him to hurry back soon, and to be careful. To go straight there and back, and that she loved him very much. We had worked out how long it took to get to the town and back. Ten minutes there, ten minuets back, and about ten minutes in the shop, providing that he would get served today. So all in all he would be back in about half an hour. I watched him walk up the path and across the road. He was wearing his trilby style hat, grey trousers and a jersey style shirt with a brown blazer over the top. The last few months had taken a toll on him, but he still looked handsome. Oh how I loved my father, how wonderful he was, and how lucky I was to have him. I watched him until he went around the corner and was gone from my sight. Standing there watching him and thinking how much I loved him made me start thinking about Isaac again. The mere thought of him brought tears to my eyes straightaway. Not a day went by that I did not think of him, and wonder what had become of him and his family. I knew in my heart that he was dead. I knew that if he were alive he would have found a way to contact me by now. I missed him so much. We had so many plans made. I often wondered if I would have ended up marrying him, or whether our friendship would have petered out some where down the line. *I guess I will never know*, I thought as I walked away from the window. I took a deep breath and wiped the tears from my eyes. "But now I must just carry on," I said to myself out loud. I went into the kitchen where my mother was sitting, darning some socks. Marek was at the other side of the table drawing.

"Mama," I said as I sat down.

She looked up from her sewing. "Yes, darling," she replied.

"What do you think will become of us? Do you think that we will all be killed in the end?"

My mother looked at me horrified. "Genug." Which means "enough" in Yiddish. "I cannot believe you can even think of that. What has your Jewish faith taught you, *nothing*?"

I knew my mother was angry because she always spoke in her first language when she was annoyed.

"Mama, I'm sorry, but I can't help thinking it. There is so much death and pain out there, and even my Isaac has gone. I'm just so worried about the future."

"I know that, darling, but you must have faith. Faith and hope in God is all we have right now. You must never give up on that."

"I know, Mama, but there are so many bad things happening. I'm so afraid to think of the future. It seems like this will never end. Every day something new happens or some new law is issued, or someone dies. Like poor Uncle Reuben in that ghetto. I just can't help thinking that soon it will be one of us. I just can't take much more of it. I feel like a prisoner in my own home, because I'm too scared to go out. Now there are rumours that they are building a ghetto here too. I can't even listen to my radio any more, because they have taken that away from us too."

"Ayala, this will end," said my mother softly. "Nothing lasts forever. These bullies can't get away with this forever; their time will come, Ayala. Their time will come. And they will face the punishment for their crimes."

I put my head in my hands and wept. My mother came around the table and held me in her arms.

I felt safe and warm as she gently pulled me towards her breast. I felt like nothing on earth could harm me now. That her protection was all I needed.

"I'm sorry, Mama, I'm just feeling down today that's all. Having an off day."

"And you are entitled to it, my sweet child," she said, as she kissed my head. "You are entitled to it."

It wasn't until afterwards I had realised that I had said all of this in front of Marek, and he hadn't even heard. Oh how worried I was for my poor little brother.

I felt so much better after our talk. I loved my mother so much; she always knew how to say just the right things at the right time, to make me feel so much better. I didn't say anything to my mother, but I had not realised just how long I had been sitting there, when it dawned on me that Papa had been gone for over an hour and as yet had not returned.

It was now one o'clock in the afternoon and my father had still not returned from town. He had now been gone for two hours. Mama by this time had obviously noticed and was quietly worrying. I could see the anxiety stretched across her face but she was trying to hide it as usual. I too tried to hide my concern from my mother. But as the time went on, it was getting harder for both of us.

"Mama, where is he?" I eventually said.

"I do not know. Maybe he has had trouble finding someone to serve him, and he is trying to find a Jewish shopkeeper."

"Mama, everybody knows that they do not exist now."

"Some of them do, Ayala. There are still some."

"Even so, he should have been back by now."

My tummy was going over and I was starting to feel sick. I kept pacing back and forth to the window to look out, only to return sighing and even more anxious.

"Ayala, will you please stop going to that window? You are making me a bundle of nerves. He will be here soon, so please stop fretting."

"I'm sorry, Mama."

"Just sit down. Play a game of cards with Marek. Keep your mind busy and he will be back before we know it."

I did as I was told and played a game of snap with my little brother. I could not concentrate. My mind was dominated by thoughts of my dear father, and praying for his safe return. I imagined telling him off when he came through the door, and telling him that as he can't be trusted to go out on his own without causing us all to worry, then I would just have to start going instead.

The hours ticked by slowly. It was now six o'clock in the evening. My father had been gone for seven hours. My mother was now frantically worried. We both knew the reason for my father's absence was not a good one.

"Please God, do not do this to us. Please send Papa home soon. He is a good man. Please keep him safe." I kept repeating this over and over in my head. My poor mother by now was dizzy with worry. I told her to lie down on the sofa and try to get some sleep.

"I could not sleep. I just want to know what has happened to him. What have they done with my Jacob?" she kept saying this over and over. I did not know what to say, for I too had no idea of what had become of him. I just prayed and prayed he was not dead. *I could not bear that*, I thought.

It was now late in the evening. I had finally persuaded my mother to take a nap. I sat there thinking of all the possible reasons why Papa had failed to return. I hoped he had been taken to a labour camp. At least that way, he would still be alive. But the black thoughts of death kept rearing their ugly heads, and I just knew that my father like Isaac and Uncle Reuben before him was dead.

I decided to sleep downstairs on the sofa with Mama that first night. Marek slept on the armchair by the fire. I covered her up with a blanket and went and curled up on the other armchair, and prayed for my father to come home safely. My mother tossed and turned all night. Every now and then she would open her eyes and call for Papa. The disappointment on her face when she looked up and saw me there, telling her to go back to sleep made me weep. I fell asleep around four thirty in the morning. The shock and the reality of our situation kept my mind busy with anxiety and fear all night. The strange thing about it was that, even though I was out of my mind with worry, my mother had taken it a lot worse than I, so I had to be strong for her, otherwise we would have all gone to pieces that night. I didn't want to show her how traumatised by it I was, so I put on a brave face and just took control of the situation.

I woke up the next morning to find my mother crying. She was rocking backwards and forwards with her head in her hands. She was praying and asking God why he would take her husband. I didn't know what to say or do to make her feel any better. I suggested that I should go out and try and find out what had happened to Papa. I knew my mother wasn't in her right mind because she said that I should.

"Mama, we must be hopeful, isn't that what you told me when Isaac went missing?"

"He is dead. He is dead. I know it, because my heart tells me," she cried pitifully.

"Mama, he might have been taken to a works camp. It is happening all the time now. There could be a million reasons why he did not come home."

"My Jacob. My Jacob." That's all she kept saying over and over, rocking backwards and forwards. I was totally at a loss what to do. I just held her in my arms and cradled her, telling her it was going to be all right, just like she had done with me. I lay her back down and put the blanket over her.

"Mama, do try to have a little sleep. I will go into town and ask anybody if they have seen anything of Papa. OK?"

"Go and find him, Ayala. Please find my Jacob," she cried.

It was heartbreaking to watch my mother go through this unnecessary pain.

I waited until she was asleep, then I went to get dressed. It was a beautiful day in June, the sun was shining and it was hot. I couldn't believe we could feel so much sorrow on such a beautiful day. The strange thing was that as much as the horror and pain we were all going through, some things still stayed the same. The sun still shone. The day still turned into night. The night still turned into the day, and yet the world was ending in Poland.

I went into Marek's room before I left to go into town. I was worried to leave him alone, knowing that my mother was in no state to take care of him, but I also knew that a trip into town would be dangerous for him in his state of mind, without the fear of what would happen to him when we were out. It was dangerous for me too. But I had to find out what had happened to Papa. I had to do this for him *and* Mama. I told Marek that I had to go out.

"Can you look after Mama for me while I am away?" I asked.

"Where are you going?" he replied with concern.

"I'm going into town, to try and find some food," I lied. With Marek's present state of mind, he didn't even know that Papa was missing. He seemed to be in another world all the time. If I was to be honest, I was grateful for that, this time, as he would not have coped well knowing that our father was missing.

"Marek, will you be OK?"

He didn't answer me. He just kept on playing with his train set.

"Marek, listen to me, darling, this is important. Will you be OK with Mama while I go into town?"

"*Yes*," he answered irritated.

I told him to come downstairs and sit with Mama while I was out. Not to answer the door to anyone and be as quiet as possible. I hated leaving him, but what could I do. I had to find out what had happened to my father. We went downstairs and I double-checked Mama before I went. I kissed her gently on the lips, then went over and hugged Marek. I held him tight as if it was the last time I would see him. The truth was, if fate was as cruel as it had been of late, then I would not be back at all, but I tried to think positive. "I will be as quick as I can, OK, darling?" I said as I slipped out the door.

This was the fist time I had been out since May. I felt agoraphobic as I walked briskly along the road. My heart was thumping so hard; it was making it difficult to breathe. My hands were sweating and my throat was dry. I kept my head down as I walked along, trying not to make myself stand out.

I could not quite believe that this city that I had loved so much, this street that I had walked on all my life, was now the most frightening and dangerous place to be. *I would give anything on this earth not to be walking along this street right now.* I thought as I approached the end of my road. I crossed over to where I had last seen my father the day before. I was walking so fast with my head down that I did not see the person walking towards me until they had bumped right into me. I jumped; my heart was in my throat. I was afraid to look up, fearing it to be a Nazi officer in front of me.

"I'm sorry. I'm sorry," I said like a frightened child. As I stepped to the side to pass, I gasped in disbelief as I saw Kamila standing before me. My natural instinct was to say hello and to tell her everything that had happened, but I could tell by the cold look in her eyes that she didn't want to talk to me. She just stood there staring, looking at me like I was a piece of mud on her shoe. I lingered there for a second or two, waiting or hoping that she would speak to me. When she didn't, I put my head back down and walked away.

I did not see a shred of pity or guilt across her face as she stood there blankly staring at me. Not an ounce of affection for the years of friendship that we had shared between us. The tears were stinging my eyes and restricting my view as I walked faster and faster up the street. I could not believe that this was the same person whom I had shared so many secrets with, the same person with whom I had laughed and cried with over the years. The same person whom only a year ago had put her arms around me and said that no German or Hitler would ever take away our friendship. *How the mind forgets*, I thought. My head ached and my heart was heavy. I wondered what on earth I had done to deserve so much misery in my life. It wasn't until I got into the heart of town, I realised how selfish I had been, thinking that I was the only one going through such hell. *The whole of the Jewish race is going through hell*, I thought as I saw three Nazi thugs beating men and young boys into the back of a cattle car. *Most probably taking them to some labour camp*, I thought as I stood in the shadows watching these poor creatures being treated so wickedly. I pictured my poor father being treated in this way, and the thought sparked fear and repulsion in me. *Oh how I hate these monsters, I hope they rot in hell for what they are doing to such innocent people,* I said to myself.

The market square had changed dramatically since I was here last. The intense feeling of fear hung in the air. People walked around with their heads down. Everywhere I looked someone was getting beaten or humiliated. It was hard to believe that all this was really happening. It was sad to see people with so much dignity being treated with so much disrespect. I tried to close my eyes to it all and not let it get to me. I needed to be strong because I had to find out what had happened to Papa, but it is hard not to notice old people and young children being hurt and humiliated right before your eyes.

I walked through the square. I was looking out for people that I knew. Mama or Papa always bumped into people that they knew in the square. Mama would stand there for ages gossiping with her friends that she had met while shopping. I sometimes met some of my school friends in the market square also. If I was lucky enough to find someone I knew, then hopefully they might be able to tell me what had happened to Papa. I could not bear to go home and have to tell Mama that I still didn't know where Papa was. It would kill her. It would kill me too. I had to find Papa. I just had to. I had lost so much in this last year. I could not bear to lose my father as well.

Chapter 9

I WANDERED AROUND THE MARKET FOR hours. Looking for anybody who might be able to tell me what had happened to Papa. I couldn't see anybody I knew. Either they had been taken away or they were too scared to come out. I was just losing hope when I saw my father's friend, Elijah, walking towards me. My father and Elijah had known each other for years. He often used to come over with his wife and children and I used to play with his daughter Hannah when I was little.

"Ayala," he called as he put his arms out to greet me.

"Hello, Elijah," I replied.

"How are things, my dear?" he asked, his face full of concern and sympathy.

"Not good, Elijah," I said as I started to cry.

"My dear child, come let's go somewhere quiet, so that we can talk."

I followed him to a back street where it was quiet. It was quite out of the way, so I felt quite safe there.

"I'm sorry, Elijah, I didn't mean to cry. It's just that I don't know what to do. Papa went out yesterday and has not been seen since. Mama is beside herself with worry. Marek is acting strange and won't talk to anyone. Oh I just can't take any more."

"Oh, Ayala, I am so sorry. Your father is a good man. Your mother must be devastated. I shall come and see her soon. I hope that nothing too bad has become of him, but one does not know these days. They do not care who they hurt. Man, woman, child. It does not matter to them."

"It's the not knowing that is the worst part," I cried. "I just want him to come home."

"Maybe he has been taken to a works site. They are taking people all the time now. It will be just a matter of time before they take me."

"Do you think that's what happened?" I asked.

"Well, that does seem to be their latest kick. They are building a construction site out in the country somewhere. I know of people who have been sent there and have escaped. So maybe that is where he is."

"If he has been sent there, then he will be needed to work, so they won't want to kill him then, will they?" I asked, trying to convince myself.

"Ayala, your father is a sensible man. I am sure he will do all that is needed to save himself from their bullets."

"Do you think so?"

"I know so. I also know your father would not want you to be out on this dangerous street on his behalf. Ayala, it is dangerous for a young girl to be out here on her own. Anything could happen to you. They take women as well as men you know. You are taking a great risk. These Nazis, they are insane. They say that we are vermin, that we are not worthy of life and that we are disease carriers, but that does not stop them raping our beautiful Jewish women."

I gasped in shock.

"No," I said in disbelief.

"Ayala, go home; go look after your mother. She will need you now. There is nothing you can do for your father except pray. I will ask around, see what I can find out. I will come and see you if I find out. OK?"

"Would you really, Elijah. I would be so grateful."

"Be careful, Ayala, try to get home quickly, and don't come out unless you really need to, OK?"

"Thank you, Elijah," I said.

He kissed my cheek before turning to go. I turned round and started to make my way home. It felt good being able to talk to someone else who knew exactly what I was going through.

I felt much more positive than I did this morning. *At least I have something positive to tell Mama*, I thought as I started to make my way home.

I was walking along thinking about my father and what he might be going through. I prayed that if he was alive, that God would keep him safe. I was so deep in thought that I did not see the two German soldiers advancing towards me until they were virtually about to pass me. I put my head down and quickened my pace as they passed me by. My heart missed a beat and I was shaking like a leaf. I thought I had been lucky not to be stopped by them, until I heard, "Err, excuse me, you Jew."

I stopped dead in my tracks and slowly turned keeping my head down. I was petrified. My chest became tight with fear. *Oh God please*, I thought as they approached me. They looked identical to each other in their grey uniforms, the only way in which to tell them apart was that one was taller than the other.

"Ver are you on your way to, Jew?" the taller one asked.

"I am on my way home," I replied quietly. I was so scared I could hardly find my voice.

"Vot did you say? I cannot hear you. Speak up."

"I have been into town. I am now on my way home," I said a little louder. My voice sounded strange, like it was coming from someone else's throat.

"Ver are your papers?" asked the shorter one. I went through my pockets and produced the document.

God please let it be in order, I prayed as they inspected it. They looked at me then back at the paper.

"Lift up your head, ve cannot see your face," said the shorter one again.

I lifted my head, shaking. With tears in my eyes I looked directly at them, as if to plead with them or to find some sort of human emotion in them.

"Vot are you so scared of?" the taller one asked. "Ve are good German soldiers. Ve don't want to hurt you. Err, maybe we might vant to just play." They sniggered as one of them touched my hair with the back of his hand.

Oh my God. I thought of what Elijah had told me. Panic washed over me. I started to cry uncontrollably.

"Vot is wrong? Don't you vant to play wiv the soldiers?" asked the tall one.

I shook my head; I was shaking like a terrified bird. I started to heave as if I was going to be sick.

"Please, please," I said. "Do not hurt me. I am just a girl."

I heard them laugh. Then with out warning I felt a hard punch on my face. It knocked me over. I did not see who threw it, but it felt like a bulldozer had hit me. I lay on the ground waiting for the next punch or kick, but was shocked to see them walking off up the road laughing, and throwing my papers into the curb. I stayed on the ground, too scared to move until they turned the corner. I got up and picked up my papers. My nose was bleeding and my lip was cut. I was numb with shock and fear. I could not believe two grown men had just assaulted me. I was repulsed. I ran all the way home, and didn't stop till I got to my front gate.

I got in and shut the door. I leaned up against it and closed my eyes. Breathing deeply I replayed the scene over in my head. I couldn't believe how close I had come to getting raped or being taken away and killed somewhere. The reality of the situation I had just got out of hit me like a thunderbolt. I ran upstairs and was physically sick.

I didn't tell my mother what had happened to me on the way home. This would just add to her problems. As it was when I got in she was still no better. She was silent and distant. I felt so helpless; I didn't know what to do. I told her about my meeting with Elijah and that he felt sure that Papa had been taken to a works camp. This in itself was of no comfort really, knowing how badly the prisoners were treated there, but at least it meant that there was a big chance that Papa was still alive. I had to believe that this was what had happened to him, or else I would have gone to pieces. The thought of never seeing my wonderful father again would have driven me to destruction, let alone what it would have done to Mama. My mother was a little relieved when I told her what Elijah had said, but I didn't think she really believed it. All she kept saying was that she wanted her Jacob back.

The next couple of weeks were really hard for me. It was strange but in a way it was like the roles had reversed. I no longer was the weak and frightened child, who was constantly looking for reassurance.

I had become the strong one, trying to keep everything together. Mama was no better, and Marek still had his problems. It felt at times that I was going to crack under all the pressure, but it is strange how the body and mind reacts to certain situations; I knew I had to keep going and be there for my mother and brother, but it was hard some days not having anyone to talk to about it. One good thing that happened was that we had a delivery of food from my uncle Otto. It was a great relief to me as we were now very much out of food and the next step for me would be a trip down to the food line. A trip I very much didn't want to have to do. The only thing that did shadow our good fortune on this day was the note pinned to the box saying that unfortunately this would be the last one, as my uncle was now running low on supplies for himself. I knew I had to make this last for as long as I could, but where on earth we were going to get food after that God only knew.

It was now July and my father had been gone for nearly three weeks. I missed him so much it hurt. I kept thinking that he would come through the door any minute, or that he would call up the stairs to tell me to put my book down and go to sleep. It was strange but since he had been gone we all slept downstairs in the sitting room rather than go upstairs to our rooms. I didn't think my mother could take the pain of sleeping in a bed with such an empty space. For Marek and me, I think, it was a case of feeling safer being together. My mother was a little better. She had convinced herself that Papa was in a works camp and when he had finished doing whatever it was he was being made to do, then he would be home. I didn't believe this at all. I had not heard from Elijah, which meant that he obviously didn't find anything out, or he himself had been taken away. I prayed every night that this war would end, and that my father would come home safely. Things had changed so much in the last year. If someone had told me a year ago that I would lose my father, boyfriend and best friend I would not have believed them.

We were nearly a year into the war, and every day things in our town went from bad to worse. The restrictions for us Jews just got worse and worse. It is a well-known fact that Jewish people are known for their sense of humour. If it had not been so tragic, then I know that some of these pathetic restrictions would have made wonderful jokes for my uncles on a Friday night after so much wine. Sadly the days of celebrating the Sabbath all together for us were now a thing of the past. No longer was our house full of children and aunties and uncles. Slowly but surely our family meetings had ceased to be. Either we could not afford to eat or drink like we used to, or we were too afraid to go out. And of course more tragically because half of my family by now were in forced labour camps or ghettos. We still celebrated our holy days of course, but it was a much more quiet and personal affair, with just myself Mama and Marek. We said our prayers and lit our candles, and we always said a special prayer for Papa and Isaac. We did not go to church on a Saturday, as all the synagogues had been either burned to the ground, or were being used as latrines or brothels. The Nazis lowest form of wickedness yet. I was always encouraged to say my prayers and to learn the Torah, but my parents were never totally orthodox, they were more concerned with their children enjoying life and not have to be burdened with rules and regulations, but I prayed more now than I ever did. I prayed for my father and Isaac and for the whole Jewish population. I asked God why he seemed to be ignoring our pleas for help. I asked him what was the reason for all of this pain and suffering that we were all going through, but it seemed that I never got an answer. If there was some logical explanation for all of this, at least then I would be able to understand more, but, there was no reason or excuse in the world that would make it right to kill innocent people, especially children.

There was no reason or excuse to say that because a person is Jewish or darker skinned than the next person that it is all right to segregate them from society and label them as "a life not worthy of living." And tell them they cannot share the same trolley bus or tram. That they cannot walk on the same side of the street as the blue-eyed, blonde-haired boy. People are people, whatever their colour or creed. I swore as long as I lived that I would never judge somebody on the colour of his or her skin.

One evening towards the end of July, I was sitting with my mother and Marek over dinner when we were disturbed by a knock at the door. The slight rapping told us that this was not the local Gestapo or Nazi thug, but it still sent Marek scurrying around to my mother's side and set our hearts beating faster. I went round to the window and peered out. "Mama, it is Barak," I called from the sitting room. Barak was a friend of Papa's whom he had known for years; they went to school together and at one time Papa gave him a job when he became down on his luck. My father considered him as one of his most favourite of friends.

"Barak," she said as she cautiously came into the room. I ran to the door and opened it. Barak was there looking thin and ravaged with hunger.

"Barak," I said surprised and happy to him. "Come in."

I led him into the sitting room. Mama greeted him with a kiss.

"Barak. You look terrible. What has become of you, my dear? As if I need to ask, you poor thing." Never one to mince her words was my mother.

"What did they do to you?"

As yet Barak had not said a word. Looking tired and worn out, his face was thin; his grey slacks looked miles too big for him. His brown lace up shoes had holes at the toes. And his hands were cut and bleeding. He looked awful.

"My dear Helena, I am all right. Just a little hungry and tired, but I think I will live after a good hearty meal."

"Come, sit down, Barak. I will fetch you some soup."

"Helena, that is very kind, and I cannot refuse because I am so hungry, but first I must tell you that I have news of Jacob."

"Oh, Barak, tell me. Have you seen him?"

My mother went pale with shock. She sat on the sofa and put her hands together as if to pray to God. I was shaking and was praying in my head, but I didn't know if I really wanted to hear what he had to say or not. My mother was babbling in Yiddish. Saying, "Please God let it be good news."

"He is alive, Helena. A little worse for wear, but he is very much alive."

"Oh, Ohmain. Amen," cried my mother.

"Ayala, did you hear? Papa is alive." We both ran into each other's arms and cried. We were shaking unable to contain our emotions. The relief that I felt was like nothing I had ever felt before. I wanted to jump up and down with joy. Even Marek was jumping up and down with excitement. Which was a joy to see in itself.

"So God was listening, Mama," I said, sobbing with happiness.

My mother clasped my face in her hands. "He is alive, Ayala. He is alive."

Chapter 10

AFTER THE EXCITEMENT AND HYSTERIA OF the unexpected good news had calmed down, Barak told us of how he had been taken from his home at the beginning of the occupation, from there he was taken to a labour camp in Germany. He was treated very badly there. With beatings and punishment handed out at every opportunity.

"There was hardly any food and we had to survive on just a bowl of soup and some coffee each day," he told us.

He was at this camp for nearly six months, when all of a sudden one day he was rounded up with hundreds of other Jews and brought back to Poland. He was taken to a works camp called Belzec, in Lublin. The conditions there were much worse than the camp in Germany. It was at roll call one morning that he happened to look to his left and see my father.

"We could not greet each other until after roll call," he said. "Otherwise." Barak made a sweeping motion with his hand to indicate cutting his throat. This made me shiver and fear for my poor father.

He told us how my father was out looking for food one morning when he was rounded up in the market square and taken to Belzec.

"It was as simple as that," he told us.

"What are they making him do at his camp?" I asked, concerned and scared of what the answer might be.

"We had to build fortifications at the Soviet Union border, and build streets. Hard work. They are slave drivers. We worked 12 hours a day without hardly any food, a little bread in the morning and some foul-smelling soup. We could not protest at this, because they would just shoot you there on the spot. I have seen things there that I never want to see again. The misery of this place must be seen to be believed. There are women actually killing their own babies, rather than watch them starve."

"Oh, enough, Barak, please enough," my mother cried in distress. "I don't want to hear anymore."

I came over to Mama's side and put my arms around her. "It's all right, Mama, Papa is strong. He will not let this happen to him. You'll see."

"Helena, I am so sorry," Barak replied. "I let my tongue run away with me. Please forgive me."

"It's all right, Barak," said Mama. "It's just so distressing, and knowing my Jacob is there. It is too awful for words."

"Helena, he is strong and sensible. He knows what to do to survive."

"Was there any message from him, Barak?" asked my mother.

"Yes, he said not to worry for him, and that he loves you very much, and to tell Ayala and Marek to look after their mama until he returns."

My mother and I both stood there crying. *Oh Papa,* I thought. *I love you so much.*

"How did you get out, Barak?" I asked.

"I escaped after nightfall. It was very dangerous and risky. I only had the chance to do it because the last two weeks we have been building right beside the fence. I dug a hole about three feet long and the same deep. Nobody could tell, because it was along the same works line. So I took my chance late one night. I asked to use the latrines. And took my leave there. I have been travelling all night. I had to sleep in the forest. I am tired and hungry."

"Barak, I will cook you some soup, then you can have a bath and I will sort you out some of Jacobs's clothes. You can have a rest before going on your way again," my mother told him.

"Helena, that is very kind. But I will not stay here too long. I will have to go straight after I have had a rest. It will be dangerous for you if they find me here, and I do not want to put you to any risk."

"OK," replied my mother. "Thank you, Barak, for the news. It is what we have been waiting to hear for so long."

Barak slept for about three hours after a long bath and some soup. Mama gave him some of Papa's clothes like she said she would, and he was on his way. It was good to see a friendly familiar face, and one that brought such good news.

The revelation that my father was alive gave us all a new lease of life. Mama was much more herself. No longer did she lollop around feeling depressed. I think in her mind she expected Papa to just come home any minute, like Barak had done. I tried to explain that Barak had just been very lucky to escape like that, and once they knew that he had escaped they would be on his tail like a dog to a hare. I just hoped that they didn't take it out on the rest of the prisoners, especially Papa.

I was relieved that Papa was alive, but part of me was also more scared than ever. Knowing what Barak had told us about this camp he was in, and that was probably just the tip of the iceberg. All those stories he had told us about women killing their own children made me want to weep; it was almost as unbelievable as it was tragic. *What a disgrace to mankind these Nazis are*, I thought. *What sort of world are we living in, when women so desperate, decide to kill their offspring?*

I tried to put these depressing thoughts out of my mind and concentrate on nicer things. I was still spending a lot of time with Marek, reading and playing with him. He seemed to be coming out of himself more since the news of my father. He was much more alert and more chatty than he had been in a long time. I prayed that this would last. Sometimes it was easy to forget that Marek was there, because of his quietness. This made me feel awful because he must have been going through so much turmoil in his little head.

My role as the strong one, keeping it all together reverted back to being the sixteen-year-old daughter again. My mother was back to being up early in the morning with cereal on the table, and cooking the soup and vegetables in the evening. This was a huge relief to me in one way, as the pressure of the last few weeks had really taken a toll on me. I was tired and irritable, and having to deal with Marek these last few weeks on my own had been hard for me. On the other hand I was worried that Mama had set her sights too high with regards to my father coming home. She had got it into her head that he would be home, when all the work they were making him do had finished. I tried to tell her that, while it was fantastic that Papa was alive, nobody had said that he will be home. I didn't want to burst my mother's bubble, and nobody wanted my father home more than I did, but I was so afraid my mother's hopes would come crashing down around her. But no matter how I tried to tell her she would not listen.

I tried to tell her again over dinner one evening. "Mama, please listen to me. I just don't want you to get your hopes up. Barak never said anything about Papa coming home. He just said that Papa was alive and well."

"Ayala, Papa hasn't done anything wrong. They cannot hold him forever. This fornication or whatever it is they are building, cannot go on indefinitely. Then they will have to release him."

"Mama, nobody has done anything wrong, but that doesn't stop them taking and killing people. It is not about who is right or who is wrong. Papa is Jewish, that is all the reasons and excuses they need. I know that this is wrong, and they will get what is coming to them one day soon, but until then, please do not expect Papa to just walk through the door any minute. All I'm saying is just don't get your hopes up too high. They might not release Papa for a very long time. I just want you to be prepared for that, that's all."

"They will have to release him. Now I know where he is, I will write to the governor and tell him that my husband is an innocent man, and should be released."

"Oh, Mama. You are not listening to me."

"Yes, I am, Ayala. Listen to me. We have to be positive. I cannot go around all day believing that I will never see my husband, the father of my children again. If I did that then I think it might just kill me." My mother started to cry.

"Oh, Mama, I am so sorry. I didn't mean to make you cry. If believing that Papa will be home soon keeps you going through the day, then carry on. Who am I to judge? I was just trying to protect you, that's all."

"I know, dear. I know," she replied, patting my hand. I kissed her cheek and gave her a hug.

Poor Mama, I thought. *How she must be missing my father.* I knew how that felt, as I still missed Isaac so much. There was not a day that went by when I did not think of him, or picture his face in my mind.

I decided not to keep on at Mama any more about her hopes towards my father. We all needed something to get us through this awful time, and if that was what helped Mama sleep at night, then I would not be the one to take that from her.

It was now September, and the war had been on for nearly a year. I had just turned seventeen. It was a strange, quiet affair. There were no celebrations as such. My poor mother couldn't afford to by a present for me, which she felt awful about. It was a rather depressing event. I had no Isaac or Kamila to share it with, and most of all, my father was not here to sing happy birthday to me. My mother did make it as special as she could, with a baked cake and seventeen candles decorating the edges. It was lovely. I told her it could not have been more perfect, and that this was one thing that Hitler could not deprive us of. She liked that. It was on days like these that it hit home just how much our lives had changed, and just how restricted it had become. It made us feel so depressed and low, but no matter how low we felt now, it was nothing compared to the events that were about to unfold in our lives in the next few weeks.

One morning a couple of days after my birthday, I was in the back garden when our neighbour Eliana popped her head over the fence, and called for my mother. Her husband had also been taken to a works camp in the last few weeks and she had been beside herself. We had known Eliana for most of our lives and she had always been a good and loyal neighbour. Mama came out and started chatting to her. I went in to keep Marek occupied. About half an hour later Mama came in looking worried. "What is it, Mama, what is wrong?" I asked as she came in and sat down on the kitchen chair.

"Eliana said that we would have to leave here soon," she told me with tears in her eyes.

"What do you mean?" I quizzed.

Mama took a deep breath. "She told me that she went into town this morning, and that there are posters up everywhere ordering all Jews to relocate elsewhere, by the end of October."

"Relocate to where?"

"To the Jewish quarter. That is what they are calling it."

"I don't understand. Why do they want us to move?"

"I do not know, Ayala." My mother was starting to become irritated.

"I'm sorry, Mama, but I don't understand. That's all."

"All I know is what Eliana has just told me. We have no choice but to go. They want all Jews to live in the same place, away from the rest of the city. That is all I know."

I thought about this a while. "Maybe it might not be as bad as it sounds."

"What do you mean? What is worse than being kicked out of our own home?"

"What I mean is, at least we will be among our own kind, people we can talk to, and we won't be hiding like frightened animals any more."

"Well, I don't like the sound of any of it. It is just another rotten rule that we have to abide by. I am going down to the council tomorrow. I will not be moved from my own home, on account of these monsters."

"Mama, I do not want you going into town. It is dangerous. I will go instead."

"No, Ayala. You have done too much already, darling. I must do this. I want you to stay and look after Marek."

"But, Mama, Papa said that we should all go together or not at all. Remember?"

"Yes, darling, I do, but Papa is not here at the moment, is he? So we must do what we feel is best. Now I don't want you or Marek to go into town. It is so dangerous. I will go. It will be fine."

I could do nothing but agree to her suggestions, even though I hated the thought of her going into such dangerous territory, but if I had to be honest with myself, I did not relish the thought of going back there. The last visit into town was still very fresh in my mind.

The next morning Mama got up and left for the town.

"I don't know how long I will be," she told us. "The last time I went there with Papa, we were there for hours, so many people lodging complaints. So do not worry, Ayala, OK? Just look after Marek and remember not to answer the door to anyone."

"OK, Mama. I won't."

She kissed us goodbye and I watched her walk up the road, just like I did with Papa that fateful morning. I just prayed that Mama would not meet the same fate as my poor papa.

The day passed slowly. I was watching the clock every minute and praying that Mama would return soon. I was so scared for her. I played football with Marek outside in the garden. The weather was much milder now that it was autumn, but it was still warm enough for a kick about outside. When he had become bored of that, we came in and played with his train set. It was now four o'clock and I was starting to become very edgy, as my mother had been gone for hours now. When she came through the door, I ran up to her and threw my arms around her. I was so relieved to see her.

"Well, Mama," I asked, "how did it go?"

"Oh, Ayala," she said desperately. "It is no good. We have no choice. We have to move as soon as possible. Eliana was right. They are moving everyone into the Jewish quarter. Then they will take our house, and we cannot do a thing about it. What is more, we cannot even take all our possessions. We can only take bed linen, along with jewels and the clothes on our backs."

"Oh, Mama," I cried. "Could it get any worse?"

"I do not know, Ayala. I would like to think not, but I do not know anymore."

On the 31st October 1940 we moved into the Jewish quarter. And of course it could and was about to get much worse.

Chapter 11

The Warsaw Ghetto

THE DAY OF OUR MOVE CAME round quick. We had been dreading it. The day before we had sorted out our personal things like clothes and jewellery. We were told that we could only take the essential items that we needed. It was hard for me to decide what items I valued more than others, as I had so many things that were sentimental to me. There were dresses that Mama and Papa had bought for me, and dolls that I'd had since I was a little girl. And of course there was my beautiful pendant that Isaac had bought me on the last Chanukah we had spent together. There was no competition where that was concerned. That had been around my neck since the day I had been given it, and it wasn't coming off. I searched my wardrobe for things I thought I might need in the Jewish quarter, such as a warm jumper and overcoat. As I mulled over the coats and jumpers that I had not worn for years, I stumbled upon something which immediately brought tears to my eyes and brought painful memories flooding back. There it was hanging in all its glory; the green swing dress that Kamila had given me to wear for the school dance. I felt a mixture of intense sadness and extreme anger as I stood there with my face buried in it, still smelling of the perfume I had worn that night. I was a mixture of emotions, of sadness and grief of a happiness I had once known, and anger at such harsh betrayal from a best friend that I had once loved like a sister. My mind strayed back to the night of the dance, and the excitement of going out for the evening for the first time and how grown-up I felt. I remember Kamila telling me how lovely I looked in my dress, and how she told me I could keep it because I was her best friend. I swallowed hard and tried to fight back the tears as I remembered seeing Isaac coming across the dance floor towards me, looking handsome in his black tuxedo, and how he felt the first time we danced. *Oh, Isaac,* I cried to myself, *how I wish you were here. Oh, how I wish I could hold your hand or touch your face. It would be so much easier to deal with all this if you were here.* I was sobbing now, big wet tears staining my face and leaving wet patches on the green dress, all the months of worrying and fretting. The grief over losing Isaac and the uncertainty of my father's whereabouts just came to the fore all of a sudden. The anger over Kamila, it just became too much.

All of a sudden I heard my mother's voice behind me. "Ayala, darling. What is wrong?" I came back to my senses and just stood there staring in a sort of daze. I felt my mother's arms around me squeezing me gently and whispering in my ear, "It is all right, Ayala, It is all right."

"Oh, Mama, it is not all right, is it? Look what is happening to us. Things are just getting worse and worse. First of all I lose Isaac then Papa. Now we are losing our home and we have to go and live in a ghetto, and God knows what will become of us."

"Ayala, be strong. We have to keep strong to get through this. I know what you are saying is correct, I cannot tell you that everything will be OK, because I do not know. You are a woman now and I cannot lie to you anymore, but all I can say is that we have to keep fighting and being strong for each other. We will get through this, Ayala. We will." My mother's voice was soft and calm, almost sedative. What would I do without my wonderful mother?

"Mama, I am trying to be strong, but these last months have just been so hard, what with Papa going and Marek being so unstable. It has just got on top of me, that's all."

"Ayala, darling, I am not saying you cannot cry. You have to have a release. We all do, what I'm saying is that you have to keep strong inside."

"OK, Mama."

"I will leave you to finish what you were doing."

"Mama," I called after her. "I love you."

"I love you too, Ayala."

"Mama," I called again.

"Yes, darling."

"Have you got a pair of scissors?"

She looked at me puzzled. "Yes, why do you need them?"

"Oh, I just need to do something to make me feel better," I said.

Mama brought up the scissors, and left me to my privacy.

I turned back to my wardrobe, pulled out the green swing dress and began to cut away at it. With every slash I made, another memory of Kamila had been cut from my mind. I had my memories of Isaac; I didn't need a reminder of the person who had helped make our situation as bad as it was today. It was people like Kamila and her family who had voted for Hitler. I didn't want to be reminded of what that meant for us.

I finished my packing, which consisted of two warm jumpers, an overcoat and the blankets from my bed. I took some pictures of my father, and some of us all together. I wished I'd had a picture of Isaac too. It hurt like hell to leave all my personal things behind especially when I knew I was leaving them to those Nazi idiots.

Mama never asked what it was I wanted the scissors for; she respected the fact that as a grown-up there were things I needed to keep private. She had told me I was a woman now. I liked that. I was now seventeen, but in the last year I felt like I had grown much older. This is not the life a seventeen-year-old should be living. I was worried about Mama. She was destroyed at having to leave the house that she had spent so many happy years, the house where she had given birth to her children. She was extremely worried that when Papa came home he would not know where to find us. I told her that he wouldn't have any problems finding us, as it was common knowledge that all the Jews would now be in this part of the town. We were dreading our departure to the Jewish quarter. I knew that Nazis ran these places. I also knew what happened to the Jews in them. My poor Uncle Reuben had been killed in the Lodz ghetto just a few months before. My mother remembered this as much as I did, but we never mentioned this to one another. When I thought about it, I wondered how hard it would be. I mean, could it be any worse than our situation we were in now? We were scared to go out. We were harassed and humiliated in the street, and people who were once our friends now shunned us. Maybe being amongst our own would be easier for us.

We had left it right up until the deadline date of the 31st October before we left, simply because we were hoping in vain that by some miracle things might change before then, and we also knew that as soon as we were out, some Nazi slob would be in our house using our things and sleeping in our beds. This was our house and what right did anyone have to just come in and take it away, but there was nothing anyone could do about it.

The morning of our move to the Jewish quarter was here. We were all nervous and anxious as to what would happen. Mama was in the kitchen with Marek, when I pulled back the curtains in the sitting room. I gasped in shock as I looked out and saw hundreds of people, all with their belongings and family members marching past our house. Over the other side of the street, people were being pulled from their homes by the Nazis and thrown into the crowd. There was a lot of shouting and crying as people were being forced from their homes.

I called Mama in from the kitchen, she came in and herself gasped in horror at the scene before her. "Quick, Ayala. Let's go before they come here." Shaking and crying, we all got our bundles and bags together, and ran outside. We joined the screaming rows of people and started walking. It was so very humiliating as we huddled together and were frogmarched to the end of our street by the Nazis. It was raining and cold, which added to our misery. Marek was crying as we walked, and Mama was trying to comfort him. Every now and again she asked if I was all right. I was trembling with fear as every minute somebody else was thrown into the crowd crying.

As we neared the end of my street I looked over to where Kamila's house was. I was stunned to see her with her parents standing by their front door watching the misery of us poor Jews. I looked at her as I walked on and refused to believe that I was once a friend to this girl. I was hurting and felt so humiliated at seeing her watch us leave our street. What hurt the most was there was not an ounce of guilt or sympathy for me, or anyone in this crowd of misery and pain. I could not fathom how somebody could change so much.

Every so often we would hear someone cry out in pain as they were beaten or hit with the butt of one of the Nazis machine guns I tried not to look up as I heard the blows from their rifles. "Keep your head down, Ayala," I would hear my mother say. My poor darling little brother was absolutely terrified. There were lots of children like him who were afraid, and nobody seemed to care.

After what seemed like hours we entered the ghetto. We had to report to the Jewish council to be allocated our apartments. It was chaotic. There were hundreds of families waiting to be seen. We waited for hours. When we were eventually given the address to our apartment we headed straight for it. Marek was completely in pieces and I was emotionally drained. Mama was tired and we were all hungry. It was now quite late in the afternoon and it was starting to get dark. We got to our apartment, which was on the first floor of a block of flats. The door was open so we just walked in. We heard voices coming from inside. We walked through to the sitting room and were astonished to find that there were already at least nine people living in there, going by the made-up beds on the floor. It was overcrowded with two makeshift beds on one side next to an old disused fireplace, a cot with a baby crying pitifully on the other, an elderly gentleman sitting on a pile of clothes in the corner. There was a man and woman on the floor in the middle half asleep and looking frail, and a woman cooking over a little stove in the opposite corner of the room. It was madness. Mama apologised and said that we must have the wrong apartment. There was laughter as she said this. "Why do you have a special penthouse just for you around here somewhere?" asked the elderly man sitting in the corner of the room.

"What do you mean?" answered my mother sharply.

"We are lucky. There are only nine of us here. Next door there are fifteen," said the man. Suddenly the reality of our situation hit us like a ton of bricks.

"Oh, Gracious God," whispered my mother under her breath.

"Oh, Mama, what shall we do?" I asked her.

"I shall go back to the Judenrat tomorrow and sort something out, but tonight we will have to stay here."

"But, Mama, there is no room, and where will we sleep?"

"We will have to sleep in here with everybody else. There is some space over there in the corner, I will lay some bedding down and we will just have to sit quietly there for tonight."

"You cannot sleep there, that is Edith's place. She is at work and will be back soon. You will have to sleep in the passage," said the elderly gentleman again.

"But what about my children?" replied my mother. "They cannot sleep in a cold passage."

"Look around you. Do you see any spare room? The whole Jewish population is living in this way, this is the ghetto. Stop moaning about your troubles, woman. Just think we could all be dead tomorrow."

Marek gave a scared whimper and held on tight to Mama's hand.

"How dare you say such things to me, and especially in front of my children? You miserable old fool."

"Mama, please just ignore him. He is an old man. Don't let him bother you," I said, trying to calm the situation down.

"You are the one that is miserable. It is a hard life, just get on with it like everybody else has to," replied the miserable old man. Mama looked at him as if to kill, and gave a sigh.

"Come, you two. Let's make ourselves comfortable in the passage. We will sort this out in the morning, I promise you."

We made up our beds, which consisted of a couple of blankets each, on top of our coats. The floor was freezing cold. It was now almost November, so the winter was here in its full glory, and would only get worse as the weeks went on. We sat down and wrapped the blankets around us. Marek was tired so we let him lay flat out on the floor with some blankets over him. It was late and we had not eaten. Mama said first thing in the morning, she would go and find a soup kitchen and get us some food. So this was our new home. Our resettlement as Hitler so politely put it. *What was to become of us now?* I thought as I sat there in that freezing cold hallway snuggled up to Mama to keep warm.

We are destitute, and we have no money or food. What would my poor father do if he knew we were living like this? It would probably kill him. I looked at Mama, who was sitting staring into space. Today had aged her. Today they had made my mother and my brother, the people I loved most in the world, homeless and frightened. They had taken our home and marched us to this morbid, frightening place. Mama said she would sort it out tomorrow and find us somewhere else to live. She knew as well as I did that there was nowhere else, as the miserable old man had said. This was it. This was the ghetto.

Chapter 12

1941

JANUARY DESCENDED UPON US ONCE AGAIN. We had been in the ghetto for three months. Life was extremely hard and depressing all round. Christmas and New Year doesn't exist in the ghetto. We didn't even have a candle to light for Chanukah. It was soul destroying. It was worse for the children as the holiday season is a time for them. It was tragic. As we both knew Mama did not find us anywhere else to live. She was laughed out of the council offices. So we resided here at the one bed roomed apartment that housed all eleven of us. It was absolute hell. It was heavily overcrowded, with four children including a poor little baby girl that was constantly hungry and crying; an elderly couple; a young woman on her own with her two small children, a four-year-old boy, and a twelve-year-old girl; two middle-aged men; and of course Mama, me and Marek. We all had our own stories of sadness and grief. There was not one person in our apartment that had not lost someone to the war. The apartment was constantly cold and damp with no heating or electric. Because of the overcrowding there was a constant stream of people coming and going all hours of the day and night. We were still sleeping in the cold passage. The smell of so many people living so closely together without proper cleaning facilities was overbearing. We tried to stay out of the apartment as much as we could, but the fear of being out on the street was worse here than it had been in our old town.

They had built a ten-foot wall around the ghetto, which from the end of November had been sealed shut. So now we were cut off from the world. They had guards and police at every gate and entrance, there were Nazis or SS as they were also known everywhere you looked, and at every turn. There was constant feeling of terror. It is impossible to comprehend the feeling of unbearable fear and anxiety at every waking moment. There were beatings and shootings all the time. The sound of gunshots going off was something one became accustomed to in the end. At first the mere sound of anything that sounded remotely like a gun sent us scurrying into a corner with our hands above our heads, and left us shaking and fearful, until the next shot rang out. Now it was just a part of our daily lives. We just got used to it. Food was another big problem. We were allowed about three hundred grams of sugar a month and about two hundred grams of bread a day. It was not enough to feed one person let alone three of us. We were constantly queuing at the soup kitchen for a small piece of bread and some vegetable soup. Smuggling was rife in the ghetto; I did not have the courage or the means or contacts to do this. People could not possibly live on the meagre rations that were being handed out. So smuggling in food was the only option. The punishment for this crime was death, but it was the only way for people to survive. Hunger was the driving force for everybody's crimes. It was terrible to see old people and children, begging on the street or selling off their sentimental valuables, just for a piece of bread. People were becoming weaker and more desperate through hunger all the time. After another long wait at the soup kitchen one day, I told Mama my decision to find employment. There were plenty of factories in the ghetto; these were owned by the Germans, but run by Jews. The wages were tiny because money had no value in the ghetto. Mama was totally against this at first, telling me that no way was she going to let me risk my life in some factory; working my fingers to the bone for a piece of bread.

"But, Mama, we are getting thinner by the day, and we need to eat. We must keep our strength up. We cannot rely on the soup kitchen, Mama, it may not always be there," I told her one afternoon.

"Then I must go, Ayala. It is not fair to put so much responsibility on your shoulders. I will worry about you, and besides if it were not for this wicked war, you would have a nice job doing something you love instead of working in a factory for a small ration of food."

"Mama, we have no choice. This is the situation, and we must just deal with it. It is hard I know, but we have to do what we can to survive."

"My Ayala, how you have grown into such a beautiful sensible woman. Your father would be so proud of you." She started to cry.

I put my arms around her, and could feel how thin she had become over the last few months. I was worried about my beautiful mother. She had not eaten in two days. The last time we had gone to the soup kitchen, there had been hardly anything left, so she had given Marek her share. This made me all the more determined that finding a job was the only option.

"Mama," I said. "I am going to get a job and there is nothing you can do to stop me. I do not want you to go, as you will need to look after Marek; you know what he is like if you are not here." She objected until she was worn out, but it was no use. I had made up my mind.

The next day I went round the factories and just when I was all about to give up, I found employment in a sewing factory, making uniforms for the German army. It was backbreaking work, and the conditions were unbearable with broken chairs to sit on all day and an old sewing machine that didn't work properly. The hours were long and hard, from six in the morning till seven at night. The wage was barely enough to feed a small cat, but it was something. A small lunch was supplied at the factory, so I ate this, and that was my meal for the day. With my tiny earnings, I bought some food from the smugglers to feed Mama and Marek.

Marek was a constant worry to us. He went back to being quiet and withdrawn; he was such a sensitive and nervous boy. It broke our hearts to see him this way. He was very tearful and clung to Mama like glue all of the time. The children in our apartment tried to involve him in their games and would talk to him, but he never budged, he just wanted to be near Mama or me. The fear for all of us was overpowering, even for us adults, but to a ten-year-old boy it must have been terrorising. We tried to do our best to make him feel better, but what could we do when we were constantly scared out of our wits ourselves. It was awful.

The situation in the ghetto was changing every day, with new rules and regulations; just as it had been on the outside. People were miserable and sad all of the time. It was a place of pure anxiety, loss and grief. Hunger was the biggest part of that misery. Food was the constant topic of conversation; it was becoming harder to obtain food all the time. We were all becoming much thinner and weaker every day. It occurred to me one day exactly what they were trying to do to us all. They were systematically trying to kill us off through starvation and slave labour. The realisation sent shock waves right through me, leaving me numb. *Why, oh God?* I thought. *Why?*

One day coming home from the factory, I saw a sign outside a shop advertising a concert in Mirokski Square. I decided that we all needed to get out and try and have some fun. After these last few months I thought we deserved it. I told Mama about my plan.

"Ayala, this is not a time for fun, we should be concentrating on where our next meal is coming from, not gallivanting around going to dances."

"It is not a dance, Mama. It is a concert, with opera singers and musicians. And we are not gallivanting, we are just getting out of here and trying to relax a little, that is all."

"Huhh. How can one relax with those murderers on our backs, watching our every move all the time?"

"Relax. Ha," interrupted Abraham, the elderly man who lived in our apartment.

"Oh, shut up, Abraham. I was not talking to you," I snapped back sharply. "And do not talk like that in front of my brother."

"Young people these days. Have no manners," he grunted as he shuffled out of the room.

"Do not take any notice of him. He is just a miserable old man," the mother of the two young children in our apartment said. "And you should go, Helena. Go and enjoy yourself. You deserve it."

"OK, I will go," she gave in. "But only if Marek is OK about it. I do not want to put him under any extra pressure."

"I'm sure he will be fine," I replied excitedly. "Where is Marek, Mama? I just realised he is not here."

"He is in the apartment next door. He has made friends with the little boy in there. It took me such a long time to convince him that I would not be gone when he came back, and I have had to go in there three times to make sure he is OK."

"Mama, I am so pleased. It is about time Marek made a friend; he needs a release just like we all do."

The concert was a breath of fresh air. The music was good and it was nice to get out of the stinking apartment, and do something normal. We decided that we would do this again as long as health and vitality allowed. It had been a long time since we had been out as a family, but then we were only half a family now, as my father was not there to join in the fun with us. This was sad for us, and I could see Mama thinking the same thing. It had been a long time since that day when Barak had come to the apartment and told us that Papa was alive, almost a year. I had wondered recently if Papa was still alive and if so where he would be now and what sort of condition he would be in. I know Mama had these same thoughts, but we never really spoke about them. Sometimes in a way I was glad he was not here. He would have been totally broken up to see us living like this, like a family of alley cats, living in a cold passage. I missed my father so much. Sometimes I tried to picture his face and was horrified to find that I could not remember it. This upset me greatly, and I had to resort to looking at the photograph that I kept in my pocket. I treasured this picture as it was the last one I had of him and me together, it was taken on my fifteenth birthday in the back garden of our house. He is smiling and we are arm in arm. I almost stand as tall as him, as I was tall for my age at fifteen. Oh how I hoped to see my wonderful papa again someday.

June was here now and the weather was sweltering. The ghetto and its inhabitants had taken a turn for the worse. There was now a curfew enforced. All inhabitants must not be on the street between seven pm and seven am. The penalty for not obeying these rules was death. This was a blow to us, as we enjoyed our nights out at the concert. The Germans enjoyed taking any little piece of enjoyment away that we had. But in the end people got used to rules being enforced and things being taken away. The physical situation in the ghetto was also getting worse by the day. I had lost a lot of weight since I had been in the ghetto; Mama had lost considerably more, which worried me so much. I had started to save some of my lunch from the factory to share with her when I got in. She scolded me for this when she found out.

"Ayala, you must not deprive yourself of the little food you are given. You are losing too much weight as it is. I will not let you do this to yourself."

"I am fine, Mama, stop worrying. You need it more than I do. You have lost much more weight than I have, and besides I am young I can afford to lose a few pounds," I said, trying to make light of the situation.

"Cheeky girl," Mama laughed. "I am serious. I do not want you to do it. You need to keep your strength up."

"And so do you, Mama." I looked at my mother. I was becoming increasingly alarmed at the amount of weight she had lost recently. She looked old and her beautiful long hair now had wispy streaks of grey in it. Marek too had lost a lot of weight; he was never a big boy for his age as it was. There were lots of children like Marek now. It was heart wrenching to watch. I thought I had seen all there was to see in this poverty-stricken part of town. Until one day on my way home from the factory, I came across something that to this day will remain with me till the day I die.

I was coming home from the factory one evening. I was rushing as I was late and it was nearly past the curfew time. Nobody walked in the ghetto, everybody rushed to get into work or out, otherwise punishment would be the severest. As I was rushing along I noticed what looked like a small bundle lying on the ground outside a pharmacy shop. It was small and wrapped in a brown coloured blanket. Nobody seemed to be taking any notice of it; people were just walking by so I thought nothing of it at first. Just as I was approaching it, I saw it move. I looked closer and to my utter horror; there lying on the ground was a tiny little boy, he looked to be about four years old.

He could have been older or younger; it was hard to tell as he was so emaciated. He was lying on his back with his right arm outstretched; he was breathing heavily, but still trying to say something. I could not make out exactly what it was he was trying to say, but I knew that he was trying to beg for food. I gasped in shock. I could not believe what I was seeing, his tiny boy in the throws of death. I just stood there stunned. I was crying and shaking. His face looked like an old man, thin, his eyes were sunken in and were darker than anything I had ever seen. His little body was contorted and bent in an awkward position; his eyes were just staring, as if they had already died. I bent down and touched his face. I knew that he was taking his last breath. Everything around me just seemed to disappear, as if we were the only ones on the street. I stroked his forehead and told him in a gentle voice to close his eyes.

"It is all right, little one," I said, sobbing with grief. "I will not leave you to die on your own. I will stay here with you." He must have understood everything I had said because with that he closed his eyes while I was stroking his face, and took his last breath. I held my breath, as if it was I who was dying. I was crying bitterly, great big sobs, my chest heaving in and out. My tears and emotions were uncontrollable. I stood up and looked around me. I was back on the street again with people walking by, as if there had not been a little boy in the street that had just died. I could not believe that people just didn't care, that they didn't even stop and hold this boy's dear little hand as he took his last breath. I do not know if it was shock or just disgust, but all of a sudden I started shouting at people.

"What is wrong with everyone? How can you just walk by, as if nothing is happening? How can you watch a child die, and not even be moved by it? What has gone wrong with the world?"

I grabbed hold of someone's arm, a man rushing by. "LOOK!" I screamed. "LOOK AT THIS. THIS IS A DEAD CHILD. DO YOU NOT CARE? THIS COULD BE YOUR SON!"

All of a sudden the man pulled his arm away. "Stop it, young girl. You will get us all killed. Go home. Go on your way. There is nothing you can do for him now." Then he just walked off. Just then I could see two German soldiers who were standing by the entrance to a coffee shop. They started to look over and became interested in what was going on. I knew what would happen to me if I stayed there. I bent down and removed the blanket from under the dead child's body. I gently placed it over his face. I took one more look at him and said a prayer. I then went on my way, still with the dead child's face firmly in my mind.

Chapter 13

THE IMAGE OF THE LITTLE BOY was firmly etched in my mind for a long time. I could not get his little face out of my head. A thousand questions I asked myself following that night. *Where were his parents? Why was he just left to die like that on the street? And where had people's compassion and sympathy gone? Had Hitler managed to take that as well?* I had never seen a dead body before, never watched someone die right there in front of my eyes. It was a strange but surreal experience, but I'm glad with all of my heart that I did, even though the picture haunted me like a ghost that could not rest. I'm glad that I was there to hold his hand.

Mama cried, Esther cried. We all cried together when I told them what I had seen that night. The strange thing was that I was not hysterical or even shaking when I got back to the apartment. I think I had let all my anger out on the people in town, but I think it was mainly the shock from it all. Mama said she was so proud of me. "My darling, you are a very special person. God has chosen you to do his work here. I know that now. You have such courage. Papa would be so proud."

"Mama, it does not take courage to watch a child die. I just knew I could not leave him. I don't understand how all those people could just walk by without a care in the world. It is so wrong."

"I think people are just scared, Ayala. They know what will happen if they try to intervene with anything. The SS will kill or shoot you for any reason. You were very brave, Ayala, but maybe a little silly too. You risked your life."

"Mama, I didn't even think about it. I just could not walk by. I just couldn't. He was so little; he had nobody there for him, so I had to do it."

I started crying again. The more I tried the more I could not find a good enough excuse or reason as to why children had to suffer in this war. I kept thinking back to the two German officers that had been standing by the entrance to the coffee shop that day. How long had they stood and watched that little boy suffer? Why did it not move them beyond tears? I wondered if they had children themselves, and if they had, did they go home each night knowing full well the atrocities they caused. Did they not realise or care that this little boy was somebody's son or grandson? Of course they didn't. They were not men. They were machines. They had no feeling or any human decency. They were a shame to the human race. They were a shame to all men. I could not understand how God could create such evilness. It was totally beyond me.

"Ayala, you must try and stop thinking about it, you did a wonderful thing, but there is no more you can do now, so fretting and getting yourself all mixed up will not change anything."

"I know, Mama, but it is hard to forget."

"You will never forget, Ayala, but you will learn to live with it, and just get on with your life at the same time. You will."

Mama was right, I had to get it out of my head, but I knew that it would haunt me forever.

Sadly the prospect of getting any such thoughts from my mind was very small. The incident with the little boy was not an isolated one. During the next few weeks, events in the ghetto turned. All of a sudden everywhere you looked, people seemed to get weaker and weaker, they just turned into zombies, shuffling along trying to put one foot in front of the other. Those that were too weak just sat on the street, where they fell. All along the kerbside were bodies lying either dead or dying from hunger and thirst. Most of these poor victims were children, having been too small to fight the hunger for too long. The elderly were also vulnerable to this wicked twist of fate. I am ashamed to admit that after a while, seeing bodies of children lying dead on the street, or being carted away in a wheelbarrow on top of other dead children became part of the ghetto life. When we saw such things, we just had to look away, for there was nothing we could do about it. If a Nazi saw someone intervene, they would just shot him or her on the spot. So shamefully I became one of those passers-by, who just looked and walked away, but the things that I saw in that place of hell still haunts me to this day. I may have looked away but the images that I saw will be a permanent photograph in my mind for eternity. It is like having a built-in photo album in my head that never closes. Along with the emaciated bodies and dead children, I had become an unwilling witness to the mass of shootings and barbaric treatment that were handed down to many of the inhabitants of the ghetto. Again this became normality in the life of a Warsaw ghetto Jew. I knew that it was only a matter of time before the rifle was pointed at our heads. I came to expect it, to sort of wait for it so to speak. I had changed so much since coming to this hell on earth. I was no longer gentle and sensitive. Neither was I shy or afraid anymore. I could not afford to be, otherwise I would not be bold enough to beg for food, or jump the queue at the soup kitchen. Yes, I was now a beggar, one of the poor victims I had witnessed only months before. I was now a poor, poverty-stricken Jew. Oh how Hitler would revel in his success at turning vermin into vermin. I soon would be motherless and brotherless if this went on any more, which I knew it would do. There was no end in sight of this misery.

I was frantically worried about Mama; she had lost so much weight that she just lay on the bedding in the hallway all day long. I did not know what to do. I cried myself to sleep every night, wondering if this hell would ever end. Marek too was desperately thin now, and he had developed a hacking cough. The situation in our apartment was getting desperate. We were still lying in the damp passage. The apartment was still overcrowded, and the smell was nauseating especially in the sweltering heat. Abraham, the elderly man in our apartment, was sick; he had constant diarrhoea and was being sick all the time. We all knew that he was not long for this world; he was so frail and weak. We had told ourselves that when he died we would have his place in the sitting room. We would also have his blankets, and clothing. See that's what they turned us into. They turned us into people who were not moved by death anymore; in fact, the death of someone, as long as it was not your own, was seen as a blessing, because one could always use that person's belongings, such as their ration card or clothes and blankets. It was not unusual to see the dead bodies on the street naked, for as soon as a person died so the scavengers came out of hiding, and would strip the body of every last item, even down to underwear. That is what they turned us into; grave robbers. Vermin into vermin.

Halfway through the summer, my worst fears came to the fore. My little brother Marek got very sick. We were all so worried for him. His cough had got considerably worse, and he was being sick, and running a high fever. We woke up one morning to find him limp and lifeless under his blanket. Mama was shot to pieces with worry. "Marek, darling, wake up, it's Mama."

Marek just lay there motionless. He made a small groan in the back of his throat, but did not answer.

"Mama, what are we going to do? He looks so sick. Oh God, Mama, I knew he wasn't right. I knew that this was going to happen. I just knew it. Marek, wake up. Marek it's me, Ayala. Come on, darling, wake up now." Still he said nothing, just lay there groaning. "Oh, Mama, what shall we do? What shall we do?"

"Ayala, for God's sake calm down, you are making it worse. Just stop babbling, I need to think!" Mama shouted at me agitated. I gulped back the tears; I hated it when Mama was cross with me.

"OK, we need to get him to a doctor. I don't think we can wait."

"But, Mama, how will we get him there? The hospital is about five blocks away. He will never be able to walk it."

"OK, I shall go outside and look for a wheelbarrow or cart. I will ask someone. They may lend me one."

"Maybe Marek's friend next door. Maybe they will have something. I will go and ask." I went to the apartment next door, they could not help us. Then I went out onto the street and asked anyone I could find on the street for a cart or wheelbarrow, people just shook their heads, and some just ignored me. After a while I went back to the apartment and told Mama I could not find anyone to help us.

"Then we will have to carry him ourselves. We need to get him there soon." Mama was crying, and pacing up and down.

"Mama, it is blocks away. We cannot carry him there in this heat. We are too weak for that. We will never make it."

"Yes, we will. Now come on, Ayala, we haven't got much time. He is very sick. Please." Mama started to pick him up. "Marek, darling, we are going to get you to a doctor, OK, darling? It will be all right."

"Mama," groaned Marek. "Mama."

"What is it, darling?" Mama replied with tears streaming down her face.

"My tummy, Mama. It hurts."

"I know, darling, but we are going to make it better."

"Mama," I said concerned. "Do you know how far the hospital is from here? What if we get stopped, or we can't carry him any farther?"

"Well, what do you suggest? Leave him here and just watch him waste away."

"Mama," I cried. "I'm just worried that's all."

"I know, Ayala. I'm sorry. Let's just try, OK?"

"OK, Mama."

We left for the hospital with Mama carrying Marek. It was a stifling hot day without even a breeze to cool us down. We took turns to carry Marek, changing over when he began to feel heavy in our arms. He was so poorly. I was desperately worried for him. He looked so bad. He didn't even know what was happening to him; every now and again he would wake up and moan or cry. He looked so frail; his little legs were just skin and bone.

We had been walking for about an hour by now. In normal circumstances the journey to the hospital would only take twenty minutes, but carrying a sick child, and being so thin and weak ourselves, it took double the time. We had to stop every couple of minutes to catch our breaths.

Eventually we got to the hospital. We could not believe how many people were in there. There were two people to every bed. It was awful. Marek looked worse than ever, he had gone deathly pale and was completely unconscious. As soon as we got there, a young nurse took Marek to a bed at the end of the ward. It already had a little boy in it, who also looked deathly sick. The nurse put Marek in at the other end. We followed closely. Not taking our eyes of him for a second. The hospital was packed full of sick and dying people. The nurse examined Marek then undressed him and put him into bed.

"What is wrong with him?" Mama asked anxiously.

"Well, he is running a fever, and his is very malnourished. The doctor will be round in the morning, to give him some tests."

"Does he have typhus?" asked Mama. "Oh God, please don't say he has typhus," she said, making the sign of the cross over her chest.

"It is possible, there is an epidemic in the ghetto at the moment, but I won't know for sure until the doctor sees him."

"Oh, dear God," Mama cried.

"Go home, and come back in the morning. I'm sure we will have more news for you then."

"We're not going anywhere," I said abruptly. "He is my little brother, and we shall not leave him."

"Please," begged the nurse. "If an officer walks in here, and finds you idly sitting by, you know what will happen."

Mama shook her head in disgust. "So a mother cannot even sit with her sick child," she said, in her strong Yiddish accent, which always came out more when she was upset.

"Come on, Mama," I said, putting my arm around her bony shoulder. "It isn't the nurse's fault; she is just like us, trying to obey the rules. Let's go home and we will come back first thing in the morning. At least Marek is in the right place."

We bent down and kissed his hot cheek. He didn't respond. Just lay there asleep.

We didn't sleep at all that night; our thoughts were full of Marek. I thought of my father a lot and wondered how he would react to all that has happened to us. I wasn't so sure if he was even alive anymore. I asked Mama a few days ago, and she told me that she prayed with all her heart that her beloved Jacob was alive, but she felt in her heart that he was dead. She didn't cry or show any emotion. She just said it as blunt as that. It wasn't that she didn't care anymore; it was a matter of trying to protect her from any more pain.

Morning finally came. We got up and went straight to the hospital. It was another blisteringly hot day. There were more dead bodies on the street and more zombies walking around half dead. We were becoming one of those zombies now, as we had not eaten a thing in two whole days. We looked terribly thin. We were not as fast on our legs now either, so walking was hard for us. *I will have some of Esther's soup today*, I thought. Esther was an angel; she hardly had anything herself, just enough to feed her and her two children, but she always offered us a small bowl, which we always declined. Esther's financial situation was a little better than ours. Her husband thought ahead and left her quite a bit of money to survive in the event that he was taken to a labour camp. She hid it under floorboards of her home and then brought it here. She hid it someplace in the apartment, so that nobody could steel it, this helped her get things like vegetables and bread. The price of bread in the ghetto was phenomenal, so her money must have been going down quick, but today I told Mama, we were both going to have some of Esther's soup, and we would also go the women's soup kitchen on the way back from the hospital.

My stomach was turning over as we got to the hospital. I felt nervous and afraid as I walked down the ward. I noticed that Marek was not in the bed that we left him in yesterday. Mama noticed the same time. "Ayala, he is not here."

"Maybe he is having the tests that the nurse talked about," I said.

We stood by the bed waiting for someone to come through. Suddenly the nurse we had seen before appeared.

"Where is my son, nurse? Is he having tests?" my mother asked nervously.

The nurse stared at us blankly, and then put her head down. I started to tremble. My heart was pounding. "Please, nurse, tell us what is happening. Where is my brother?" I asked, now panicking.

The nurse looked up with tears in her eyes. "I regret to inform you but your brother passed away in the night. There was nothing we could do."

I felt like somebody just hit me with a spade across the face.

"I'm sorry," my mother said slowly, trying to take it in. "You have made a mistake. You cannot be talking about *my* son."

"I am so sorry, Mrs Bergman, we did our best, but your son was very sick."

The nurse said this with such sympathy and compassion. I just burst into tears. Sobbing, I stood there as the waves of shock went through me. Then I heard my mother screaming as she fell to the floor and passed out.

Chapter 14

THE NEWS OF MAREK'S DEATH WAS the hardest, most devastating news that we could have ever imagined. It would not sink in. Mama was hysterical with grief, totally demented. The hospital gave her a sedative to calm her down. I took her home and Esther made us some soup. She too was shocked and saddened by the news of Marek's death. Mama would not drink hers. All she kept saying was, "Marek, Marek. My baby boy." I tried to console her as much as I could, but I was too wrapped up in my own grief. The hospital told us that Marek had died of typhus, an epidemic that was now taking the lives of many of the ghetto dwellers. This was due to the terrible sanitary conditions and overcrowding in the ghetto. The thought that we might now get this as well was on our minds, but we did not care. After Marek's death I honestly did not care if I lived or died. Death would have been my saviour. *Who wants to carry on living like this, like sewer rats, who nobody cared for?* I thought. *Where was the rest of the world? Did they not know what was happening to us here? Why had nobody come and tried to save us?* It was like the world had turned its backs on us. The worst most devastating part of it all was that we could not even afford to give my darling baby brother a proper funeral. We had absolutely no money whatsoever. They had taken away everything we had, even our wishes to bury my Marek in a decent grave with the respect he deserved. Instead of that we had to bury him in the hospital garden, in an unmarked grave with just a rose to decorate the top. We were lucky to even have that. It was not the usual procedure to bury someone on the hospital grounds, but the young nurse took such pity on us that she risked her life to be able to make this happen. I was very grateful to her for that. We said our prayers and asked God to look after him. The whole thing lasted about ten minutes, and then we went home. We couldn't even hold a wake for the poor little mite.

Mama was hysterical and quite made with grief for Marek. I was totally numb. Part of me couldn't quite believe that I had actually lost my baby brother. Sometimes I would wake up in the night, and think that it had all been a bad dream, then suddenly reality would hit me, and the pain and grief would start again. I thought how my father would take the news if he ever came home, but he was most probably dead anyway. If he was alive then this tragic piece of news would kill him.

I missed Marek so much, even though he was a quiet little boy, the apartment was still and empty without him. His death was so tragic, but I know that it would have been such a release for him too. He had spent the last few years in absolute terror of the Nazis, scared to move and living as Mama's shadow. *You have nothing to fear now, my darling. Nobody will harm you now*, I thought. Who are these Nazis? What demonic hold do they have over everybody? They are just men at the end of the day. What gives them the right to presume that they are superior to everybody else? How I hated them. How I hoped that they would burn in hell for the pain and suffering that they had caused us all. If there was a God at all I hoped that he was planning their punishment, and I hoped that it would be soon. *God*, I thought. I wasn't even sure that there was one anymore. What sort of God would let people suffer like this? What sort of God would let children die the way that Marek did? Or suffer the hunger and pain that I saw every day on the street. The shootings and beatings, just for trying to eat. No I don't think that there was a God after all. If there was then he must have been a German God. I decided then and there I would no longer pray to him. In all my life I never did think that I would live to see the things that I had witnessed in the last few years. And in all the things that I had seen, nothing could have prepared me for the death of my beautiful little brother.

It had been three weeks since Marek's death. Since then Abraham had died too. He was old and could not fight the hunger any longer. People were dropping down like flies now. The summer heat and the sanitary conditions of the ghetto produced the most horrendous smell, that with dead bodies lying in the street made the situation a thousand times worse than it had already been, if that was at all possible. We had moved into the sitting room now, so at least we no longer had to sleep in the cold passage. *Why could this not have come sooner, when Marek was still here? At least he would have been a little more combatable in his last days*, I thought as I moved our belongings into the sitting room.

Mama had not moved from the sitting room for three weeks now. She was eating a little, but that was only because I fed her, and made her eat it. She would not speak, only nodded or shook her head when she was spoken to. I was worried, but at the same time frustrated because she was all I had left now, and I needed her to talk to. Over and over I tried to get her to talk to me, but to no avail.

"Mama, please, you have to start to get better, otherwise you will just give up all together and you need to be strong," I said one afternoon.

"I'm OK, Ayala. Just look after yourself," she told me.

"I need you to look after me, Mama. I can't do this on my own."

"I do not want to get better. I just want to die and be with my Marek and Jakob."

I could not believe she had just said that. I swallowed hard and blinked away the tears that were threatening my cheeks.

"So what about me then? Does that mean you do not want to be here with me?" I cried.

"I do not know what I mean, Ayala. I just know that I do not want to be here in this hell any longer."

I stood there and cried. My mother never even looked at me. I was hurt beyond words.

"So what you are saying is that you don't care if you leave me here on my own to face whatever it is they have in store for us. As long as you are OK."

"I am hurting, Ayala. I am grieving for my son. Allow me that. Do not take that away from me please," she cried.

"I'm not saying you cannot grieve for Marek, Mama, but I am grieving too. I too lost him. I too miss him, just like you do. I wish I could just give up and die, but I wouldn't because I wouldn't want to leave you here on your own. And it hurts me so much to hear you say that you just want to be with Marek and Papa, because it means you don't want to be here with me." I was sobbing hard now, I could not hold it all in.

"A mother should not have to outlive her child. She should not have to bury her baby, Ayala. One day you will have children of your own, and when you do, you will understand that."

"I do understand, Mama, you must be going through hell, but I am still

93

here, and I need you to help me through this." I tried to control my emotions, but the tears were flowing down my face like rain on windowpane.

Just then Mama came over and put her arms around me. We held onto each other and just cried and cried. It seemed like we were sat there like that for an eternity. "I am sorry, Ayala," Mama said at last. "Of course I would not leave you, not for a minute, but sometimes in life things are so painful, it is easier to give up than to face any more pain. I just cannot accept that I have lost my child. I will never get over that. Losing Papa was bad enough, but to lose Marek too." Again the tears flowed, and the sobs came. It was good that Mama was letting all the pain she had bottled up out.

"Mama, I will never get over losing Marek, but for now we have to fight to survive. If by some miracle we survive this hell, then when it is all over we will grieve for him properly. Until then we must concentrate on keeping alive."

Mama looked up at me with a look of admiration in her eyes. "Whatever happens in life, whether I live or die, one thing I will always be proud of is the fact that I brought up such a wonderful daughter. I am so proud to be your mother."

I was broken up with emotion at these words. I hugged her tight. "I love you, Mama, with all of my heart."

"And I love you with all of mine," she replied.

Mama seemed a little better after our conversation. Of course we both felt the pain of Marek's death around us all of the time. At every moment and in everything we did, Marek was always there in our mind, but we had to concentrate on trying to survive, that was the most important thing to us. The ghetto was still as ravaged with hunger and death, and getting worse all of the time. Smuggling was more rife than ever; even though the penalty for smuggling was death, that did not stop the children trying to get over the ghetto wall. That's what hunger does to you; makes you so desperate that you do not care what the consequences are. Even death.

The saddest part of ghetto life was the clever way that the Nazis made us turn on each other. The hunger was so bad that if one had a piece of bread, one had to hide it straightaway, otherwise the sight of that bread would bring out all the people hiding in the shadows, just waiting for someone to walk by with food. They would just rip you to pieces for the tiniest piece, like wild animals scavenging for crumbs. Out they would come in their droves fighting each other for the scrap of bread. I begged for food most days when I was not at the factory, but I never attacked for food, as hard as it was; I never allowed myself to become a slave to the hunger, but it is something I had to stop myself from doing.

Another tragedy hit us one morning in the late summer. The baby girl of our apartment died of starvation. It was heartbreaking. I do not know how she lasted as long as she did. Her mother was crazy with grief. It was heartbreaking to hear her crying for food all the time. In a way it was a blessing and relief for her, for she was no longer in any pain. My mother was a tower of strength to the baby's mother, for she knew all about losing a child. So there it was yet another victim to Hitler's murdering game.

Chapter 15

THE AUTUMN CAME WITH HOWLING WINDS and torrential rain. It was unusual to have such bad weather at this time of the year. Usually it was quite mild. It was late September and the cold winds and rain didn't usually start until November time. It was the last thing any of us needed; to be freezing cold, starving and sick before the winter had even begun, but the good hand of fate was certainly missing for us Jews; that was something we all agreed on. At the end of September I turned eighteen. A milestone and a reason to celebrate and be happy, but of course turning eighteen in the ghetto meant nothing; it was just another miserable day of shootings, beatings and general Nazi abuse. Mama tried to make it special for me by singing Happy Birthday, and plaiting my hair. Singing Happy Birthday was quite sad as neither one of us felt happy; even the tune was flat and lifeless as Mama sang it, but she tried her best and she promised me that as soon as this was all over then we would celebrate all the birthdays I had missed.

"We shall have a great big party and invite all the family and we will sing Yiddish songs all night," she said with a pitiful tone.

"Yes, and Papa will come home. He will surprise us all by coming through the door in his trilby hat and he will shout, 'Hello, princess,' and I will run and jump into his arms, just as I did as a little girl."

"Yes, then he will look over at me and open his arms; and I will go running into them crying and sobbing; and he will tell me he will never ever leave us all alone again," my mother said sadly. "Then Marek would come out from behind a curtain and shout, 'Surprise; here I am,' and there will be tears of joy; and we would all fight over who would hug him first. Then everybody would go, 'Oh, look at him, the little love,' when he fell asleep on my lap," said Mama emotionally.

I cried as I pictured this. Me, Mama, Papa and Marek all together again. We both knew that this was just a fantasy; we knew that Papa was dead. I had come to terms with that a long time ago, but it was nice to pretend sometimes. I dreamt these images a lot over the last few months. When we were sleeping in the passageway, I had never dreamt at all. Now we had moved into the sitting room, I would have the same dream every night. They were real and vivid, with bright colour.

I would dream that I was in our house and it was a Friday night on the Sabbath. All my aunties and uncles were there, and there was music and lots of laughter. Then Mama and Papa would appear together holding hands and singing and looking so happy. I would see my little Marek and he would be next to Mama, as he always was, smiling at me from across the room. In my dream I would put out my hand to touch him, but every time I approached him he would turn away and shake his head. I would then start getting very distressed at this, as I wanted to touch him so much. Just as I start to cry with frustration, Isaac would then appear, pulling me away telling me that it is not my time. I didn't understand what he meant and would wake up crying and sweating. Mama would wake up too and have to calm me down, by telling that it was just their way of trying to contact me to tell me they were happy and at peace. She would then go on to tell me I had the gift of second sight, just like my Auntie Dora. It was just like my mother to exaggerate. A typical Jewess, but this would make me feel better anyhow. It was a nice dream in one way as everybody is so happy, but it was disturbing in another as I could not speak or touch my little brother and I really needed to do that.

One morning, not long after Ariel had died, I woke to find the most terrible sight. Her mother Perle was dead. She had hung herself with the cord from her dressing gown in the corner of the sitting room. She could not take the grief and pain of losing her baby anymore. She looked horrific with her eyes still open and her tongue hanging out. Mama screamed when she first saw her, but I just stared. I felt numb and emotionless. It was not that I did not care; it was because I had seen so many dead bodies now, and had lost so many of my own that I don't think I had enough room in my heart for anymore grief.

I helped Mama get her down; we lay her on the floor. Mama took a blanket from her bed and covered her face, making the sign of the cross as she did so. The other residents just looked upon the whole scene as if they were watching a movie, like me with pity, but unemotional. We sat and thought about what we would do with her body. There was no way we could bury her. I suggested that we inform the Judenrat, but was quickly told not to otherwise we would not be able to use her clothes and ration card. "Is that all anybody thinks of when somebody dies in this place? Ration cards and clothes," I said with anger and bitterness. "It makes me sick."

"We are starving, and cold, we have to survive somehow," said Saul, one of the younger residents left in the apartment.

"I am starving and cold, but I cannot take the clothes of a dead woman's back. Her ration card maybe, but not her clothes, and I will not stand here and let any of you do it either."

"Then you cannot be a desperate as you look then," replied Saul with spite.

"How dare you talk to my daughter like that, you stupid man," argued my mother. "You are just a vulture, waiting for burnt offerings. Go away and mind your own business."

"Mama, ignore him, he is just ignorant," I said, trying to calm the situation down.

"And stupid," piped up Esther.

Knowing that he wasn't going to win an argument with three women, the young man huffed and went back to his side of the room.

"Look," said Esther. "I do not agree with the things that some people resort to, but we are cold and we are hungry. I do not agree to taking the clothes of the poor woman's back, but I'm sure her blanket and ration card will not hurt."

Mama and I looked at each other. "Maybe you are right," replied my mother. "I mean, I am sure she would not want us to be cold when we could have her blanket."

"OK, so who will take charge of her ration card?" asked Esther.

"I will," I replied, "and I will make sure I share it out fairly between us. Although there will not be much, but I will do my best."

"OK, what about her other clothes? The ones in the suitcase over there." Esther pointed to a small blue case in the corner of the room.

We went through it and found two jumpers and a long black skirt, with some tights.

"OK, we will take this, but not the ones on her back," I said with authority.

"OK, so what do we do with her body?" Mama asked.

"We cannot leave her here, and we cannot dump her body on the street with all the other piles of bodies. It is not right. Where did she bury her baby? Maybe we could bury her there," I asked.

"She gave the body to the orphanage," replied my mother. "They buried the baby there."

"Can't we take her there? And she can be buried with her baby," I suggested.

"They only take small children," answered Esther.

We sat there for what seemed like hours, going over and over different places where we could lay her to rest, but every one we thought of was out of the question, unless we wanted to be killed in the process. Eventually we came to the decision that we would have to put her on the street. We hated the idea, but there was no other choice. We picked her up, and carried her outside. I looked for a clear area where she would not be trampled on, or put on top of anyone else. We lay her down outside an old building. She was still wearing the gown that she had died in. Mama put the blanket back over her face, and we said a prayer and walked away.

Just as we were about to turn the corner, we saw three children of no more than ten years old. They lifted the blanket off her face, stripped her of all her clothes and ran off, with the blanket as well. And there she lay; naked just like the other poor souls who had died. We stood there shocked, but not surprised. This is how you survive in the ghetto. This is what they had turned us into. Vermin into vermin.

The apartment which once housed all twelve of us was getting smaller and smaller with each passing month. With people dying around us all the time, there were now only eight of us left. It was still terribly overcrowded in comparison to the size of the apartment. The smell was still horrendous, and people were still dropping down like flies from hunger or diseases such as typhus and dysentery. On top of all that we now had lice, which kept us awake day and night scratching us to death. There was no end to the misery that surrounded us all. It was a demonic waiting game. Waiting to eat, waiting to catch this disease or that disease, waiting to be stopped by the Nazis and shot. Waiting to die. We never knew if there was a tomorrow. For most people there wasn't. For me I was getting tired of all the fighting. It seemed that we had been fighting this enemy for so long now. There never seemed any hope of a positive outcome. Never any news of the allies coming to save us. It was a soul destroying endless nightmare. I was getting to the point where I could not care less if I lived or died. I was so thin and bony, a shadow of my former self. It was now painful to walk, and even to bend down and pick something up was too much for me. My work at the factory began to suffer. Every day people on the factory floor collapsed and died, but up until now I had managed to fight it, mainly because I didn't want to leave Mama on her own and the will to live inside me was strong, but just lately I didn't have the strength to fight it any more. I came home from work one evening feeling more tired and weak than usual. I had not eaten all day, as I had missed my meal at the factory because I was told I had to finish a batch of orders. This was common practice, but today I just could not afford to miss out on another meal, but unfortunately I did. I got to the apartment and fell down onto the bedding on the floor. Mama noticed straightaway that I was not well at all.

"Ayala, good heavens, child, you look so poorly. Are you feeling sick?"

"No, Mama. I am fine. I'm just tired that's all," I lied. I started to cough, and I was beginning to feel weaker all the time.

"Well, you do not look fine. You are pale, Ayala, I'm worried about you." Mama came over and felt my forehead with the back of her hand.

"You are running a fever, Ayala, we have to get you to the hospital," she cried.

"Mama, I am not going to the hospital. I am fine," I protested between coughs. "Besides, it is past the curfew hour so we cannot go."

Mama looked worried. I didn't know what to say to ease her fears. I was feeling very sick, but I did not want to cause her any more worry. Secretly I did not want to go to hospital, because I feared I would not come back. I never told Mama this, of course, but I was very scared. I feared I had typhus; as I was running a high fever and my head hurt something awful.

"OK, but if you are no better in the morning, Ayala, then you will go to the hospital. Do you hear me?" asked Mama.

"Yes, Mama," I replied. "Just let me close my eyes and get some sleep, OK? I will feel better when I wake up."

"Not until you have some soup," demanded Mama.

"OK, Mama."

The last thing I wanted now was to eat. I felt so bad, but if I told Mama that she would have had a fit. I drank the soup and closed my eyes. I was freezing cold. The last thing I remember is Mama bathing my head with a flannel and praying over me. I knew that I must have been dying. Then everything went black.

Chapter 16

I WOKE UP; THE FIRST THING I saw was a white ceiling. I thought I had died. *This must be heaven,* I remember thinking. *Everything is so bright.* I lay there feeling confused. Then I heard Mama's voice. She was crying and thanking God in her strong Jewish accent. "Oh, thank you, God," my mother was crying. "Ayala, you are alive. You are alive."

She was planting big wet kisses all over my face. The next thing I knew a young nurse coming over and putting a thermometer in my mouth. It was all so confusing. After a while I started to come round a little, my mouth was dry and sore. I could hardly speak. I felt so weak.

"Mama, what is going on? Where am I?"

"It's OK, darling, you have been very sick. You are in the hospital."

"What is wrong with me?" I asked concerned.

"You have had a really high fever, and severe malnutrition. I thought you would not make it."

"Do I have typhus, Mama?" I asked scared.

"I don't think so, darling. You have just been very sick through lack of food."

"How long have I been here?"

"About a week," replied Mama.

"Have I been asleep that long?"

"Yes. I thought I was going to lose you as well. I couldn't take it if I lost both my children." Mama started crying uncontrollably.

"It's all right, Mama, do not cry. I'm not going anywhere." I held her bony hand. It felt frail and light in mine.

Mama went on to tell me how I fell asleep after the soup she gave me. How my temperature rose dramatically and I started hallucinating. Esther and Mama both sat up with me all night fanning me down to bring down my temperature. I was still very bad the next morning, so they brought me to the hospital together with Saul. They had to carry me there, just like we did with poor Marek. I was unconscious all week, until they managed to bring down my temperature. Mama told me how I was shouting and crying for Marek and Papa and Isaac for the first two days. Mama said it was such a frightening time for her. Poor Mama, she had been through so much; we all had, but to lose your husband and your child must be the worst thing that can happen to a woman.

It is hard to believe that just three years ago we were a normal family living a normal everyday life; then bang, our whole world turned upside down. If somebody had told me three years ago that we would lose our home, our father and brother and that I would see things that I would not imagine in my wildest nightmares, I would have told them that they were sick minded. Tears came to my eyes as I thought of all the pain that we were all going through. As I lay there in my hospital bed, I told myself that if I do survive this hell, then I would tell the world just what these monsters have done to us, and that it will never be forgotten.

I was released from hospital after a few days of wakening. I was weak and tired, but at least I had some food inside me. The one good thing about being in the hospital was that I was fed regularly. It wasn't a lot and was only bread and soup, but it was something. I was terribly concerned about Mama. I do not know how she was still going, with hardly any food inside her and being so thin and gaunt all the time. It worried me terribly. I knew it would not be long before she too became sick, and that frightened me so much. I do not know what I would do without my beautiful mother.

The winter was here in full force. It was now December; snow lay thick on the ground like a white blanket. The worst part of being in the ghetto in December was the cold. It got into your bones and froze you from the inside out. More people died in the winter than in the summer. We would literally fall over dead people lying in the road. The winter made everyone so much more desperate. It was hideous to see people watching the dying lying in the street taking their last breath ready to run over and strip them of every piece of clothing they had on. They were not even allowed their dignity in death. I have seen people killing each other over a slice of bread or a coat from a dead man's back. That is what surviving the Warsaw ghetto does to you. Turns you into bloodhounds. I have seen children as young as three or four holding tiny babies in their arms as they lay dying on the frozen ground. Their parents having died or been murdered some time before. I have seen children checking each other's hair for lice, their filthy black skinny fingers reminiscent of monkeys in the jungle delousing their young. Hitler called us animals, the lowest form of life. He was right. That is exactly what he managed to turn us into.

As for Hitler and his murderers, they walked around the ghetto day and night, killing beating, terrorising us all. The sick games they played on the innocent victims, the twisted pleasure they got out of giving us false hope or lying to us. The barbaric heinous things they did to the children will live with me till I go to my grave. I remember one day on my way to work I saw a young woman on her way somewhere with her child in a pram. All of a sudden two Nazi officers stopped her. I was in earshot of the conversation and could hear the officers talking to the baby in the pram.

"Oh, vot a cute little baby ve have," one of the officers said.

The woman looked on in terror.

"Ah vot a pretty girl you are," said the other, putting his hand in the pram and tickling the baby under the chin.

The woman stood there frozen on the spot. My heart was pounding. All of a sudden, without warning, I witnessed one the most heinous things I would ever see in the ghetto. One of the officers took the baby out of the pram and started throwing it up in the air and catching it. The baby was giggling, thinking it was a silly game. The woman started screaming in terror. The other officer motioned to his friend to throw the baby to him. My heart was breaking as I stood there and watched the woman screaming as her baby was being used as a football. I started to run, as I could not look on any more. Just as I took my leave, I looked back and saw one of the officers throw the baby up in the air and let it drop straight to the floor. I looked away before the baby hit the ground, but I heard the thud as it did so. The young mother was kneeling over her dead baby on the floor. Demented with shock, and screaming like nothing I have ever heard in my life before. Then I heard two shots ring out as they shot the mother dead. I did not see this, but I knew that is what had happened, because the screaming stopped instantly. This sort of barbaric, sick torture was common in the ghetto. What a disgrace to mankind these Nazi murderers were. How could God make such evil? I asked my tortured soul. Maybe they are the work of the devil. No God in this world would ever make such evil. Would never let babies die in such wicked ways. The tears were pouring down my face now as I thought of all the children I had watched suffer and die; of Marek and how he just wasted away before our eyes, and the little boy on the street whose hand I held as he took his last breath, and of all the children shot up against the wall, trying to escape this hell. Oh how my heart was heavy, how old I felt for my eighteen years. Where had my soul gone? How my mind was scarred with all the pictures and images constantly going round my head. If I survived this hell, I don't know if it would be a good thing or bad thing. I knew I would never be the same person as I was before I came here. Something inside of me had died. The person I was before had died.

The New Year brought with it its own new misery. Mama was sick; she had a terrible cough. I could not help but be reminded of how Marek coughed so much when he became sick. It was bitterly cold, the snow was coming down thick and fast, and trying to keep warm in this hellhole was impossible. Mama was lying on the floor with her jumpers on and blankets wrapped round her up to her neck. Mama was so thin now that I honestly didn't know how she would survive any longer. I think it was her spirit that kept her going more than anything. It is amazing how the will to live is so strong, when we are faced with the most extreme circumstances. I worried for Mama so much. I was determined that I would not let my mother die like my brother. I had lost too much in this wicked war to allow yet another person I loved to die on me.

I made a decision to do something that I said I would never do. I decided that I would have to start stealing to survive. I had to do something for Mama. I decided not to tell her, because I know she would not allow me to do it. I hated the thought of stealing the food from another person's starving belly, but it seemed the only way to survive, and besides this had happened to me on so many occasions.

I got up early one morning and waited for the curfew to be lifted. I went outside and walked around for a while. My tummy was going over and I felt sick. I had never stolen anything in my life before. I watched while people went about their business. I hid behind a corner just behind a bakery shop. I decided that the first person to come out of the shop would be the one I would steal from. People were generally on their guard with food as stealing was so rife, but I knew there would be the odd one that would come out of the shop holding their bread for all to see. I waited for what seemed an eternity for someone to come out holding their bread. It was freezing cold. The temperature was below zero on this morning. My feet were frozen solid. I had my brown lace up boots which now had holes in them, with my thick warm winter socks underneath; my feet ached with the cold. I waited and waited and waited, until suddenly out she came, holding her bread and just about to put it down her coat to conceal it when suddenly out I ran and snatched it out of her hand as quick as a flash. I heard her swear at me as she chased me through the street. In and out of the people I ran as I tried to get away from her. I had already concealed the bread in my coat before anybody could steal it off me. I turned the corner and ran down a side alley. I waited there for a while until the coast was clear. Out of breath and shaking with adrenaline, I started walking back towards the apartment. I was starving hungry, but I turned my back on the temptation, as I so wanted Mama to eat something and get better. I entered the apartment and saw Mama lying on the bed on the floor. She was awake and looked a little better than she did the night before.

"Mama," I bent down and kissed her cold cheek, "I have a surprise for you," I said as I pulled the bread out from my coat.

"Ayala," gasped Mama. "Where on earth did you get that?" She smiled.

"Never you mind," I said. "Just eat it, OK?"

"But, Ayala, you didn't steal it, did you?" asked Mama.

"Would I do such a thing?" I said with a look of surprise.

"Ayala, I have told you before, do not risk your life for me."

"Then whom shall I risk it for?" I answered. "Mama, I did not steal it. I came across it, OK, so just eat it and stop arguing."

Mama retreated her argument and dived into the bread like there was no tomorrow. The look of the doughy gluey bread made my mouth water and my stomach ache, but there was no way I was going to take a mouthful of it away from my dear mother. Stealing became easier and easier after that. At first I felt guilty at taking something that somebody desperately needed, but it was a case of doing what you could to survive. Stealing, the same as smuggling, was a way of surviving; it wasn't nice, but it had to be done. If you didn't do it, then someone would do it to you. It wasn't personal, just a way of keeping alive. One could not go into a shop and buy food anymore. Money had no value in the ghetto. Life had no value in the ghetto. Just how little life mattered here was about to become tragically obvious to us all by the time summer came. Life here was hell on earth, one had to live it to believe just how bad it really was, but nothing on this earth could have ever prepared us for the events that were about to unfold.

Chapter 17

1942

THE SPRING BROUGHT THE WARMTH AND a little sunshine back into our miserable lives, although nothing could compensate for the restrictions and misery that our lives had become. The ghetto was now like a graveyard, with people walking around dying on their last legs. The amount of bodies now piled up on the streets was unbelievable. All naked and decaying. The whole place reeked of misery and death. Mama was a little better. She had got over the worst of her illness, and was up and about again, although she was extremely weak and fatigued all the time. Stealing for food had become a way of life for me. Since the first time I had done it, it become easier and easier for me. I still hated doing it. It was low and degrading, but it was a way of life in this hell of a place. It was not always a success, some days I would not find anyone to steal from, as everybody was on his or her guard where food was concerned. Sometimes I would wait all day for that one potato or small loaf of bread only to have it stolen from me the moment my stealing hands had touched it. It was soul destroying and tiring, but it was the only way to survive.

I no longer worked at the factory, as for some reason they had sacked everybody and only kept a few on. I was highly suspicious of this, but what could I do? Now I no longer had my daily meal, which was something I lived and dreamt about all the time. That is what starvation does to you; makes your mind think of nothing else but food. Every conversation, every thought, every dream you have is about food. It is mind-bending torture. Mama and I would sit and talk endlessly about the meals she used to cook at home, and pretend what she would cook tomorrow. It was sad.

It was now the beginning of the summer and Marek had been gone nearly a year. It seemed impossible to us that he could have been gone for that long already. It was also hard to believe that we had been in this hellhole for over a year and a half and we were still alive. Struggling and fighting off death all the time, but still alive. We missed our little Marek so much. Never a day went by without a conversation or passing comment about him between us. Some days were harder than others, some days the struggle to survive was so strong that it overtook everything else and there was not enough space in our heads to think of anything else but to survive the next hour. Other days we thought of nothing else apart from Marek and we would cry on and off all day. It was an emotional roller coaster. I knew we had not yet grieved properly for my little brother, and I knew that if we survived this hell, then it would hit us like a ton of bricks and we would mourn forever, but until then we just had to keep on surviving.

I still thought of Isaac, and I still hoped in my heart that he might be alive somewhere on this wicked earth, but I knew deep down that he wasn't. I still missed my father too. I hoped that he was also alive somewhere too, but again I knew this was not the case and I could not afford to give myself false hopes. I know it would most probably have been easier for me to believe that he was alive somewhere, as this would have given me something to fight for, but I just could not lie to myself like that. Life was hard for us all in the ghetto, and we had to have a realistic outlook rather than live with our head in the clouds. We had to be prepared for whatever they had in store for us, no matter how bad it was.

At the beginning of the summer, there had been some very frightening rumours circulating around about the Lodz ghetto. Some of the inhabitants were saying that the residents there were being sent to a concentration camp in Poland called Chelmno and being gassed or shot and thrown into mass graves. At first no one believed a word of this, as it seemed so out of this world.

"They wouldn't do that, they couldn't. It is just wild rumours. If they are being gassed, how can they be telling people what has happened to them?" Others would look and say, "Oh yes, how can they tell people if they are dead." And people would laugh and pass it off as a rather sick joke. Then the rumours kept recurring, only this time it was: "I know someone who has escaped the Lodz ghetto. He was put on a train and sent to Chelmno. He managed to escape before he was put into a van filled with gas. He says they are killing hundreds of people every day, including children and babies." The laughter stopped at this and people would look at each other and say, "Stop it, you are frightening us. Do you think they will do that to us here?"

I was inclined to believe the rumours. I as well as everybody else had seen the evilness that these Nazis displayed. I would not put anything past them. The thought of being shot and thrown into an open pit or gassed to death put a new wave of fear in me. One cannot imagine the horror that goes through the mind at such thoughts. I felt sick to my stomach every time I pictured myself dead on top of a pile of bodies. I felt the colour drain from my face every time I thought of my poor mother begging for life. The pictures inside my head were making me insane.

"Mama, do you believe all these rumours people are saying about the Nazis gassing people in Chelmno?" I asked one day.

"Ayala, I do not know what I believe anymore. I know that we cannot carry on like this for much longer. I mean how long can they keep us living like this for? They must be planning something for us. What that is, I do not know. I would like to think that they have plans to resettle us somewhere else, but I do not trust them, and I do not know what it is they have up their sleeves."

"Mama, I am scared."

"So am I, my darling. I am scared for you. Not for myself. I have lived my life, but you are young. You have so much to offer the world. I have nothing left to give. I have lost my son and my husband, but you have all of that to look forward to."

"Mama, don't say that," I cried. "I would not want to live if I didn't have you. And that hurts me to think that you do not value your life. I know you have lost Papa and Marek, but I am still here and I still need you."

"My Ayala, I love and need you too. Please do not think that you are not important to me. You are my world and I would do anything for you, but you are stronger than you think you are. If I was not here, you would survive because you are strong."

"No, Mama," I sobbed. "I would not want to survive. I would not want to be left on my own in this world."

Mama came over and held me close. I could feel her bony frame as she pressed me towards her. I felt like a child again as she stroked my hair and rocked me backwards forwards.

"It's OK, Mama's here," she soothed. "I will do my best, Ayala, not to leave you on your own," she cried, "but, Ayala, you have to be prepared for the fact that I might not get out of here alive."

Mama looked at me with guilt in her eyes, as if she was confessing something to me. My heart ached with pain at the words.

"Mama, please," I sobbed. "Please don't say that. Even if you think it is true. I could not bear it."

"No, Ayala. You have to hear it. I know that you don't want to. I cannot believe that we have come to this, but we have to prepare for that fact now."

"But, Mama, the things people are saying, it might be all rumours. Please, Mama." I was sobbing and shaking.

"Ayala, even if it is, how long do you think we can live like this for. Something has to give soon. All I am asking is for you to prepare yourself, OK?"

"I will never prepare myself for that, and I will never accept it. They have taken everything away from us. EVERYTHING! I HATE THEM SO MUCH!" I was shouting and hollering; this uncontrollable anger just rose from the pit of my stomach. I wanted to tear the apartment to pieces. Mama tried to hold me down. She was weak and found it hard to control my anger as I shouted and punched and kicked anything that was in my way.

"Ayala, calm down. Stop it. You will attract the wrong kind of attention to us."

Mama was panicking. Still I would not stop screaming and shouting.

"Ayala, please stop," Mama pleaded.

All of a sudden I felt a hard slap across my face. This brought me back to my senses. I stared hard at my mother. I couldn't believe she had just hit me. All of a sudden I collapsed to my knees and just broke down. I was crying so hard I did not think I would stop. Mama knelt down beside me. She just held me and didn't say anything at all. I don't know how long I had been there on the floor with Mama beside me.

I fell asleep on her lap, just as I had done as a little girl and woke up sometime later on my bed wrapped up in my blankets. Mama gave me some soup and then I went back to sleep. I slept round to the next morning. I slept like a baby. I do not remember the last time I slept for so long. In the light of things, this was very surprising. Mama and I never mentioned what happened between us. It was too emotional for both of us. I knew that she only slapped me to calm me down and to stop any unwanted attention coming our way. She also knew that I would never hold it against her for that. The pressure and strain that we were all under was enough to send the most saintly person to the brink of madness. I got up and went over to Mama and gave her a hug.

"I love you, Mama," I said.

"I love you too, my beautiful daughter." She looked deep into my eyes and held my gaze for what seemed an eternity. She had tears in her eyes. I felt the tears welling up in mine. I had to look away for fear of breaking down again. I don't know what it was about this day, but I felt that I was starting to lose my wonderful mother. The look in her eyes told me that she knew her time was coming.

That is why she tried to prepare me yesterday, I thought, as I left the apartment for another day of stealing some poor soul's food. *Oh God*, I prayed, *I know I said I would never pray anymore and I'm so sorry for that, but please spare my mother. I have lost so much; please let me keep my beautiful Mama. I don't want to be left alone in this wicked world.* I spoke to him in my head. I prayed that he would not take the only person in the world that I had left. *God, if you spare my mother, I promise I will start to pray again. I'm sorry for all the things that I said. I was angry, but I didn't mean it.* As I spoke these words in my head, I felt that God had heard them. I felt that he had taken pity on me at last and was going to answer just one prayer for me. I felt a small ray of hope as I walked through the piles of bodies on the floor, through the half-dead people shuffling past on the street. Stepping over the dying children too weak to move away from the side of the road, too weak to stretch over for that small piece of bread that some kind person had dropped for them. How could anyone feel hope in a place like this? I wondered, as two men were being chased down the street only stopping when a round of bullets hit the back of their heads. How could anyone possibly even think of a positive outcome in this horrific mental asylum?

Just as I was approaching the market square, I saw people mulling around a notice board in the square. People were crying and looked panic-stricken. As I approached the poster my heart hit the pit of my stomach. There it was; what we had all feared. A written notice from the Judenrat for all unproductive Jewish residents for resettlement in the east. The only people exempt from this new threat were the factory workers, hospital workers and the Judenrat itself. The notice ordered people to be at the Umschlagplatz, for transport onto the trains by four pm on the 22nd of July 1942. It went on to say that anybody not complying with these orders would face punishment by death. The notice did not state where we were going or what plans they had for us there. My whole body shook from head to toe. I knew that this was it. The rumours were true. This was the beginning of the end for us all.

Chapter 18

I RAN BACK TO THE APARTMENT to tell Mama the latest news. All thoughts of finding food today were soon forgotten as I made my way through the crowds of people running around trying to find work in every factory. The notice stated that factory workers were exempt. I joined the circus of people running around frantically trying to find a job. I knew in my heart that most of us would not be saved from the trains to the east. We only had one day in which to do it. The deportations started the very next day. I myself was disappointed beyond words that I no longer held my job at the uniforms factory. This would have spared my own life for a while at least, but what of my poor mother's. I knocked on every factory door I could find, but with no luck. I was determined that there was no way that myself or Mama would be getting on any train to the east, even if it meant risking our lives further by hiding in the ghetto somewhere. I walked and walked until I could physically walk no more. I knocked on every door I could find, but I could not find any employment anywhere.

I walked home scared and angry with myself in failing to save our lives. I walked through the door to find Mama and Esther talking about the news that was circulating the ghetto like wild fire. Debating and pondering on the latest development in our misery. Some people welcomed this new piece of news on resettlement, thinking that nowhere could be worse than the misery and hell that we were all living in here. I totally didn't trust the Nazis with anything; or believed a word they said. *How can one trust murdering child killers?* I asked myself. *There was no way in hell that I was getting on any train to anywhere*, I thought as I sat down next to Mama. I would rather take my chance here.

Mama was neither surprised nor worried about the news. I think she had come to terms with the fact that something had to give sooner or later. I told her that there was no way we would be going anywhere, that we would stay and hide here.

"We have nothing to lose," I told her.

"And what if this place is better? What if they have just been trying to find somewhere for us to settle all this time?" Mama asked naively.

"Mama, you have seen the evil and wicked things these monsters have done. How can you be so naïve about it? Of course they are not settling us somewhere. They want to get rid of us. Think about all the hate and abuse they have handed out over the last few years."

"Ayala, I am tired. I don't think I have the strength to hide or live in fear anymore than I am doing already. I just don't have it in me."

"But you have to, Mama. Who knows, the war might be over soon. We may not have to hide for that long," I pleaded.

"And if they find us in the meantime we are dead," she answered.

"And if we go, then we will surely die," I responded back.

"Ayala, we do not know what we are turning our backs to. This might be our chance to get out of this mess, even if it is on a works camp; it will be better than this."

"Mama, I don't care what I have to do, but we are not getting on any train to anywhere."

"I am going," said Esther. "I need to get my children out of here. We have nothing to lose. We are dying anyway."

"Esther, you need to do what you feel is right, but I have very strong feelings on this, and I will not go, and neither is Mama."

Mama looked up and laughed. "She treats me like a child. Sometimes I forget who is who."

"I just want to survive this war with at least one of my family left," I answered, not seeing the funny side of Mama's joke.

I sat there all night with Mama and Esther. Neither one of us could sleep. The whole ghetto tonight would be fighting the tiredness with fear and trepidation, I thought as I sat there desperately trying to find a way to save us from the trains. We sat in silence, each of us with our different thoughts. I was thinking about Marek, and how I missed him, and how much I was glad he was not here at this time. He would have been terrorised beyond words. Mama was thinking about him too, and Papa. Esther kept looking over at her sleeping children, with tears in her eyes. I looked at them too. I prayed that somehow the Lord would spare them from the Nazis' guns or gas chambers.

I fell asleep around five o'clock in the morning. Mama and Esther had fallen asleep sometime before. I knew that the morning would bring tears and carnage, but I never in my life expected what was about to unfold for us before our very eyes. In the two years that we had been in the ghetto, we had seen things that only our eyes would believe. To tell someone of the horror we had witnessed on this death plain would have had us committed to a mental asylum. But even though we had seen things that would haunt us forever, I still did not think it possible to see anything worse than I had already seen. How wrong I was. I thought my life had changed for the worse, just being in this hellhole, but it was about to take another twisted turn. The depraved evil that these Nazis would commit had not even yet begun.

We woke to the sounds of screams and shouting, as doors were smashed down, and tanks rumbled by. I ran to the window and saw in the distance people being dragged and pulled from their apartments. I heard the Germans screaming, "Schnell, schnell," (quick, quick), as they ordered the poor helpless victims out onto the street. People were being thrown onto waiting cattle cars along with their possessions. They had guard dogs that were going berserk and attacking anybody that passed them by. The ferocity of the attacks in which they had no mercy on its helpless victims left me retching with sickness.

I saw people being shot; some for being too slow, some for no reason at all. Old people and children being beaten and kicked as they tried desperately to comply quickly with the orders being screamed at them. I saw people being shot down in cold blood as they tried to escape the horrific scene. Gunshots could be heard all over the ghetto; some in the distance, some closer to home. The destruction taking place was on the other side of the ghetto. I could see clearly most of the horror taking place. As yet the carnage had not reached our apartment block; it just was a matter of time. The Germans were working fast in their brutality, and were getting closer every minute. It was utter chaos.

Everybody else in our apartment, apart from Mama and Esther, had decided they would be better off on the trains. They packed up their clothes and said their goodbyes, and that was that. We had lived with these people for the last couple of years, now they were gone in a flash just like that, probably to die in the gas chambers. I ran over to Mama and Esther.

"What is going on?" they asked hysterical and screaming.

"They are gathering everybody into the square," I told them quickly. I did

113

not tell them of the brutality I had just witnessed, but they knew anyway. We could hear the screams and wails of people throughout the apartment.

"What shall we do?" Mama asked hysterical.

"We shall find a place to hide," I told her. "It will be OK." My heart was pounding and I felt my legs buckle underneath me with fear. I thought I would collapse.

"Where shall we hide? We cannot hide in the apartment. They will find us straightaway," Mama answered.

"We shall leave the apartment before they reach our block. Then we will run down the back streets and find a place to hide out, until it calms down," I suggested weakly, not really believing in what I had just said.

"That is absurd," Esther replied. "They will have blocked all of the roads off, and there will be Jewish police and guards everywhere. We will be killed in no time."

Esther was right. It was absurd. *I should have spent yesterday trying to find somewhere to hide, instead of trying to find work*, I thought. I had not anticipated the brutality of the situation. I just thought that people would take themselves down to the Umschlagplatz and declare themselves to the trains, but I should have known better. The Nazis couldn't do anything without putting fear and terror into it.

"Ayala." Mama came over and took my hand in hers. With tears rolling down her face, she told me that we have no other choice but to go and join the line. I cried; as I knew how right she was, and that there was no other way. I had failed in trying to save our lives. "Ayala, you have not failed. You have kept us alive this long. We would have been dead a long time back had it not been for your intelligence and strong will to live."

I cried as I looked into my mother's eyes. My beautiful mother. The one who gave me life. The one who rocked me to sleep, the one who nursed me when I was sick. I could not believe that I could not save her from this nightmare. I loved her so much, and I could not imagine what life without her would have been like for me all these years. I wanted to tear my hair out with the pain of what we would now be facing.

"Ayala," my mother cried. "I am so sorry."

"What for, Mama?" I sobbed.

"For not getting us out when Papa had the chance. I should have had more faith in him. I am so sorry for that."

"Mama, it is not your fault. Papa tried to get us out and he couldn't. Nobody is to blame for that. Especially you, Mama."

"Ayala, always remember that I love you. Always remember," she cried.

I sobbed out my heart as I held my precious mother close to me. I knew that she was saying goodbye. "I love you too, Mama. And I want you to know that you have been the greatest, most sweetest mother any child could have ever have wished for."

I looked at her face for what I knew would be the last time, and my heart broke. I gathered my belongings together. The notice stated that we could not take any more than seven pounds of luggage including any valuables and cash that we had. We had neither, so we just took the clothes on our backs and some bedding.

Esther's two children cried pitifully, as their mother tried to dress them. The sound of their cries and wailing as they begged their mother not to make them get on the train was pitiful. With fearful hearts and trembling bodies, we slowly descended down the stairs and out onto the square. We were crying and holding onto each other as if to protect ourselves from the abuse that was surely to find us.

We joined the crowds of wailing people that were heading in the direction of the Umschlagplatz. The scene there was worse than before, with people pushing and shoving each other, and children crying and screaming and holding onto their parents for dear life. I was holding onto Mama's hands tightly, scared to let her go. There were more beatings and shootings as the gendarmes randomly shot anyone they passed.

I cannot describe the hysteria and terror that we all went through on that first day. During the scuffle and commotion of terror on the way to the Umschlagplatz, we lost Edith and her children. Up until now we had tried to stay together, but with all the chaos, she must have been lost behind us, or shoved into another part of the crowd. All this time in the apartment we had built a good relationship, now all of a sudden in one morning that friendship was wiped out forever. I was still trying to hold onto Mama, as we were frogmarched through the streets. We tried hard to squeeze ourselves between people, so as to be hidden in the crowd, this way it was possible to dodge the shots and beatings from the SS, but they were too smart for us. They knew that people were trying to hide themselves inside the chaotic crowd. Every now and again they would come into the middle of the crowd and start shooting randomly, without reason or cause. Everybody would start screaming and running in every direction, as the bodies of the innocent victims would hit the floor in between people's feet. The blood would splatter everywhere as the poor innocent victim lay dying on the cold floor. This would make the murderers even more bloodthirsty as they liked nothing more than to see the reaction of the innocents with blood on their faces. Mama was screaming hysterically. I could not calm or pacify her in any way as I too was screaming and running for my life as well. As if things could not get any worse for us that morning, something happened that I had been dreading and fearing for the last two years in ghetto.

115

As we were being dragged across the road towards the Umschlagplatz, Mama fell over. As I bent down to help her up I felt a searing pain in the back of my head. I heard Mama scream as I realised I had been hit across the head by a Nazis truncation. I tried to ignore the pain as I kept on running. All of a sudden I saw my mother fall down again, this time from the boot of a gendarme. As she tried to get up again, he kicked her to the floor. He was screaming all sorts of filthy abuse at her. I was screaming as he continued to kick her down every time she tried to get up. All of a sudden his attention was turned elsewhere. I helped her up and we kept on running. Mama was in a lot of pain, but carried on running all the same. Suddenly a shot rang out in the crowd. Everybody screamed and scampered around in all directions once again. I was screaming in terror as I ran to get away from the bullets. When they stopped, I looked around for my mother, whom up until now had been holding my hand throughout. I span round in circles scanning everyone in front, behind and to the left and right of me. A new wave of panic took over me as I searched and searched for my mother.

I could not see her anywhere. Seconds turned into minutes as I ran in and out of the crowd calling her name. I did not care for the German gun or boot as I desperately tried to find her. There were hundreds of people in the crowd; she could have been anywhere. We got to the Umschlagplatz. There were thousands of people there already, standing around waiting to be placed on the trains. I must have run up and down every row, but could not find my beautiful mother. There were just so many confused and demented people there. Eventually minutes turned into hours. I fell down onto the floor and with my head buried in my hands I sobbed and sobbed, until I thought my heart would burst. The pain was agonising. I felt detached from reality as I realised that I had finally lost my wonderful mother.

Chapter 19

I SAT ON THE PLATFORM, MY eyes red and sore with tears. I felt like a thunderbolt had hit me. Nothing felt real after all I had seen that day. The realisation that I would probably never see my mother again left me with no more fight for survival. I sank into deep depression sitting there on the floor surrounded by emaciated half-dead human beings. I sat and watched the poor helpless victims, as they were being pushed and pulled onto the trains. They were packed in like sardines in a tin. Maybe a hundred odd to a carriage. The July heat made it even more unbearable for everyone. There was not even a drop of water to quench our thirst. It was torture beyond words. Children cried as their parents held them in their arms and tried in vain to soothe them. I wondered if my mother had already been sent on to one of the trains; she must have otherwise I would have found her by now. Unless she was lying dead in the street somewhere, but I would never know that now, as I was on my way to the gas chambers, or so the rumour had it. I knew that I too would soon be on one of those trains to the east. Where east was and what it meant was of no concern to me anymore. I had lost my mother, my only surviving relative. I did not care what happened to me now.

There were hundreds of people on the platform that day. It was so confusing. There was so much commotion and hysterics as people tried in vain to save themselves from the dense carriages. Some people went on the trains of their own accord; believing that they were off to a better existence, these people were actually smiling. I had been in the same spot on the floor for hours as the trains came and went with people loaded up on them. I don't know how many people were deported that day, but it must have been in the thousands.

It was now after dark and we had been on the platform all day long. I don't know why we had not yet been sent to the trains. It must have been around midnight when we were told that no more people were to be deported that day. There had been so many people; they just could not keep up with it. They would continue their barbaric treatment tomorrow. People were crying and thanking God that they had been saved for one more day. I did not care one way or the other. I had lost everything and everyone in my life, so what was the point in living? People were running again, back to their filthy squalors they called home. My heart was heavy and my mind was lost as I slowly dragged my feet and shuffled from the platform. Walking from the station was like walking through a scene from a horror film. Dead bodies lying everywhere. Pools of blood like puddles decorating the pavement like a morbid piece of art. People's possessions scattered here and there, suitcases and clothes; it was a horrific portrait of a world gone mad. My feet were taking me in the direction of the apartment. My mind was somewhere else. Where I did not know. It was foggy and black with images of all I had seen that day. Of the beatings and shootings. The cruelty to people who could not fight back. I was demented with the images that would haunt me forever. I had completely lost my mind, as I wandered around aimlessly moaning and muttering under my breath.

As I was walking through Mila Street, two German officers were turning the corner, heading towards my direction. The streets were now deserted as the two men approached me. I could see clearly that one of them had blood splattered all over his coat. A grim souvenir of a long day's killing, probably the blood of innocent children. The other had a vicious, hungry looking dog on a long lead. My heart beat hard and my mouth went dry as the two officers approached me. The fear one feels when faced with such evil is beyond any words that the human voice could describe.

"Veer are you going to, Jew? It is past the curfew hour," said the one with the dog.

I could not answer. Shaking, I just stood there with my head looking down towards the blood splattered floor.

"I am speaking to you, you stupid Jew bitch. Answer me," he said again.

"I am on my way back to the apartment," I whimpered like a small child.

"There was no more room on the trains. They say to come back tomorrow." My voice was so small and childish; I didn't recognise it as my own.

"Veer is your papers?" said the gendarme with the blood on his jacket. There was something in their tone; that something awful was about to happen. With trembling hands I took out my paperwork and showed him. They looked at the paper, looked at me and handed it back.

"So do you know it is dangerous for a pretty Jewess to be out on the street at this hour?" Again I did not answer. My whole body was racked with fear. I was crying and begging in my mind for them to just disappear.

"I think zee Jewish bitch needs to be taught a lesson," said one of the Nazi monsters.

I do not know which one spoke as I had my head down, scared to look into their faces. My legs started to buckle underneath me. All of a sudden I felt a hand across my mouth as I was dragged into a shop doorway. I screamed as they pulled me into the shop and threw me down onto the cold floor. I lay there screaming and begging them to not hurt me. This seemed to encourage them further as one of them bent down and punched me in the side of the head so hard I nearly passed out. The other officer stood by with his dog that was barking furiously, and laughed as he encouraged his friend to carry on. My ears were ringing from the punch and my eyes tried to focus as he kept punching and kicking me in every part of my body. I was screaming and crying in pain.

"PLEASE, I BEG YOU! PLEASE, PLEASE, HAVE MERCY ON ME!" I begged, but this just infuriated him more.

All of a sudden the one with the dog came and bent over me. His friend stepped aside as he sat astride me and started tearing at my clothes. Horror washed over me as it dawned on me what was about to happen. He ripped off my clothes so hard and furious, he was scratching at my skin. The other officer was holding me down, as his friend proceeded to assault me. They were laughing and screaming at me the whole time. I lay there naked, trying desperately to hide myself from their demented faces. I had been screaming so hard that my voice had given way, and I lay there trying to beg them to stop, but nothing would come out. All of a sudden I realised that the screaming and begging was just making the vile situation worse for me, and that no amount of begging would ever make them stop. I stopped trying to scream and just lay there, as they both abused my body. The pain was unbearable as their hands pawed at my beaten skin. I thought that if I stopped crying and screaming then I would not be adding to their pleasure, as this seemed to make them all the more frantic in their abuse of me.

I lay there and prayed that death would come. I prayed that they would just hurry up and kill me. I knew that this was what the end result of this vile invasion of my body would be. They were still screaming obscenities at me as they attacked my body. I just lay there and cut myself off from it, as they robbed me of my innocence. It was easy after a while. I pretended in my mind that this was not happening to me, but all the same the tears were still rolling down my cheeks. I do not know how long the attack lasted for; to me it seemed like hours. At last they finished their filthy act, and got up.

I lay there whimpering and moaning. I was completely devastated at what had just happened. How could they put someone through so much pain and torture? And not have an ounce of pity or guilt about it. How could they listen to the screams and pleads of an innocent person and not care what torture they are putting them through. I lay there in utter shock. I was muttering and mumbling nonsense. I had completely lost my mind. I waited for the bullet in my head or some sort of barbaric act to finish off their demented, brutal invasion of me. I waited and waited, but it did not come. I prayed that they would kill me; to end the pain and torture, but they didn't. All I heard was, "I bet you enjoyed that, didn't you, you filthy Jewish bitch?" As they walked out of the shop. Naked and bleeding, bruised and battered from head to toe, I was in utter shock at what had just happened to me. I think I was more shocked that they had not killed me. I couldn't move; my body had become paralysed with pain, my mind gone.

As I lay there, my mind became a picture book of the events of the day. The twisted sick images kept playing over and over in my head, of all they had done to us. The shootings and beatings, the old people they shot for being too slow. The screaming mothers trying desperately to protect their terrified children. The street beggars being dragged away and thrown onto the waiting carts, and the children, oh the children, the images of their poor pathetic faces as they were taken from the Dzielna Street orphanage screaming in terror is something that I will never forget. And my mother, my beautiful sweet mother. Where was she? Was she still alive? Did she get deported on one of those trains?

What would I do without her now? She would have been beside herself to know what I had just been through. Oh how I wished I had got on that train with her. At least we could have died together. My mind was tormented as I lay on that cold floor. I put my hands up to my head and squeezed it tight, as if to try and stop the images. Scenes of the vile attack on my innocence permanently etched in my mind. I could still smell their filth on me, and it made me sick to my stomach. I sunk into a deep depression as I realised that my life had come to a point of no return. I had lost every living soul in my beautiful family. My darling baby brother, my beautiful father and my sweet mother. There was nothing left to live for. No one left to live for. Even if by some miracle I did survive this hell on earth, how would I ever live with all

I had seen? How would I live with myself after what had happened to me tonight? That is something I knew I would never recover from. The physical scars may heal, but nothing would ever heal the scars inside my head. I had been violated in the most extreme way. I knew that I would never get over that. I felt the cold tears sting my eyes as I thought about all I had lost.

I decided that I wanted to die. I didn't have to think about how I would do it. It is easy to commit suicide in the ghetto. All I had to do was to walk out onto the street after the curfew, or climb over the wall, or go out without my badge on and death would come, just like that. It was so easy. I was still lying on the floor some hours after the attack. I was comatose; I knew this was the end for me. I fell into a deep sleep; the dreams that came were vivid and colourful. They were not of all the horrors and evil that I had endured, but of the happy times I had shared with my family. The holidays and birthdays we had shared together. I dreamt that I was with Isaac, down by the park where we used to go. Isaac was making me laugh with his wonderful humour, and we were holding hands. We were so happy. I saw my father; we were at the beach on one of our holidays we used to go on. He was chasing me around and I was laughing as he picked me up and threw me into the sea. Mama was there laughing and telling Papa not to play so rough. Marek was sitting on Mama's lap; in my dream he was still a baby and he was giggling with delight at watching us fool around. Then all of a sudden Kamila was there coming towards me, as she tried to approach me I turned my back. She kept saying she was sorry for all she had done. I woke to the sounds of my own sobs. I was calling out my mother's name. I felt like an abandoned child. I could no longer suffer like this. I could no longer be a party to the devastation and evilness around me.

"Today I will end it all," I told myself. "Today I am going to die."

Chapter 20

I WOKE UP FREEZING COLD AND naked on the shop floor. Daylight was streaming through the windows, and I could see clearly now the end result or their horrific assault of me. My whole body was black and blue with bruises. My head felt swollen, and the pain was like nothing I had ever felt before. My legs were a mass or cuts and bruises, and ached something terrible. I knew it was still early in the morning as there was nobody about, apart from the funeral carts being pulled along, heavy laden with the night's victims of Hitler's murdering game. I knew I had to get out the shop before it opened up. I looked around me and realised I was in a coffee shop. From where I was had been lying I could see that there was not an ounce of coffee or current bun left in there.

Slowly I tried to sit up. The pain in my body was like nothing I had ever felt in my life. Racked with pain I stretched over to reach for my dress, which was lying under a table where it had been left after being ripped from my back. Crying, I managed to pull my dress towards me. Lifting my arms to put it on was excruciating, but I managed to do it. My dress was ripped to shreds from the vicious way it was torn off my body. It hardly covered me at all. It had rips and slits all over it. I cried as I remembered my ordeal. I tried to shut out the images as I slowly tried to stand. I grabbed hold of the counter to secure my balance as I stood on my sore feet. My head was spinning and a wave of nausea rushed through me as I stood there trying to gain my balance back. I took deep breaths and waited for the nausea and dizziness to pass, before I left the shop. I didn't know where I was going or what I was going to do; all I knew was that I'd had enough of the misery and pain, and that today I was going to end it all. I didn't care anymore. I looked forward to the end of the suffering. I smiled as I looked forward to seeing my family again, all waiting for me to join them. My father would be smiling with open arms, and my beautiful mother would be with him and next to her would be my little Marek. My Isaac too would be there, and I would be happy again. I wasn't scared of death anymore. I had seen too much of it. After living in hell the way we had done all these years, death is a remarkable relief and a wonderful release. No I could not wait. I didn't know how I was going to do it, but I knew it would be easy. There was always somebody in a grey uniform that would quite happily put a bullet through your head on any street corner you turned.

I waited for the dizziness and nausea to pass. When it did I made my way to the door. The curfew was still in operation at this hour, which meant that I should not yet be out on the street, but I did not care. I secretly hoped that some German officer would pop up out of nowhere and shoot me dead. Then it would be all over and done with, as easy as that. I stepped out of the shop and walked back down Mila Street and out onto the square. The pain was unbearable and intensified with every step I took. I don't know how my bruised and battered legs were holding me up. I could not stand the pain much longer. I knew today was the day I would end my life, that was definite, but how and where I would do it was another question. If I was to be shot by a gendarme, then I would want it to be somewhere fairly quiet, not in full view of everybody especially children. The residents of this poor town had seen enough death. If I could save them from seeing one more death, then I would do it.

As I was walking through Mirowski Square and wondering how and where I was going to end it all, I heard someone call my name. I spun round, then round again in a full circle as I heard again my name echo across the empty street. I was shaking with fear. The thought of anyone coming near me after last night sent shock waves of terror right through me. I trusted no one now, and would not give anyone else the chance to abuse or hurt me like that again. I thought I must be hearing things, but as I started to walk off I heard it again. Once more I turned around, and there in front of me was a man. I knew his face, but could not put a name to it.

"Ayala, is that you?" he called.

He was short, very thin and very grey looking. He must have been around forty or fifty years old. He was wearing a cream-coloured cloth cap and he was pulling an empty funeral cart that must have just been emptied somewhere. He left the cart and came over. I shrank with fear, like a frightened child about to be spanked. I was shaking and crying as he approached me. Mumbling, I hid my face from his view and tried to face the other way. I turned and started to move away, but my legs were slow and heavy with the pain and they would not carry me with any great speed.

"Ayala, my dear child," said the man who was now facing me. "It is you, my dear, isn't it?" he questioned, as he put his arms out to greet me.

In terror I put my hands up towards my face and sunk my head in my neck; like a tortoise hiding in fear.

"Please," was all I could manage to say.

The man pulled his arms back, seeing the state of fear that I was in; he now became gentler in his approach.

"It is all right, my child," he said calmly. "I will not hurt you. Do you know who I am?" he asked gently.

Something in his tone made me feel slightly more at ease. Slowly I raised my eyes up to quickly look in his face, and then quickly looked away again. It was a kind warm face, friendly and so familiar. I knew that I knew this person, but just could not remember his name. Again I looked up into his face once more, and then it came to me. I remembered who this familiar face was. It was Barak, Papa's oldest friend. The one who had been with Papa in Belzec.

"Barak," I whispered. "I'm sorry, I…"

"It's all right, my dear. I understand," he whispered back. "What are doing out on the street so early? It is very dangerous."

"I do not care anymore, Barak. I have lost everybody. I just want to die," I cried desperately.

Barak's eyes filled up with tears. "Everybody?" he questioned cautiously.

"Marek died and Mama disappeared yesterday. I do not know where she went. I think she was put on the trains to the east," I sobbed.

"Oh, my dear child, I am so sorry." Barak was shaking his head, and was visibly crying.

"Ayala, please come with me. If you get caught out on the street at this hour, it will be the end for you."

"I do not care; I have nobody and nowhere to go. I just want to die, Barak."

"Ayala, please do not talk like this. You are just a girl; you cannot give in like that."

"Barak, I have seen and been through so much. I am not a girl anymore.

I am an old woman. I cannot live with all I have seen. Please just let me go."

"OK, Ayala. Come with me, just for a little while. I promise I will not try and talk you out of anything you want to do, but at least come back with me. I have some coffee and a slice of bread. You can rest for a while then I will let you go. I promise."

"Barak, I do not want to rest. I have made up my mind. There is nothing left to live for."

"Did you ever find your father, Ayala?" Barak asked me out of the blue.

"No we did not. He never came home, and he never knew what became of us," I answered sadly.

"Then what would I do if by some miracle he survived this war, and came back and tried to find you? How would I feel, knowing I saw you today knowing what you intend to do, and done nothing to prevent it?"

"Barak, how can you say such a thing? That is cruel. My father is dead. He would have come to us by now if he wasn't."

"How do you know that? Have you had proof? He could still be alive somewhere, working in a concentration camp. There could be a thousand reasons why he did not get home. There is a war on, Ayala, but no matter what, we must not give up hope."

I thought about this for a moment. I was so confused. My thoughts were muddled and my head ached. I didn't know what to do.

"Ayala," Barak said quietly. "Please come back. Just for a while. I promise I will not try to talk you out of anything, but just give me a chance. I owe it to your father, whether he is alive or dead."

I thought about this for a while, I was so confused. "OK," I gave in. "But only for a while, OK?"

"OK," he replied relieved.

We got back to Barak's apartment. His wife was there with their daughter. I remembered her from when I was a child. The apartment was on the other side of the ghetto. Quite a way from where ours was. It was filthy dirty, with wet grime all over the walls, damp and the smell was overpowering. It was small and up until the first deportations had been busy housing ten other people. Barak told me that he had two jobs in the ghetto. Clearing the streets of the dead in the morning, and working for a leather factory during the day. This had saved them all from deportation on the first day. Barak was under no illusions that as soon as he was not needed anymore then it would be their turn, but he was grateful for the extra time he was given. I told Barak how I had searched all over for a job when the deportations began, but had no luck whatsoever.

I drank some coffee, which didn't taste that bad at all. It had been a long time since I had a drink, let alone coffee. I didn't ask where he had got such a luxury. One does not ask such questions in the ghetto. Barak did not ask how or where I got my injuries from. He also paid no attention to the condition of my clothes, which was a dead giveaway that something bad had happened to me. I was grateful for his ignorance at this. Barak's wife Bosmat was kind and thoughtful. She did not ask any awkward questions. She just sat and talked to me gently about recent events and what her plans were for herself and her family after the war. I liked her positive attitude. It is hard to believe that one could still be positive after all we had seen and heard. I told Barak about Mama's disappearance, and how she was there one minute and gone the next. I cried fresh tears as I relived the worst day of my life, and the thought of Mama on that train scared and frightened. Bosmat came over and put her arm around me. At first I flinched as she made contact with my arm, then slowly I felt more combatable as she sat there and soothed me. She was a wise woman, and although she did not say it, she knew what I had been through. I could tell by the way she was with me, cautious in her approach and very gentle.

"You must not give up hope, Ayala. We do not know for sure if they are actually killing people in these places. For all we know your mother may be sitting somewhere right now going through exactly what you are; worrying if you are alive or dead," she said, trying to convince me.

"What good have these Nazi beasts ever done for us? Can you really say in your heart that they are actually sending people off to a better existence?"

Bosmat looked at me and sighed. "I do not know, but I have to be strong and stay positive, because no matter what they throw at us, no matter what they do, I will not let them win. They can beat me down, but I will always get back up, and that is what you must do too, Ayala."

"I do not care what they do to me now. I have come to the end of the road. They have taken my mother, the only person in the whole wide world I had left. Now she is gone, I just want to die and be with her."

"And what if you go and kill yourself? And you get up there and she is not there. Then what will you do? You cannot come back down again. What would your mother do without you?"

"My mother is dead, Bosmat. I know she is. So that is all there is to it." I cried more tears as I pictured my mother in my head.

"You do not have proof of that, Ayala. That is all I am saying. Why do you not wait until you are at least sure, before you make a decision like that?" interrupted Barak.

I felt so confused and tired. It was true; I did not have proof that she was dead. I just presumed that she was. After all they had killed everyone else I loved. I asked if I could get some sleep. I told them I would be up and out before the nightmare of deportations started again. I didn't want them risking their lives further by my being there.

I thanked them for all the help and kindness they had shown me. Then I lay down on the floor and fell into a deep sleep.

Chapter 21

IT SEEMED I HAD NOT BEEN to sleep for long when I was gently woken by Bosmat. "I am sorry, Ayala, but the deportations will be starting again soon and the Germans may come here today."

"It is OK, Bosmat," I said sleepily. "It is not your fault. I will go now." I could hear the rumbling of trucks in the distance and doors banging already. I felt sick at the thought of having to go through all the hell again.

"Ayala," Barak called. "I need to talk to you some more, we don't have much time so I will be quick, OK?"

"OK," I answered curiously.

"I could not just let you go, Ayala, knowing what you intend to do. I would not be able to face God if I let you take your own life."

"Barak, I—"

"Shh, child, let me finish. I went down to the leather factory this morning, before my shift started. I met a man there that I know, and I have arranged for some work for you, and for some papers to be drawn up. I have to go back in one hour and pick them up, OK?"

"What work, Barak? I don't understand, and what papers?"

"It will save you from deportation, Ayala. If you work for the Germans you won't have to be deported just yet. All you have to do is show them your papers and they will not send you on the trains."

"What do these papers say?" I asked confused.

"They say you are an essential worker to the war effort. They say that you work in the leather department making boots for the German army. Whenever you get stopped, you will show them your papers, and tell them that you are an essential worker."

Tears stung my eyes as I looked at this kind old man. "Why would you do this for me, Barak?" I asked, choking back the tears.

Barak took hold of my hand. "You are just a girl. You have had no life, and I know your father would have done the same for me. Like I say, I owe it to him, but I must know, Ayala, that you will not do yourself any harm. I have to know this."

I put my arms around him and hugged him tight. I felt uncomfortable about it, but managed it just the same. All of a sudden I did not want to die anymore. I felt that I had been given another chance. "Barak, I promise I will do all I can to survive this hellhole. I still feel very sad and depressed that I have nobody left, but I listened to what Bosmat said to me and she is right; Mama could be alive somewhere, and if I killed myself I would never know. So I will carry on, with the hope that Mama and Papa are still out there somewhere. I will use that to get me through."

"That's my girl," cried Barak. "Your parents would be so proud of you."

"How will I ever repay you for all you have done for me?" I said with emotion.

Barak looked at me with admiration. "Stay alive, Ayala," he replied. "Stay alive."

Barak came back an hour later with my papers. We all worried the whole time he was gone. We sighed with relief when he came back through the door. While he was gone I sat and thought about the last twenty-four hours. About Mama going and about the horrific attack the night before. I thought about how close I had become to actually taking my life. I would not have been scared to do it. Death would have and still would be a huge relief to me, but I thought a lot about what Barak and Bosmat had said to me and I realised that they were right about Mama and Papa still being alive somewhere. They made me look at things in a different light.

I decided that I did not want to die. As Barak had said, I was still a young girl. I had not yet lived my life. I had never been married, never had children, and never travelled abroad. All I had known for the last few years was misery, pain and the Warsaw ghetto. It was strange that only hours before I had made up my mind that I was going to die. Now death was the furthest thing from my mind. I knew I had to survive. I knew that I was going to survive. There was no way that they were going to beat me now. I was not ready to die. They had taken too much away from me, and enough was enough. They would not take one more thing from my life. On the night of the attack I was weak, and vulnerable. Now I emerged stronger than ever, ready to fight for my life. I knew that there was no way I would ever get over the things I had seen, and the things that had been done to me, but for now I had to concentrate on surviving and finding my mother and father whether dead or alive. I owed this drastic change of heart to Barak. Had I not seen him that morning, I would have gone through with my plan. I owed my life to this wonderful man.

The deportations started again. Everybody had to make their way to the Umschlagplatz. Those who were exempt from deportations had to show their papers. When my turn finally came I showed my papers with sweat dripping off my head. I was sure they would see my paperwork and just send me to the trains anyway. I could not look the officer in the eye through fear of being sent to the trains. He took my paper then looked at me and handed it back. There was so much going on around us that I don't even think he read it. He pushed me aside and went onto his next victim. I cried with relief as I ran all the way back to the apartment. That is what happened every day, the same procedure, the same fear of being sent to the east. There was no let up in the misery and suffering that they caused. Still the innocent victims were dragged and beaten to the trains. Still the children cried and suffered.

The deportations lasted for seven weeks; in that time the ghetto inhabitants were racked with fear, misery and the constant strain of trying to survive the deportations. Some weeks into the deportations, the Nazis and their Ukrainian helpers would round up Jews randomly in the streets or shops, regardless whether they were exempt from resettlement or not. This put a new wave of fear into every ghetto resident. Although the curfew was still in full swing, people would no longer go out onto the street, unless it was extremely necessary. No more did one see the street beggars or people trying to barter for food. Or the children half dead through starvation. The ghetto, unless chaotic with people being sent to the east, was now like a ghost town, without a soul to been seen, day or night.

The work at the factory was hard and the hours were long and tiring, but it saved me from being deported. I was still ravaged by hunger and lice. I got one small meal at the factory each lunchtime, which consisted of soup and a small potato, it was hardly enough to keep me going but it was something. I decided to stay with Barak and Bosmat. We all felt safer when in numbers than on our own. I was so grateful of this, as I did not want to go back to the apartment and be on my own. There were too many bad memories there for me, and I knew that wherever I looked I would see Mama and Marek. I cried for Mama every day. I thought about her constantly and was forever wondering where she had been sent to that day, and if she was still alive. My heart and soul ached to see her again. I missed her so much. My hatred for the Nazis grew stronger with every passing minute. Since the night of the attack, I would look at every Nazi I saw and blame him in my head for what had been done to me. Every time I saw one of these vile men, it would bring back terrible memories of that night. I would relive it over and over in my head.

Nighttimes too were a problem for me, for although I did not sleep that well anyway, when I did I would relive that night the moment my eyes would shut. I would wake up screaming and crying. Bosmat would come over and calm me down by telling me it was all right. She never asked about my dreams or why I was having them, but she knew. She just pretended that it was all a part of what I had seen in the ghetto. She was a lovely warm person, with thick dark hair, and a kind round face. She was like a mother to me, and when she soothed me after one of my dreams, she reminded me even more of my poor departed mother. Her daughter Sarah was also a source of inspiration to me. She was around about my age and we got on well with each other. We would tell each other secrets and talk about all the things that young girls talk about. It was refreshing to have someone my age to talk to after so long in the ghetto with only grown-ups to chat with. This made our time in this awful place a little better to deal with.

Towards the end of August, the situation in the ghetto had come to a peak. With the deportations, people were being rounded up all the time, either being taken off the streets or having their apartments broken into by the Germans. Once they were in they would wreak havoc and fear into the poor helpless residents. They would torture and shoot people at will. No longer did papers or work exempt us from being sent to the east. Anybody who was anybody was being sent away. We waited day by day for our turn. The waiting was tormenting.

More people were going into hiding, as now it was common knowledge that the rumours were true; people were being gassed at concentration camp called Auschwitz. And Treblinka. Both were as bad as the other, whichever one you were sent to meant death either way. When I first heard this I sobbed my heart out knowing that my poor mother had been sent there. I was beside myself with grief, but as Barak put it, "We do not know yet, she may still be alive somewhere. Do not give up hope." But it was hard not to give up hope in the Warsaw ghetto.

Barak sat us down one day and told us that he felt we should now start thinking about hiding ourselves. At first I was scared, for the punishment of such a crime was certain death. I told Barak that I needed to find out what happened to my mother.

"If I don't go, how will I ever know?" I said as we sat there talking.

"You will know, Ayala, if we survive this hell, then you can begin the process of finding her, and the rest of your family."

I knew he was right, but I was so frightened of being caught. "OK," I said. "What choice do we have?"

"Good, so we are all agreed then," he replied.

"Where are we going to hide?" asked Sarah.

"I have secured somewhere for us. It is in the factory, but we must keep very quite about this, OK?"

"Where in the factory?" I quizzed. "Surely that is the first place they will look."

"It is in a bunker above the factory floor."

"Will we be safe there, Barak?" asked Bosmat.

"I hope so, Bosmat, but who knows. We have no choice."

"How will we get in?" I asked.

"Well, we will make our way up to it at the end of our shift. For us it is easy, because we work there, but Bosmat and Sarah will have to be more cautious. They will have to smuggle themselves in when the coast is clear."

"It all sounds so frightening," said Sarah.

"You will be fine. As long as we are all sensible, nothing will go wrong. I have thought this through for long enough. Now we have to decide when we will go."

"I say we should do it as soon as possible," I suggested. "Get it over and done with."

"OK, let's say tomorrow. Do we all agree?"

We all agreed. That night none of us slept. It was a nerve-racking waiting game. I just wanted it to be over and done with. The morning of the move came. We went to work as usual. When our shift had finished, we went up to the bunker. We waited for Bosmat and Sarah to turn up. Our hearts were beating and I was nervously rocking backwards and forwards in my chair. It seemed we had been waiting for hours. All of a sudden the hatch door came open and there they were, safe and sound. So we had all made it. Now we were on our next survival journey. Trying to survive the bunker.

Chapter 22

THE BUNKER WAS QUITE SMALL, HARDLY big enough to house all four of us. In it were four makeshift beds on the floor. A small table and one rickety old chair. It was not big enough for any of us to stand up in, especially me, as I was so tall. The roof was at an angle, so we had to stoop when standing. That was as straight as we could get. I was under no illusions that when I did finally leave here, I would have a permanent stoop. There were no windows in the bunker. The only light that we had was through the slates in the roof. When the sun was shining it was actually quite light in there. It was not the ideal situation of course, but it was better than facing the trains to the east. I was impressed with Barak though, as he had made it as combatable as possible. Silence was the main theme to our new home. As the bunker was in the attic above the factory floor, we had to be extremely careful not to make any noise during the daytime. Even at night when nobody was there, we still had to be on our guard. We constantly lived on our nerves; hoping and praying that no one would come sniffing around.

Boredom was another fact of in the bunker. The days were so long. We couldn't stand up or stretch our legs. We had to whisper every time we spoke. We tried to amuse ourselves playing games like Eye Spy or Chinese

Whispers. At other times we would sit and talk about life before the war, and about our families. I found it extremely painful to talk of my family. I missed them all so much. I envied Sarah because she still had all her family around her, and sometimes this hurt me to watch them as they prayed together and hugged each other. The one good thing about being in the bunker was that no longer did I have to face the roundups, and no longer did I have to see anymore dead and dying bodies lying on the street. Food was another problem, as it always was. Being in hiding meant that none of us would get any food whatsoever. Now we were not working on the factory floor, we didn't even get our daily lunch of watery soup and potatoes. Barak brought provisions for the first few weeks; he had some coffee and bread and some vegetables that he had smuggled in from the Aryan side. This would not last long so we had to sit and figure out a way to acquire more food when the last provisions had run out.

After being in the bunker for about three weeks, we had completely run out of food. "What are we going to do now?" asked Bosmat.

"I will have to go back down to the wall and get some more provisions," answered Barak.

"No, Barak. You will get killed. It is too dangerous," replied Bosmat.

"We have no choice. How are we going to eat? We will all starve up here if I don't."

"But how will you get down without being seen?" I interrupted.

"I do not know yet. I think maybe I will have to go after dark. I cannot go during the day, unless I want to be caught by the factory workers."

"And if you go at night, you will be shot for not obeying the curfew rules," said Sarah.

"I will just have to be extremely careful and not get caught. If I go around midnight it will be more quiet. I might have more of a chance."

"Oh, I do not like it. I think I would rather starve than have you risk your life like that, Barak," said Bosmat, full of concern for her husband.

Barak went over and put his arm around her. "It will be all right, my sweetheart. I have got us this far, have I not? There is no other choice. We will all starve otherwise."

I looked on with envy as I watched Barak comfort his wife. It reminded me so much of Mama and Papa. I felt the tears sting my eyes, as I watched this emotional display of affection for each other.

"When will you go?" I asked.

"I will have to go as soon as possible. Maybe tonight."

"Please, Barak, be careful," cried Bosmat.

"I will, my dear. I will."

We all waited till nightfall. The waiting seemed agonising. The time ticked by so slowly. I was afraid for Barak. He was so brave, risking his life to put food in our bellies. I prayed that he would not get caught. It must have been around seven o'clock as the factory workers started leaving the building.

"Just another couple of hours then," whispered Barak.

We sat there looking at each other, not really saying much. It was now dark inside the bunker and we could not see a thing. Nobody spoke as we waited for the hours to tick away. My nerves were shot for Barak. I could not imagine the fear he must have been feeling as we all sat there waiting for the time to arrive. Suddenly Barak spoke. It was something that none of us were expecting.

"I want you all to listen to me carefully, OK?" He spoke deep and serious. "If for some stroke of bad luck should befall me, and I don't come back, then I want you all to make your way tomorrow morning to the trains."

"What are you saying, Barak?" replied Bosmat in shock.

"I am not saying that I will not return, but we do have to be realistic. There is a chance that I may get caught, and I don't want you waiting around here for me. The chances are that they will find you eventually, and I think that you should take your chances on the trains."

"I will not, and I don't want you talking that way. You will come back. I could not bear it if you didn't." Bosmat was now crying quite hysterically. Barak tried to calm her down.

"Bosmat. This is just a precaution, just in case I do not return. Please come to your senses and listen to me. I'm telling you this just in case."

"Well, I don't want to hear it, Barak," sobbed Bosmat.

"OK, my dear. OK," said Barak, not wanting to distress his wife anymore.

"And why would you want us to go to the trains? Do you want us all to die?" questioned Bosmat, not letting the conversation drop.

"Of course I don't, you silly woman," snapped Barak back. "We do not know for a hundred percent that is what is happening there, but I know you will not survive here without me. So I think you would stand a better chance there, than here starving to death."

"I am so frightened for you, Barak," replied Bosmat, in a much softer tone."

"And I am scared too, but we must be positive. If I am extremely careful, I will be OK."

No more was said after that. We continued to sit in the dark in silence. Finally the time came. Barak whispered to everybody that it was time. We all shuffled about nervously, as Barak bid us all farewell, told Bosmat and Sarah that he loved them, and then took his leave. We watched as he opened the door to the bunker, took to the stairs and was gone. We sat there in silence. Quietly praying that he would make it back. I tried to lighten the situation a little by suggesting that we play a game of Eye Spy.

"But it is dark and we cannot see anything," said Sarah.

"I know, but we can pretend we are in a big house, OK? That will make it more fun. I will say what room we are in, and you have to try and guess what the object in that room is."

"OK, then," sighed Sarah unenthusiastically.

"Bosmat, you're not getting away with it either. You have to play too."

"Do I have to?"

"Yes, you do, so come on."

"OK, OK," she reluctantly replied.

We sat and played imaginary Eye Spy for what seemed liked hours, but in fact was only about one hour. We sat and talked quietly for a while, then when all conversation had run out, we sat quietly in our thoughts. We all knew we would not sleep tonight. How could any of us sleep knowing that Barak was out there risking his life for us? I sat and thought about Mama, and Marek.

Then my mind drifted back to before this crazy nightmare began. When we were all together, living in our lovely house. My mind drifted back to Isaac, and how in love with him I once was. *It seems a lifetime ago now*, I thought as I tried to picture his face in my head. I couldn't quite remember his face. At one time I would have been angry and frustrated at not being able to conjure up such an image, but now it didn't seem to matter to me as much. I still loved Isaac, but it had been so many years since his disappearance and so much had happened in my life that the events of this nightmare had forced me to move on. I was just a girl when all this started, just sixteen years old. I was nearly nineteen now. How I had managed to survive for this long could only be described as a miracle.

My thoughts drifted back to Marek. How life was so cruel to him. How he had suffered. He was just a child, why did God not spare him? I remembered how terrified he was all the time, and how he would not let Mama out of his sight. I thought back to all those years before when I came home and found him on the stairs crying, because he had heard Mama and Papa talking about the Germans. I remembered how I comforted him, and told him it was all wild rumours. Dear God if I had known then what was just around the corner. I don't think anybody ever imagined the horror and despair that awaited us. Oh how I missed my little brother. How I missed his big smile and gentle manner. How I missed the sound of his laugher and his inquisitive nature. I sat there sobbing underneath my breath, as I thought how much I hated those demented murderers.

I wondered how long they could possibly get away with eliminating our population. Why had nobody come to save us? Why had the world turned its back? Surely they must know of the atrocities happening to us here. I cried more tears as I thought of Mama, of how scared she must have been on that train to nowhere. I knew that even as scared as she would have been I knew she would still be worrying for me more than herself. I missed her so my heart ached. I missed our chats we used to have late at night. I missed her sensible advice she used to give me. I even missed being in the apartment with her. God how I hated those murdering beasts. How I hoped that they would suffer for all they have done. They have destroyed a whole population of people. We should not be living like this. We should not be hiding away like criminals. We are not vermin or disease carriers, or criminals. It is they who are the sewer rats. They who are vermin. And they who are the criminals. And it will be them one day that shall hide their faces in shame for all they had done. I was disturbed from my thoughts by Sarah.

"Are you awake, Ayala?" she whispered.

"Yes, I am just sitting here quietly thinking, that's all."

"What are you thinking about?"

"I was just thinking about my family and how much I miss them."

"I'm sorry, I didn't mean to pry," she said regretfully.

"No, no. You were not prying, honest."

"I sometimes forget what you have been through, with losing your family and all."

"That's OK, I just wish it was as easy for me to forget," I said.

"I could not imagine what it would be like if I lost all my family. I don't know what I would do. You are a very brave girl, Ayala."

"I am no braver than anybody else," I replied. "I have just had to face up to the situations that I have been forced into, that's all."

"Well, I still think you are brave," she answered back. "Ayala."

"Yes."

"How long do you think he has been gone now?"

I could not lie. I had noticed Barak had been gone for quite some hours now. "I think maybe…"

Just as I was about to tell Sarah how long Barak had been gone. The door swung open and there in front of us was Barak. We all jumped up, hitting our heads on the way. We all cried as we hugged him tight. "I told you I would be back, didn't I?" he said cockily. "And not only am I back. I come bearing gifts as well."

We stood there with our mouths open as Barak emptied his coat, which contained potatoes, vegetables, and tined meats, everything we could have dreamt of. I couldn't believe it. For the first time in years. I actually smiled.

Chapter 23

WE ALL TUCKED IN TO THE food that Barak had found as if it were our last meal. It was almost dawn as we sat there and ate for the first time in days. To see so much food was like all our birthdays had come at once. Barak told us how he found the food items in the empty apartments. The poor victims had been taken away by the SS against their will and had left most of their belongings behind. Barak told us of his guilt at taking somebody else's food, but as we told him, they would no longer need them; God rest their souls.

"I could have got so much more," he told us. "Every apartment was open or had doors blown off. I could have carried on like that all night, but I did not want to tempt fate. I just got what we needed, then came straight back."

"Did anybody see you, Barak?" asked Bosmat scared.

"Would I be here now if they did?" Barak answered with a chuckle.

"I suppose not," replied Bosmat, feeling a little silly at the question she had just asked.

"I did see others though," said Barak.

"What do you mean?" I asked curious.

"There were more like me. Trying to loot every apartment. You could see them hiding in the shadows. Waiting for the right moment to seize what they could. At first I thought they were Germans, but when you looked you could see their thin shadows and their stooped frames."

Barak told his story as if he had been on an adventure. Anyone else listening to him would not have guessed he had just risked his life, risked being tortured, shot or sent to the east for trying to put food in our bellies. I had so much admiration for him. After all he did not have to risk his life for me. I was not his family, just a friend. I was so grateful to him for all her had done for me.

"How long do you think the food will last, Papa?" asked Sarah.

"If we are careful. It will last at least a week. We must be very sensible."

"Then what will happen? Will you have to go out again?"

"Yes, unless the war ends. Otherwise I will probably have to go back down and find more food. Although, going by tonight, I was lucky to find anything. So many people trying to survive. I got there just at the right time tonight otherwise there would have been nothing left."

"I do not want you to go down there again, Barak," cried Bosmat. "I worried so much for you tonight."

"I know, my dear, I know. Let's just pray that the war ends soon then."

And we all agreed on that one. The light was starting to come through the slates, which told us that it was now dawn. We were all so tired. We retired to our beds and fell asleep. It was gone midday when we all woke up. That is how life went on for us in the bunker. Life was slow, boring and nerve splitting. Before we knew it we had been in there for three months. I had not been outside in the fresh air for a long while now. It seemed strange, but I did not care less. The longer I did not have to see a German or any more dead and sick people; the better it was for me. I did not care that I had not stood up straight in three months, nor did I care that the longer I hid the harder it would be to come out. I just knew anything was better than living like vermin under the noses of the SS. Barak's ventures down into the ghetto were a weekly thing. Sometimes he would not find anything, other times he would come back with a loaf of bread or half-eaten potatoes. He never did find as much as he did on that first night. "Beginners luck," he used to say. Obviously the real reason was that the Germans had become wise to the scavengers and would take the food as well as the people when they invaded their apartments, also the amount of people in hiding meant that there was always somebody there before Barak and had taken the last little crumb.

The worry was always the same. Sometimes he would be gone for an hour, other times it would be two or three. And as the first time, we would get excited and hug him with relief when he came back. There was no consistency to it. Bosmat made Barak promise that he would only make the journey, "down into hell," as she put it once a week. Barak could do nothing but agree. Sometimes our provisions would run out before the week was up, and we would feel extremely weak with hunger by the time the night of the journey came round.

It was now well into the winter and once again we had the added worry of the cold. Being in the upper part of the factory with nothing to keep us warm apart from a few thin blankets was extremely hard. The cold would seep into the bunker and the air would freeze. We would huddle together to try and keep warm, but this was of little help. Barak told us that he would keep his eye out for some warm clothing or blankets on his next trip. The trouble was that every trip started to become more risky and with less and less provisions every time. The deportations had now finished. They had only lasted seven weeks, but in that time they had managed to empty the ghetto of at least three hundred thousand people. The last weeks of the Aktions, as they came to be known, were the most brutal. We could see a lot of this through the gaps in the roof. And we could hear every murdering shot, every pitiful cry and the running of feet in terror of the wicked Nazis. Every time I heard a gunshot or screaming it always reminded me of the first day of deportations, and that last time I saw Mama. It also brought back vivid memories of the horrific night in the coffee shop on Mila Street. *When would this ever end?* I constantly asked myself.

It was now December and most of the ghetto dwellers had now been sent to the east. Even the factory workers and hospital staff were no longer exempt. I will never forget the day that they came to take the factory workers away to the railcars. They came in unexpectedly, with their brutal aggression and animalistic behaviour. They dragged everybody away from their machines and out onto the street. People were trying in vain to show them their papers. Women were crying and screaming for their children. It was horrible beyond words. The Nazis just took their papers out of their hands and threw them down, whilst pushing the poor victims to the floor. Some would never get up, as they were shot right there on the spot. We could see all of this through the gaps in the roof. Bosmat would tell us to come away and not to watch such evil.

We would all sit there terrified of the inevitable footsteps that would eventually come up to factory attic. The Germans were well aware of the ghetto people's hideouts, and they were very good at sniffing out such places. These footsteps soon came. We all sat there frozen with fear as the sound of their Nazi boots came up the stairs and closer to the bunker. We could here them moving about and throwing things around in their anger. I totally believed that this was it. It was all over. The door to the bunker was completely concealed, but to a professional murdering Nazi it would be dead easy. We did not breathe for what seemed like an eternity. Looking at each other from across our side of the bunker, the fear of capture was etched on all our faces. Sarah had tears running down her face. Bosmat stood next to her husband, looking down at the floor, silently praying under her breath. Barak stood with his arm around his wife's shoulders staring straight ahead, not even a blink of his eye made a move in fear of being heard. My heart was beating so hard I was sure it would be heard. We stood there for so long waiting for them to disappear; we were actually rooted to the spot.

Finally after a heart stopping time, we heard them say, "There is nobody here."

We heard their footsteps descend the stairs and out onto the street. We collapsed on to the floor with relief; we could not believe that we had not been found. We sat there in silence for a long while after, trying to come to terms with what had just happened to us. This happened to us on a number of occasions and every time I thought I would die of fear.

The New Year descended upon us. It was miserable and depressing, as it ever was. This year was worse than any other for me. I missed my family like crazy. I tried to be positive and believe that Mama was still alive somewhere. But now everybody knew for sure what was happening in the east. My hopes were waning, but I had to believe something to get me through this, otherwise I would sink into a suicidal depression again and not ever come out. I was nineteen years old now, but felt and looked like an old woman. I remembered the last time I caught a glimpse of myself in a reflection of a shop window. I was horrified. I was filthy dirty. My once beautiful long thick hair was now thin and lank. I was emaciated with hunger and I was running alive with lice. I itched and scratched on every part of my body. I felt so ashamed of myself. My nails had started to fall off through the constant hunger and lack of vitamins. I had not had a bath in years.

Apart from food, which was our constant source of conversation, a long hot bath was another thing we constantly dreamt of. I would have given up anything for a long soak in a nice hot bath. It was heinous what they had turned us into. Now on top of everything, we all had a constant slouch because we could not stand up straight in the bunker. My back and neck ached all of the time. After the factory workers had been taken away, we decided that we would have to take an extra risk and go down to the factory each night to stretch our legs. At first none of us wanted to take the risk, but we all ached so much after being shut up for the last six months. We talked about it, discussed it at length, like we did with everything, and finally managed to agree, that for ten minutes each night we would all go down into the factory and get some exercise.

That night we waited until it was very late in the evening before we made our way down. I had been confined in such a small space for so long that the thought of going out into a large open space filled me with intense fear. After a rather nasty panic attack and changing my mind every five minutes, I finally managed to do it. It was wonderful to be able to stand up straight, but also quite painful. My spine had got so used to being in one position it had actually set. When I did finally try to stand straight, it was extremely painful, but still nothing could take away the feeling of being out of the bunker.

Our eyes hurt at trying to look around at things some distance away, as we were only used to having a nearsighted view of the world. After ten minutes we climbed the stairs and went back into our hovel. We only ever allowed ourselves ten minutes and no more. It would have been easy to give ourselves another five and another, but we could not afford to become complacent. After that first trip, we thought of nothing else apart from our next trip down to the factory floor. It is strange, but one does not realise the importance of freedom. It is taken for granted. When it is taken away from you, you suddenly realise just how much you want and need it back. That was what being in the ghetto and the bunker did to us. Made us realise just what we had before, and how lucky we were to have it. Going down to the factory floor every night brought all those thoughts and feeling back to the fore. Of course the danger of being caught was very high, and we were constantly on our guard, but it was just so good to be able to stretch our legs at last, and dream that we were free. I think all in all we must have made at least twenty trips down into the factory, until one evening fate dealt us another cruel blow. Our isolated, miserable little lives as we knew were about to come to an end.

Chapter 24

1943

AFTER ANOTHER LONG AND BORING DAY in the bunker, the time came for us to venture downstairs once more to stretch our aching legs. The silence of the factory floor, once noisy with the machines and people working, was now a graveyard. Quiet and creepy. What made it more eerie was the knowledge of why there was nobody there anymore. It had now started to snow and was freezing cold as we descended the stairs to the floor. Once there we stood looking around us as usual to make sure nobody was watching. We shuffled around trying to get the blood to circulate around our stiff bones. After the ten minutes were up, we were just about to climb the stairs up to the bunker when suddenly the door to the factory burst open. We swung round, hearts beating furiously as we came face to face with four gendarmes. Staring wide-eyed with shock, nobody said a word. Our breathing was hard and heavy, as it dawned on us what was happening.

"Vell look what ve have here," said one of the gendarmes, sneering.

"Ya dinner," said another, and they all laughed.

We stood there trembling so hard our heads would not keep still. I felt sick and I was now sweating. I could not believe that we had been caught.

"So ver have you all been hiding then?" asked one of the gendarmes.

None of us spoke. We just kept our heads down. The fear we all felt was indescribable.

"Are you all stupid or something?" asked the Nazi again. "Ver have you all been hiding?"

With shaking hands, Barak pointed up towards the stairs leading to the bunker. "Up there," he finally answered.

"So, ve have a clever Jew, eh?" he laughed.

Two of the officers stayed downstairs with us while the other two went up to the bunker. A thousand thoughts were going through my head at the same time. I was convinced that now, finally, I was going to die. They were going to kill us at last. I wondered how they were going to do it.

Would they shoot us? Would they beat us to death or would they send us to the east. I looked over to Barak and Bosmat they were holding each other tightly. Sarah was crying uncontrollably and holding onto her mother's hand. Barak looked up at me. "It is OK," he tried to soothe. The tears started coming.

"Shut up. Do not talk," said one of the officers, as he hit Barak across the face with the back of his hand.

Bosmat and Sarah screamed as Barak fell backwards at the force of the punch. Barak came to his feet, visibly shaken. I cried as I saw this old man trying to hold onto his dignity and get to his feet. They just stood there watching and guarding us like we were criminals. Did they not know that we were scared to death, half starved and freezing cold? How on earth could we go anywhere? I looked over at one of the officers. For all I knew he could have been one of the men who had so savagely raped me that night. I never looked in their faces. Never saw their eyes. Now for all I knew I could be standing right in front of them. The images of that night came back to haunt me. *Perhaps they would rape me again*, I thought. The thought of going through that again actually scared me more than what was happening now. We could hear them laughing and screaming upstairs in our bunker. Laughing at our misery and shame. The two gendarmes came down the stairs. Again we froze with fear.

"Vell, vot shall ve do viv the poor helpless Jews?" asked one of them.

"Ve could just shoot them right here."

This caused a commotion of screams from Bosmat and Sarah. I was sobbing hard, and praying in my head. Waiting for a response. *For God's sake, just get it over and done with*, I was screaming in my head. *Just shoot us. Do whatever you need to do. Just put us out of our misery you bastards*.

"Ve could just let them loose tomorrow, without zer badges and papers. Zee how long zay last," said another.

144

"Zat is good ya," said the other officers, laughing.

"Or ve could just send them to ze trains. Zay are sure to die there. Viv not enough air to breathe and no room to move."

"Ya and ve vont have to get our hands dirty on zees filthy Jews."

Sarah was crying hysterically. Begging them for mercy. Bosmat was trying to reassure her that it would be OK. They left us standing there like that for hours, mentally torturing us with their wicked mind games. Dawn was coming and I didn't know how much longer I would be able to stand on my feet for. The Germans were talking among themselves. I was just praying that they would get it over with soon enough.

Suddenly after hours of waiting, they came over and dragged us outside. It was now snowing hard and it was so cold. They started marching us through the square. We did not know where we were going; we hoped it was to the trains. At least there may be some small chance for us. It was better than staying here and being shot. The whole time we were being frogmarched they were beating at us and pushing us to the ground. It is almost impossible to explain the thoughts and feelings that one goes through at being faced with such brutality and fear. It is hard to imagine what such fear is like unless one is faced with it. We arrived at the gates to the Umschlagplatz. By all accounts it looked like they were sending us on the trains. It was now early morning and the sun was coming up. There were already hundreds of people waiting for the trains. We looked at each other with hope in our eyes. *Please God let them leave us here, so we can get on the trains*, I thought. Just as I said this to myself, they came over and told us to go and stand in the line. We did as we were told.

"Now your misery really begins," said one of the gendarmes.

With that they spat at us and left. We all collapsed into each other's arms and cried. The relief that once again we had been spared was tremendous. We were all shaking holding onto each other. After the initial shock that we had survived yet another confrontation with the Nazis had calmed down, we stood and awaited our fate.

"I thought that the deportations had finished," said Sarah, still shaking and crying.

"They have, these are the people from the hospitals and workers of the Germans. There are probably people like us, who have been caught hiding," Barak answered.

"I am scared, Mama," cried Sarah. "We are going to be gassed. I know it."

"We do not know that; just try to calm down, darling, OK? The main thing is that we look healthy enough to be able to work," answered Bosmat, trying to foresee the situation. "Just pinch your cheeks and make them nice and rosy. Try not to slouch, keep your head held high and don't look into their faces."

"How can we not slouch, when we have been bent over in that bunker for the last six months," I answered sarcastically.

"If you want to live, Ayala, you will do it."

The line started moving. It was the same old scene. People crying and children wailing as they tried to fight the inevitable. The Nazis were pushing and shoving them into the trains. Some were kicking the old people and children into the waiting cars for being too slow. What fun they were having, watching the children cower in terror at their guns and jackboots. *What big men you are,* I said to myself as were neared the train. *What bravery you muster, to hurt young children and defenceless old people.*

We got to the front of the queue. Barak climbed in first then bent down to help us all on. The Germans didn't stop in their aggression as I climbed up. They kicked and punched us onto the train. I had been beaten so much by these people that one more punch or kick in the back didn't hurt me anymore. We were pushed in tight into the middle of the carriage. There was already about sixty people in there, and it was already a very tight squeeze. My heart started racing as more and more people climbed into the car. I wondered when it was going to stop. Children were crying pitifully as the air around them closed in. Everybody was pushing and shoving each other to try and make a bit of space. It was horrendous. The Nazis were shouting and screaming at us all to move back into the compartment more. It was virtually impossible. Bosmat and Sarah were crying. Barak was trying to comfort them, all the time more and more people were climbing into the train. Eventually the rush of people stopped. There must have been at least one hundred people in a carriage that could probably only hold about forty.

The doors shut tight. Suddenly we were in darkness. Everybody started wailing again and the children were screaming. The sound of their misery rang in my ears. There was no ventilation and the air was shut tight around us. People were being crushed at the weight of each other being so close. I was sandwiched in the middle of about ten people and I could not breathe. The tightness about me was so strong I actually thought my body was going to crush. The worst part of it all was the fact that there was nowhere for anyone to go to the toilet. A filthy bucket placed in the centre of the carriage served as a latrine. If people wanted to relieve themselves they would just have to do it there and then in front of everyone. It was degrading and humiliating. After a while the bucket would be so full that the contents would be spilling out onto the floor. The stench was disgusting and overpowering. People were fainting and being sick all the time, which made the smell even more overpowering. This was just another way to dehumanise us. We had been standing up in that carriage for hours. *Will it ever go anywhere?* I asked myself.

I could not see Barak and his family. They were completely eaten alive by the people around them. At last the train started moving, just before it did a gendarme opened the door and ordered someone to empty the bucket. That was the only time it was emptied throughout the whole journey. The train moved at a snail's pace. I was utterly convinced, as I had been so many times before, that we were all going to die. I thought about my poor mother on a train like this, suffering and not being able to breathe in the summer heat. It must have been even worse for her, for not only was she alone in her fear and misery, she couldn't stand being closed in. It was one of Mama's fears. I cried as I thought of my poor mother. How I wished she was here with me.

The train had been moving about twenty minutes now, and more and more people were starting to faint. They could not even fall to the floor, but just stayed standing as they passed out. Some people let the children near the door so as to get a small draught, but this was not of much use, as the train was moving so slowly. It was a journey from hell. People were talking to each other, trying to figure out where we were destined. They were telling horror stories about being gassed and mass graves. The children would scream more and the mothers would say, "Shut up, you are scaring everybody." This would cause a huge argument. It was a living nightmare.

My head was spinning, and at any minute I thought I was going to pass out. I kept telling myself to hold on. I consciously had to fight with myself to stay with it. I could hear Sarah crying and Bosmat talking to her. Barak was quiet and had not said a word since the train had started moving. We had been moving around an hour now and there seemed to be no end in sight to the misery that was our journey. On and on it went; where to, was anybody's guess. We were so thirsty, but of course there was no water. Every now and then the train would stop. At first we all thought that we were at our destination, but suddenly a shot would ring out, and that would tell us that some poor soul had tried to escape the carnage, and failed. This also served as a warning to us not to try the same thing.

Eventually after many hours, we finally arrived at our destination. At the start of this horrendous journey, there had been around one hundred of us. Now there was half of that amount. Everybody else had died. The journey was just too much for them. How I survived that trip into hell, I will never know. The doors opened. It was dark and the snow was still coming down thick and fast. More SS guards and their vicious dogs ordered us out. They virtually dragged people from the carriage. Everybody was crying. I looked around me. I tried to focus on where I was. There was so much going on. We were being pushed and shoved around; it was hard to take it all in. I looked up and there in front of me was an entrance that read "Arbeit Macht Frei."

"Work make's one free." I didn't understand the concept of it. Then I saw another word I had never heard of. Auschwitz-Birkenau.

Chapter 25

THE SCENE ON THE PLATFORM WAS chaotic. The Germans in their SS uniforms dragged the people from the trains. We piled out, confused and frightened. The SS men were shouting and screaming. Children were wailing. Mothers were desperately trying to hold onto them. Everything was happening so fast. It was the usual carnage of abuse, much the same as in the ghetto, but there was something very different about this place. It was a dark foreboding place. The white stone buildings were long and hollow. One could see the rows and rows of barrack-like buildings, which looked cold and unforgiving. In the middle of these buildings was a steeple-like watchtower, with guards manning it constantly. As soon as one got there, one could feel the death and depression in the air. There was a constant sweet nauseating smell that seemed to follow you everywhere you went. The most disturbing thing that I will always remember about that day was the people there.

As soon as we got off the trains, they came to unload the dead that had died on the way. I will never forget the way they looked. Totally emaciated, their eyes completely sunken in. Their bellies swollen from hunger. Their heads shaved, and wearing a strange stripy pyjama style uniform, reminiscent to that of prisoner's clothes. These totally dehumanised zombies were in the very last throws of death, waiting to take their last breath. Out they ran in their droves, like hungry animals in the night, eyes wide and staring in fear and paranoia. What had those eyes seen? I wondered. How long had these poor men been in this place? Suddenly there was more screaming as the SS officers started dragging people apart and screaming, "WOMEN TO THE LEFT, MEN TO THE RIGHT!"

Wives were pulled and dragged apart along with the children. Little girls with their mothers and little boys with their fathers. The screaming and hollering was unbearable to hear. "WOMEN TO THE LEFT, MEN TO THE RIGHT!" they continued to scream.

Just then Barak was dragged away and literally thrown to the floor and kicked as he was separated from his wife. Bosmat screamed and ran after him. An SS man ran over and dragged her back by the hair. Sarah was hysterical with shock and screaming dementedly for her father. I grabbed hold of Bosmat and held her close to me. The scene before us was like nothing I had ever seen in the ghetto or anywhere else in my life. It was terrible. The women were demented with fear and anger as they ran after their children, only to be shot down or savagely attacked by the snarling dogs in front of their own family. The tears that flowed that day would have sunk a battleship. The pain these monsters caused was unforgivable beyond words. Some women were actually attacking these monsters and trying to scratch at their faces, only to be shot through the head.

Afterwards more lines were formed. At each end there was an SS officer with a stick, pointing in the direction of the left and right. They would just look at you and point the stick saying, "Left," or "Right." It was all so confusing. I was still with Bosmat and Sarah. We could no longer see Barak, the lines were moving so fast. Bosmat and Sarah were beside themselves, heartbroken and grieving for Barak. I knew only too well what that felt like. My head was spinning and once again I tried not to faint. I thought my heart would just stop beating any minute. In a way I wanted it to, to be away from this mental asylum. Our turn came at the top of the line. I straightened myself up as much as I could, head held high. I looked him straight in the face. I knew I had to look well, for I knew that this selection was life or death. I whispered to Sarah and Bosmat to straighten up. He looked at me. My heart stopped.

"Left," he said as he pointed his stick. I went to the left. I did not know if I was in the good line or bad line. It was terrorising. I stood there and looked over at Sarah and her mother. Sarah was first. "Left," he pointed, and Sarah came over and stood next to me.

Next Bosmat's turn. He looked straight at her. "Right," he said. I could not believe it. My heart hit my stomach. We cried as Bosmat looked over at us and was ushered away with the line.

"Mama," screamed Sarah. "Mama."

I was crying as I tried to control her. "Sarah, no. They will kill you." She didn't hear me as she tried to run off. I grabbed and pulled her back. "Please, Sarah, there is nothing you can do now. Just pray."

Sarah was not listening. She was so hysterical; I could not calm her down. Suddenly she shot off and was gone in the crowd. I could hear her calling for her mother. I sobbed as I stood there waiting for the inevitable. Then I heard it. I could not see anything, but I heard the shot ring out, and then I heard the screaming. I heard Bosmat's voice screaming for her dead daughter. Then I heard another shot and more screaming. I knew I had just lost both of my friends. The only two people I had left in the world. I was stunned into silence. Suddenly I could not hear anything apart from the pounding of my own heart. I did not cry. I tried to contain myself, as I knew if lost it, I too would be dead. I could not believe that in a matter of minutes I had lost two important people in my life. I felt like I had been hit with a tranquilliser. I was numb. I came back to myself. The noise and chaos around me, the wailing and screaming was getting louder and louder, there was just no let up.

We were taken to a large room, and told to leave all our possessions and valuables on the floor. I had no possessions apart from a few jumpers that Barak had found for me, and the only thing that was remotely valuable to me was the necklace that Isaac had bought me all those years before. I left my things on the floor. We packed ourselves in tight. In this room were two women SS guards. I could not understand how a woman could do such a task, to take away screaming children. They were not human beings. They were machines. They stood there looking at us. No emotion or a sign of compassion for any of us. We were ordered to undress. Nobody wanted to do it. We all felt so conscious of ourselves. We were given our orders once more. Failure to do so would result in death. We started to undress. This brought back the memories of the night of the attack. I could see the two women peering at us as we slowly took off our clothes. It was so humiliating. It was freezing cold and there were filthy dirty pools of water all over the floor. We were now all naked, freezing cold and barefoot in the middle of winter, standing in filthy water. *Is there nothing they will not stoop to?* I cried to myself as I tried to cover my nakedness behind someone else.

Suddenly one of the guards came over to me. "Vot is zis?" she asked with vile anger.

I was still wearing my necklace. "It is my pendant," I replied in a pathetic whimper.

"I told you to take every zing off," she replied, looking at me like I was filth. With that she tore the chain from my neck and threw it on the floor. I stared straight ahead and didn't even flinch. *Does she think that I will be concerned with a piece of silver, after all I have lost? Stupid woman!* I thought. A part of me was upset at the loss of my necklace. It was the last thing that Isaac had given me, and it was the last reminder I had of home. It was sentimental, but what could I do. My precious memories were still in my head. Nobody could take that away from me. They left us there in that room for hours crying and freezing cold. Some of the women were completely shot to pieces after having their children taken away. They were muttering and talking to themselves, completely insane. Everybody was in pieces. After a couple of hours some people started to collapse. They never got up again. I tried to hold on as much as I could, but I was weak and cold. I had not eaten for at least two days now and the hunger pangs were eating me alive. I could deal with that. I had enough practice. I thought once again of my poor mother. I imagined her in this room, and the indignity of the situation. It hurt so much to think of her in this hell camp all alone. We still did not know what was to become of us.

"What line do you think we were in?" People were asking. "Was it good or bad?" Nobody knew. That was part of their sick game. To leave us in the cold, knowing that some of us would die. Keep us guessing what our fate would be. My feet were starting to freeze and I found it difficult to move my toes. I hopped from one leg to the other to get the circulation going. Naked I stood there hopping, in the freezing cold. It was demoralizing and humiliating. Just when I thought I could no longer stand. In came the two SS woman again.

"Put zees on," they ordered us, as they dropped the clothes on the floor. I picked mine up and quickly put it on. It was a black and white stripy uniform, the same ones the poor men were wearing when we first arrived. It was made of the thinnest, cheapest cotton and was miles too small for me, and on top of that it was now soaking wet. There was no way in hell this would keep us warm. Another sick joke for the Nazis. Together with the flimsy uniform was a pair of hard clogs. Again they were way too small for me. I squeezed my cold, wet foot in, and recoiled from the pain in my foot that was now shooting up my frozen legs. I knew in no time at all I would have blisters on my feet to add to the rest of my troubles. If the tragedy and sickness of the situation was not so serious, I think I may have laughed. We looked pathetic standing there in our prison issue clothes that would not keep a stick insect warm, and clogs that were far too small. In some people's cases the clothing was too big. It was pathetic. They had done a fabulous job at dehumanising us. We no longer looked like human beings, but freaks in a sideshow.

The German women stood there jeering at us. Laughing at our grief and misery. After this sideshow we were taken down to another room. It was in another block, so we had to walk back out into the rain and cold in our flimsy uniform and clogs. While walking over to the block. I stared in horror as I looked up and saw a large brick chimney spitting its contents over the whole camp. I felt uneasy and suspicious at this large flume of smoke. I tried to close my mind off to the thoughts that were now burning in my mind. I followed the row into the block. Again it was a large room with no windows, and a wet floor. We were even more scared now, as we still did not know whether we were going to the gas chambers or a works camp. It was horrendous. Again we packed in tightly. There were more women SS guards and we were ordered to stand in a line. Another woman officer came in; she gave us some solution to put on our heads. We were confused, but followed the orders anyway. The solution stung like hell, and smelt awful. We were told this was to kill the lice. After this the woman with the solution along with the two other SS guards came down with razors in their hands. My heart stopped as I realised they were going to shave our heads. My turn came. I felt sick as she grabbed my head and pulled it back. With one great swoop of her masculine hand, she began to viciously shave at my head. I cried as I saw my once beautiful hair fall to the floor. I tried to tell myself that it was just hair and it would grow back. If I survived. She ripped and scratched at my head; there was no water or soap, only the smelly disinfectant that was used to clean my head of lice. I stared straight ahead, not caring if she saw me cry or not.

Afterwards I looked around at the other women, everybody all looked the same. Like clones in the same clothes and the same hair. I only had to look at the person next to me to see what I looked like. We were a pathetic sight. Like freak shows at a circus. Next the most bizarre thing happened: they came in and tattooed our arms. It was painful and sadistic as they scratched numbers into our skin. We were so debilitated; we did not even question why we were being tattooed. I thought that it was just another sick joke for them, as they knew it was against the religion of the Jews to have any body art whatsoever. Again after this we were left standing around, not knowing was coming next.

After more hours of waiting and standing on our cold feet, we were taken to some barracks. It was now dark and very late in the evening. At last we were told what was to become of us. We stood outside the barracks and a fat German SS officer came and told us, "You have been assigned verk duties. Tomorrow you vill be told vot it is you vill be doing." We looked at each other with relief.

"So we are workers at last," somebody said.

We were led into the barracks; on the way in we were given a large dirty bowl, and a coffee mug. We were assigned a bunk each. I could not believe my eyes when I saw how many women were sharing one bunk. Some there were two to a bunk, some there four. I was dumbstruck. I felt awkward and hesitant when I got to my bunk. The woman in there opened her eyes as I approached the bed.

"I am very sorry," I whispered. "I didn't mean to wake you, but I have been assigned this bed too."

"Wake me, what in here. Nobody sleeps here, my child. That is something you will learn fast."

She moved over to let me climb in. There was absolutely no space whatsoever. She told me we had to top and tail. I got to the end of the bed and slowly slid into the thin sheets that served as covers. I tried to lay down, but being so tall my feet were hanging out the end. I was bent at an angle and was so uncomfortable. This was not a bed; it was a concrete slab with some straw on the bottom and a thin sheet on top. It was horrendous. *The woman was right*, I thought. *I will never sleep here like this*.

I shuffled about trying in vain to make myself more comfortable, but the bunks were so close together that every time one person moved over, everybody else had to move over, so in the end I stayed in the one position. I lay there like that all night. I did not sleep a wink. It was hideous. What was worse than anything was the lice. The bunks were full of them. All night long they crawled up and down my legs biting at my skin. I wanted to scream out loud. After so many hours lying there scratching, I turned to my neighbour next to me and apologised.

"I am so sorry for keep disturbing you," I said.

"That is OK," she whispered. "That is what life is like here. Welcome to Auschwitz," she said.

Chapter 26

MY FIRST NIGHT IN AUSCHWITZ WAS the most horrific experience I have ever endured. I lay in the same uncomfortable position for hours. Sleep never came, as I lay crooked on a concrete bed with lice as big as flies eating away at my skin. The smell of the place was overpowering, the disgusting stench of sickness and death mixed with diarrhea made me constantly retch. My head was full of thoughts of the day's events. The brutal act of the Nazis, the death of Bosmat and Sarah was an utter shock to me. It had not sunk in properly that I had lost yet more special people to me. I thought of Barak, and where he had been taken. I wondered whether he was dead or alive. The tears flowed yet again as I thought of this kind man taking me in and saving my life only to be murdered for his kindness. I didn't believe he was still alive, no more than I believed that my mother was still alive. One minute in this soul-destroying place told me that nobody survives here for long.

My thoughts strayed back to everything that had happened to me that day. Standing in the freezing cold water; having my head shaved. The train journey. It was utter madness. The lives of us poor Jews had been left in the hands of criminals and murderers. I thought that the ghetto was hell on earth. This place made the ghetto look like home. *So this is what east meant*, I thought as I lay on the concrete bed looking up at the white ceiling. *If there is such a thing as hell on earth, then this is surely it*, I thought once again of all the dear people lost to me, and I could not understand why I had so far survived. Was it just luck? Or was it that for some reason God needed me to survive. I couldn't quite make up my mind. I wondered what the next day would bring in this evil place. Would I survive it? Would I care if I didn't? Of course not. I knew as soon as I arrived here and saw the poor victims of this evil school of hard knocks, that death would be a huge release. Death did not scare me. After all I had seen and endured; death would be an escape.

The way in which I may die is what frightened me. I did not want to be gassed or shot, or die of an epidemic, like my poor Marek. Marek, just the thought of his sweet name immediately brought a sob to my throat. He was such an innocent. How could anyone hurt an innocent child? I missed him so much. Even if I did survive this hell, how would I ever forget? How would I live without my family? I would be alone with all my memories of them, and all my memories of the torture I had been through. Did I really want to survive?

Slowly I heard the voice of death calling me again. Encouraging me to end it all. I had no Barak to rescue me this time. No Bosmat to advise and comfort me, no Sarah to play Eye Spy with. I put my hand up to my face and wiped away the tears, as I did so I felt the top of my head and cried with anger as I felt my scalp bald and scratched to pieces. *Why do they hate us so much? Why do they enjoy inflicting so much pain and suffering?* I asked myself. How I hated them. How I would never forgive for what they had done. If I did decide I wanted to live, then it would be to see justice rain down upon them. That would be the only reason I would want to survive this war. To see them suffer.

I looked around the large room to see if anyone else was awake. I was astonished to find that most of them were fast asleep. I could not believe that anyone could sleep in such conditions. It was unreal. Just as I was thinking this, the lights came on and a loud alarm woke everybody from their sleep. Armed SS guards came running in ordering everybody out into the square. I got up with everybody else and went outside. My neighbour told me not to forget my bowl and cup. I did as I was told and followed everybody out into the square.

"What is happening?" I asked, as I was running.

"Roll call," answered somebody.

I did not understand what this meant. We were ordered to stand in a line. There were rows and rows of us. Hundreds and hundreds of people. It was freezing cold and it was still the middle of the night. Daylight had not even begun to break yet, and already the abuse and suffering had started. SS officers walked down the lines counting every head. Nobody spoke; the silence was eerie as the only sound one could hear was the clicking of their boots as they slowly walked up and down inspecting everybody as they counted. Every now and then they would spot somebody whom was not pleasing to the eye, or somebody who looked too old or weak or sick.

"How old are you, Mother?" they would ask. If they did not believe the answer or the answer was too old, too young or for no reason at all they would send the person to another line. The bad line, as it would come to be known.

Sometimes they would just shoot at someone there on the spot. If a person was found talking, then they too would be killed. The methods of killing were never the same. Sometimes they would shoot. Other times they would let their vicious dogs loose on some poor unsuspecting victim, and their screams could be heard all over the camp. The roll call system was another way to beat us down, dehumanise and push us as far as we could go. It was terrible. Hours and hours every morning and evening we would have to stand around being counted and chosen for death. If they lost count, they would start all over again. The worst part was to find somebody missing. This would result in mass killings. Everybody in a certain group or line would be executed. They way they did this would change from day to day. Depending on who was in charge. Sometimes if it was somebody particularly deranged, then they would go down the line shooting every other person to their left or right of them. At other times they would just shoot into the crowd randomly shooting at people. It was a constant soul-destroying game of Russian roulette.

Every day people would collapse after being on their feet for so long. Some of them never got up again. Others would catch pneumonia and die. Some people just dropped dead from exhaustion. The mortality rate at this hell on earth camp was extremely high. People would drop dead all day long. I wondered how long it would take me to become like the zombies I saw when I first arrived. I knew it would not be long.

After roll call we would be given our breakfast. This consisted of watery coffee and a piece of bread. Out they would come, those poor emaciated souls, with the soup and coffee on a table and set it up in the corner. The rush of people trying to get to it was pathetic. They would fight and kill each other for a slice of stale bread. That is what hunger does to you. If you were too slow, you would starve. The Germans were clever people, for not only did they systematically kill us off, they also starved us to the point that in the end we were killing each other for the sake of a slice of bread. The bread and coffee was utterly disgusting. At first I gagged when I tasted it, but after a while the taste became the most delicious thing in the world. When one is starving, one will eat anything. To watch us all scavenging for food in this way would have been identical to watching animals in a zoo. That is what they turned us into. It was barbaric.

Although I knew in my heart that my mother was dead, it did not stop me asking anybody who would listen if they had heard of her. I would give them her name, age and so on, but I never had a single lead. The most disturbing part of it all was the response I would get. Some people would point to the burning chimney and say, "That is where your mother is."

I recoiled in horror when I first heard this finding it impossible to imagine my poor beautiful mother dying in such a way. Eventually I stopped asking. My mother was dead and that's all there was to it. I just had to accept it. I learnt a lot in that first week in Auschwitz, and I learnt fast. I had to if I wanted to survive that little bit longer. I learnt not to ask for anything in any way. If I was sick, I had to hide it as much as I could. I would scrub my cheeks furiously to make them appear red and healthy. If I wanted to use the latrines during work hours, I would just have to wait until the end of the day and go with everybody else. The latrines were a hellhole in themselves. With just a large hole on top of wooden blocks. There was no privacy or intimacy; one just had to go there and then with your neighbour watching. It was disgusting. I learnt fast that wherever I went, my bowl and mug had to come with me. Even in our so-called beds, underneath the pillow they would go. If not they would be gone, once gone there was no chance of getting another one. If one had the courage to ask for one, then one was suicidal.

Shoes were another lesson soon learnt. After half a day of working hard digging trenches, my feet were so sore and swollen I was actually screaming in pain. The blisters on my feet were the size of golf balls, the pain incredible. I knew I could not ask for a new pair; that would mean a severe beating or death. I knew I could not take anymore of the agony, so I decided to ask someone to swap with me. I found someone that had a small foot who had a large shoe, and I swapped. It seemed that I had started a craze; now everybody was swapping their shoes. It felt good that I had helped to ease some suffering in such a big way.

The things I saw in that camp were like nothing on earth. It was the end of the world here. We were tormented souls; crazy with the horrors we had seen. The ghetto was a place to be feared, but here was something else. One had to witness it to believe it. People would literally be here one minute and gone the next. The suicide rate was extremely high. The Nazis knew what their evil and sickening deeds were doing to people's minds, so they built an electric fence and told us to run into it when we had had enough. This would save their bullets, they would tell us. The fence was constantly decorated with dead bodies. After a while in this death camp it became common knowledge among the inmates that this was an extermination camp. The end of the road.

The rumours in the ghetto were true. They did gas people here. They would take people to the "Bath House," as they put it and make them undress; about 100 victims would be shoved in tight into a room. Then they would turn on the gas. The showerheads on the ceiling were there to fool people into thinking they were being deloused. The gas would be turned on and out through the showerheads would come the gas. After twenty minutes they would all be dead. Men, women and children. Because of the amount of people in the room and the tight squeeze, the poor victims would be still standing after they died.

The most tragic part to all of this was the children. Once the mothers heard and smelt the gas, they would try to hold the children in up to the shower heads so they would die straightaway and not suffer. After this, to try and hide their wicked crimes, the Nazis would burn the poor victims in an oven. There were rumours that some of these poor people would still be alive when they were sent to the ovens. How did we know all this? Because there were inmates here whose job it was to take these poor helpless victims to the gas chambers, then it was someone else's job to watch them burn. This made me think again of Mama, and how she must have suffered. I wondered too about my father and if he was sent to the gas chamber somewhere. Then I thought of Marek and for the first time I was actually thankful that he had died in the ghetto. The thought of my poor baby brother dying like that tore my heart to pieces.

I decided not to make any friendships here. We were all in the same boat, and we needed each other very much, but also there was a lot of backstabbing. People would betray one another for a small potato. It was madness. I also didn't want to get close to anyone else for fear of losing that person to the Nazis. I'd had enough of grieving. I also believed I was a jinx. Everyone close to me so far had died, and I had so far survived. I didn't want to put anyone else at risk. I decided I was to be on my own. Now until my death or if fate allowed even after liberation. That was the way it was to be. Forever.

Chapter 27

THE SUMMER HAD BEEN AND GONE and it was now October again. My twentieth birthday had been and gone and I didn't even know it. I did not care. Birthdays meant nothing. Life meant nothing here. I had been here ten months and I was still alive. Not many people survived that long here. I knew I was living on borrowed time. To say every day was a bonus would not be the right words for somebody existing in a place such as this, but it was pretty amazing that I was still here. I'd had my share of sickness and disease, but so far I had managed to fight it off. There was a constant epidemic of dysentery and typhus and people were dying of it all the time. I don't know how I had escaped death so many times. I was just as thin and emaciated as everybody else. The food rations were disgusting and small, and there was always a reason for the SS not to feed us on some days. I was constantly hungry and thought about food all of the time. The main topic of conversation in the barracks was food always. That is all we dreamt of. The work was a sickness in itself, it was backbreaking, degrading and hard to the extreme; the days were long and hard from four in the morning till seven or eight at night. This system of slave labour killed hundreds of people every day. The SS guards liked nothing more than to beat and kick us workers for being too slow or stopping to stretch our aching backs. People dropped down like flies on the trenches. Once this happened the SS would pull out their pistols and shoot them in the head, just to make sure they were dead. This happened all day on and off. After a while we just got used to it. I had seen so many bodies in different states of death that it meant nothing to me anymore.

I was still looking for my mother. I knew in my heart she was dead, but I think somewhere deep inside me needed a reason to stay alive. I had stopped asking people about her, but I still went on looking. I searched every face I passed, every dead body I looked at from top to toe. Every new arrival I tried to glimpse at before they were sent to the gas chambers. I never stopped looking.

It was now the New Year 1944 and the war had been active for five years. If I died now then at least I would have survived five years of hell. It was hard to believe the war had been on for five years. It was even harder to believe that it had been five years since I had seen my father, two years since I had seen my mother, and three years since Marek had died. I thought about the rest of my family. My aunts and uncles, my cousins. Were they all dead? Were they in a concentration camp somewhere being tortured, abused and murdered? I felt all alone in the world as I remembered my family and all the happy times I had spent with them, all the holidays we had celebrated. I would never see or enjoy those times again. There was so much I missed, not just my family, but everyday things that one enjoys and takes for granted, like music or reading a good book. The sound of laughing. I had not heard somebody laugh for years. Trees and flowers or just a walk in the park and music, oh how I would love to hear music again. The SS played music here all the time, but it was usually when they were killing someone or rounding up poor victims for the gas chambers. This music I never want to hear again. Things, which seemed so normal and everyday at one time, were now a million years away from where I was.

I looked around me. Nothing grew here. Nothing was born here. There were no children here, no flowers or trees or grass. Nothing existed here only death. It was as if they had built their very own version of hell, or as if somebody had dug deep into the ground and pulled it up from its roots. Hell on earth. Words were not strong enough to describe the evilness of the place. It was beyond any form of human words. There was no end to barbaric treatment and torture the Nazis displayed. There was no level of wickedness that they would not stoop to.

Another common practice here was also the experiments. At first I did not believe it, but as time went on I saw more and more evidence that this was true. They particularly liked children and babies to experiment on. What sort of experiments they did nobody exactly knew, but they were wicked and cruel. The children never survived them. As soon as they had satisfied their evil curiosity, the children would be put to death. Adults were another matter. Some of them would survive another day, telling anyone who would listen what had been done to them. It was sickening. Some people were put into freezing cold water with ice in it and made to stand for hours. Others would be subjected to injections and medicines that would make then extremely sick. There was no end to the torture and inhumanity that they put us all through. I prayed every night that I would not be the next victim of the murdering doctors.

There was some unusually good news floating around the camp in the spring of 1944. People were starting to talk of the end of the war. I didn't listen to such gossip. I had done so before and been disappointed every time. The topic of the end of the war was as popular as the topic of food, but in April something happened which was to give us all hope, something we desperately needed. While working on the trenches one day we heard the sound of aircraft fire. We looked up and flying above our heads were American planes. The SS ran for cover, leaving us all outside to take their bombs, but we didn't care. We threw ourselves on the floor, hoping and praying that after everything we had been through, we would not be killed by the allies. Everyone was so excited.

"At last they have come to help us. At last we will be saved," people were shouting.

This was one in the eye for the scum of the SS. Now they knew how it felt to be persecuted. It felt great. It gave everyone such a great sense of hope. This bombing continued all the way through the summer. The Germans were nervous. There was talk of liberation and the Red Army advancing towards the east. It looked at last that the end was finally in sight. How long it would be until they actually liberated us nobody knew, but it *was* in sight. The SS were no less brutal in their actions and the terror and torture went on regardless. The gassings, roll calls and general abuse to the inmates went on regardless of the bombings. The roll calls got worse as time went on. They were humiliating and degrading. To ensure the prisoners were fit and healthy for work, they would make us run up and down in front of Nazi doctors naked to see how thin or weak we were. When they were bored with that, they would order us to do strenuous exercise routines like standing with large rocks or stones in our hands while bending and straightening our legs. For the healthiest person this would be exhausting, so to starved and beaten prisoners it was almost impossible. If a person looked too thin or too pale and could not keep up with the exercise, they would send you to the gas chambers. It was as simple as that. What was worse than all of this was to see a person you once knew and respected before the war, like a doctor or schoolteacher standing before you naked and looking pathetic. The Nazis loved nothing more than to make us feel humiliated. I do not know how I survived these selections. Every day I expected it to be my turn.

The winter was here again, the cold got into our bones and made the hellish situation we were in so much worse. I prayed even harder now that the war would soon end. The Russian army were advancing nearer and nearer all the time. The end was so near. There was high excitement and talk all over the camp, talk of liberation was more popular than the topic of food. Everybody just hoped and prayed that they would make it. The Germans were now very worried, knowing full well that the war for them was all about over. The SS knowing what was to become of them now tried desperately to hide their vile crimes by destroying all the evidence of their murderous acts. Of course they used the poor Jews once again to carry out the dirty work.

During December I was sick once again. I was in the camp sick bay. Normally I would have been sent straight to the gas chambers, but for a miracle they were no longer in operation. I had been sick for about a week. Dysentery and frostbite had taken a hold on me, and I was near death once again.

After two weeks I had improved somewhat, and was now able to sit up in bed, I pretended that I was still very sick, to save me from the hard labour. Now that the gas chambers were no more I felt I had gained an advantage so to speak. I knew that the Soviet Army were now very close, so I tried to stay in the hospital for as long as I could. The New Year rolled in and I had still managed to keep myself in the sick bay. With the Soviet army so close, the SS had other things to worry about, and their attention was diverted to other things. This made it easier for me to stay in the camp sick bay. The sick bay was full of sick and dying people. I prayed that this last bout of sickness would be my last.

With liberation being so close, I started to think about what I would do after all this was over. I had no family to turn to; they had all been killed in this sick and meaningless war. I knew I would never be the same person I was before. I still didn't even know if I wanted to live a lonely existence, with no family or friends around me. Where would I live? Where would I go? I knew there was no way I would stay in Poland after everything that had happened. I thought about my aunties and uncles. Were any of them lucky enough to have survived all this? *Surely I can't be the only one*, I thought, as I lay there in bed. I felt guilty that I had survived up to this point, when others had died. *Why me, God?* I asked myself. *Why would you let me survive and not my little brother?* What sort of life can one lead after going through what we had these last few years? How can I ever forget what I had seen, and what had happened to me? How could I ever get over the death of my parents and my little brother?

I thought about our old house where we used to live, and how happy we all were. I cried as I pictured my parents and Marek in our house. I looked around me at the dying and injured people, and could not comprehend how far I had come from the young girl I used to be and the secure and loving home I had once shared with my parents, to come to this point, sick and lonely without a single person left in the world. *Did I really want to survive after all this?* I questioned myself. I thought about Barak and the kindness he had shown me. I knew he had not survived. He was an old man and frail from living so rough in the last few years. I knew that he had died soon after coming into this hell on earth. I thought about Bosmat and Sarah. A whole family wiped out in a flash. It didn't seem real. It was as if all this had been a bad dream. *Oh, how I wish it were*, I cried to myself.

Then I thought of Kamila. I had not thought of her in such a long time. I closed all thoughts on her a long time ago, but now I found myself sitting in my sick bed thinking about her. Wondering what she was doing. What sort of privileged life had she led, since she had helped Hitler to murder half the population of Poland? My tears were streaming down my face now as I thought of our friendship and how she said we would always be best friends and how much I loved her. I remembered the day I knocked on her door, and the way she spoke to me, as if we had never been friends, like she really hated me. Then I remembered Mama, and how she comforted me in my grief over Kamila. I thought of my father and how he comforted me when I lost Isaac. I wondered if I would ever find out what had happened to all of my family, or would I spend the rest of my life trying to fit the pieces in, like a horrific puzzle. I wasn't even sure if I wanted to know the real truth of what had happened to them. *Maybe it would be best to imagine that they died in a more humane way*, I thought. Could I live with the knowledge of what had really happened to them? Could I sleep at night wondering what their last thoughts were? If I did survive these last few weeks here, then what would the future hold for me?

I looked down at my body, all broken and torn from the years of suffering. I did not look my 21 years. I looked and felt like a hundred years old. My skin was dry and cracked; my back had a permanent slouch. My hair was thin and short, no longer the thick locks I used to have. My teeth had started to fall out through lack of calcium. I was not the pretty young teenager in love with her boyfriend that I once was six years ago. If Isaac was alive somewhere, would he even want me; now that I looked like an old lady? Would I want him? Would I want anyone to touch me after what had happened to me on the night I lost my beautiful mother?

I was frightened of the future. I was frightened of what sort of person I would become once I had left here. I was not the sweet naïve person that I once was. They had turned me into an animal, scavenging for food, a lice infested bag of bones, a thief and an orphan. Whether they would win this war or not, they had certainly succeeded in turning us into the vermin that they had accused us of all along. I remembered the children in the ghetto, delousing themselves like animals in a zoo, those poor innocent children. Out of everything I had endured in this evil existence, nothing would torment my mind as much as the images of those poor children. The suffering they must have gone through. The pain they must have endured. *Why did they have to hurt the children?* I cried. *What harm could an innocent child do to anybody?* I lay there wiping away the tears as the images of everything that had happened covered my mind like a blanket. The next thing I knew I was asleep, dreaming of my family and the life I had lost forever.

Chapter 28

AT LAST FREEDOM WAS HERE. ON the twenty-seventh of January 1945 the Soviet Army liberated us. We cried when we saw them. They cried when they saw us. The feeling was exhilarating. Some of the inmates were hugging them; others were just sitting in silence, thinking about what they had lost. For some, liberation had come a little too late. The scene that the Red Army stumbled upon was like nothing they had ever seen before. These were hard men who had fought a war for the past five years, but had not in those five years seen anything like what they saw on that day at Auschwitz. The army was asking all sorts of questions about what had gone on at the camp. Of course the SS were nowhere to be seen, having fled the place some days before, taking most of the able-bodied inmates with them, dragging them for miles in the snow only to kill them when they could no longer walk. Again I was lucky; I avoided death once more by staying in my sick bed for as long as I could.

The liberators listened in stunned silence of the stories we had to tell them, of all the torture and abuse that had happened to us. Of the gas chambers and the death or our families and children. Some were visibly moved; others were shocked and angry. They were kind and sympathetic, giving us warm blankets and medical treatment for our injuries, and to top it all off they gave us food, proper food, real bread and sausages. We had not had meat in years. Some people got chocolate and nice tasty coffee. Some of the inmates cried at the sight of such a luxury. It had been years since we had eaten anything healthy and tasty. We ate like there was no tomorrow. For me personally I could not quite get my head round the fact that at last we were free. I was relieved, but not happy. Like most of us there, I had no family to return to; they had killed all my family off, so for me I felt that freedom had come a little too late. I kept saying it over and over in my head "Freedom."

"Freedom," but it would not sink in. *What does freedom mean to me?* I asked myself. *I will never forget and will always be haunted by the images of all that had been. Is that freedom? Or would I always be a prisoner of my own thoughts?* I did not know.

The next few days were a mixture of different emotions for everybody, one minute we were ecstatic to be free, and the next there would be extreme anger and bitterness for the loss of our loved ones. It was an emotional roller coaster for us all. The Russians' reactions to what they saw at Auschwitz were also a mixture of different feelings. Some of the soldiers actually cried when they saw the evidence of the gas chambers and the crematorium; they were shocked beyond words. Others just stood and shook their heads in disbelief at the thousands of possessions taken from the prisoners, from jewellery and shoes to thousands of pairs of glasses. What was particularly sickening was the children's toys and bales of human hair they found in the warehouses. They could not believe what their eyes were showing them.

They filmed some of the things they saw, as a constant reminder of what they had seen at Auschwitz. I hoped and prayed that they would show the world what they had seen, for that footage would serve as a voice for all those who had died who could not tell of their torture. The Russians could not believe how we had survived through all of this. They praised us for our bravery. We told them we were not brave; we had no choice but to live as animals, in filthy squalor being beaten and tortured at every waking moment. But still they admired us for our strong will to live.

We were examined by doctors and were given treatment for our wounds, but no doctor or medicine would ever heal the wounds in our heads. I could not understand why I had survived. I felt extreme guilt that I was still here, when millions of others had perished. I asked God over and over in my head why he had chosen me to live, but not my brother or my parents. I didn't know whether to thank God for allowing me to survive or blame him for my family's fate. I was confused with God. I still didn't know if I wanted to survive on this earth without my family, but I was proud of myself that I had survived this vile era of abuse and torture. I had lost all of my family and friends, I had been raped, beaten and abused and had faced death at every moment, and I was still here; scarred and frightened of the future, but I was still here. I was strong and I knew that if I could survive this, then I would survive anything that life threw at me. Nothing in my life would ever compete to what I had been through these last few years; nothing would ever be as bad as this again. I was a survivor, whether or not I wanted to survive from this point on was another question, but I had survived this and I am glad they did not beat me. I wondered what would become of the Nazi murdering squads now. I hoped they would get the justice they deserved, but where does one start to build a case against a whole nation of people? Some of these people had murdered so many they would not even remember most of them. I knew for a fact that I would not see my attackers justified, as I did not even know who they were or what they looked like. I felt cheated at that.

How would I ever know if the murderer of my parents would ever get justice? I knew deep down in my heart that most of these vile men would just slip back into society and would get away scot-free with what they had done. That was hard to take. Some of the prisoners swore that now they were free, they would spend the rest of their lives hunting down the murderers of their wives and children. The sad part about it all was that we were free, but we would always have to live with constant reminders of what we had been through. We only had to lift up our sleeves to see the number on our arms to remind us of what we were, and where we had been. The physical scars would always heal, but the emotional and mental scars would be there for the rest of our days.

More tragedy was to come tumbling down on us after our liberation. With the relief and shock of our sudden release a lot of the inmates sadly died. This was partly due to the fact that after being starved for so long their bodies could not take in so much food at one time. Heart attacks and death by shock accrued for days after the Russians arrived. This seemed even more tragic than the events that had taken place over the few years. To survive all that time, only to die on the day of freedom was something I could not quite understand. Was God having his last laugh at us? Or was it just another tragedy in the lives of us poor Jews? People were starting talk about where they would go now that they were free. Most people, including myself, did not have anywhere to go. We were sent to a misplaced persons' camp. We stayed there hoping that someone would come and find us, a family member, or a friend. In a lot of cases nobody came. I knew that nobody would come for me, I had prepared myself for that a long time back, but I had nowhere else to go, and I needed time to gather my thoughts on where my next journey would take me.

I had been at the misplaced persons' camp for three months now. I had gained some of my weight back, and my hair was slowly growing. I still had a slouch from the time I had spent in the bunker, but I was feeling physically better all the time. I was still quite weak, and my nightmares had started again, but I was on the mend. I had made a few friends whilst in the camp, but I did not want to get to close to anybody, after being in the ghetto and losing everybody around me had made me a loner. I knew that this was how I would always be. I started thinking seriously about where I was going to go. I could not stay here forever, and I needed my own space. After years of living so closely together with strangers made me claustrophobic and I needed to have lots of space around me. The problem was I had no money whatsoever, and I needed money to survive. I started thinking about our old house. I wondered whether it was occupied. I knew that the Germans were no longer there, I didn't even know if it was still standing.

Some of the inmates had gone straight back to their homes before the war, some did not have a home to go back to. I was one of them. But for those who did they sold up and moved away, as far away as possible from Poland and all the memories it held. I wondered if I could do the same. I mean I was twenty-one now and the soul survivor of the family. I was surer than ever now that my mother was dead. *She would have come to find me by now*, I thought. I thought about it for some time and investigated the possibility of selling my parents' house if it was still there. I was told this would be OK providing they had made a will and testament. This was not a problem, as I knew that they had. When the war had started that was the first thing my parents did. I decided that as soon as I was fit enough I would make the journey back to my parents' house. This was a journey I would not be looking forward to, but it had to be done if I was to survive on my own.

After my fourth month in the camp I decided that I was now fit enough to make the journey. I was dreading it, walking back down the street that we had been taken from, going past Kamila's house, and walking into my parents' home, knowing they were no longer alive. I knew it was going to be one of the hardest things I would ever have to do.

I got up on the day of my journey. I felt sick to my stomach at having to make such a trip, I got dressed and out I went. I left very early in the morning as I didn't want to be among lots of strange people going to work. I also wanted to be back at the camp before it got dark. I was so nervous and frightened, as this was the first time I had been out in the real world on my own for five years. The last time I walked out on the street I was wearing a yellow star, waiting to be stopped or shot. The fear was still the same. Every time I heard a loud noise or a German voice I trembled in fear, and shook from head to foot. It was hard to break the habit of six years of hiding away your face for being Jewish. I came to the train station and waited. With a thumping heart I waited for the train.

Suddenly, all the images of that train journey to Auschwitz replayed itself in my mind. I could hear the children screaming and I could smell the vile odour of death and the smell of the bucket that served as our latrine. Over and over the images flashed, like a picture book turning its pages over. So many times I decided to change my mind and not get on the train, but I was strong and I knew I would get through it.

Eventually the train came along and I stepped on. I sat down and closed my eyes. With deep breaths I sat on the edge of my seat and awaited my destination. When I arrived in Warsaw I could not believe the destruction that had taken place. There was not one building standing, it looked like the end of the world. I walked up the road from the train station. Along one side of the road was the ghetto wall, which was now half fallen down. I could see some of the buildings inside or what was left of them. I shuddered as I walked past. I felt the lump rise up in my throat and the tears sting my eyes. My heart was beating fast as I remembered all the horrors I had witnessed there.

Flashes of images came back to me once again of that dreadful day when I lost my mother and the night I was brutally raped. I remembered the death of my beautiful brother, and all of the wicked acts of brutality I had endured. I felt so angry I wanted to stand in the middle of the street and scream, but I didn't; I kept on walking. Before I knew it I was at the top of my street. I had to stop and gather myself. It didn't feel real that I was actually here, after all this time, five years. I had palpations and I could not stop myself from trembling. *I should go back*, I told myself. *I can't do it. Yes, you can*, said the little voice inside my head.

My feet were stuck to the floor as I argued with myself whether to go or not to go. I was so confused. I don't know how long I stood there, but eventually I decided that I had come this far, and a small part of me wanted to see my house, to go back to the past, when things were good. *Maybe just once*, I told myself.

I started walking along the street. Not much had changed, the houses seemed to be intact, so that was something. At least I knew that our house would still be there. I remembered the times I had walked this street with Isaac and Kamila, again the tears started to flow. Then I remembered being dragged down this same street by the Nazis, and Mama and Marek being so scared. I pushed the images out of my mind and concentrated on walking. I walked along with my head down, another habit that would be hard to get out of. I was walking fast now, not wanting to attract attention to myself. It still felt strange to be out walking, without the worry of the SS attacking me or not having to look over my shoulder all the time. At first I still did this, but after a while of telling myself that I didn't have to do that anymore I stopped doing it.

I was walking along, with a thousand thoughts inside my head and the memories of the past coming back to me like ghosts in the night, when all of sudden I heard someone call my name. I knew the voice straightaway; it was nervous and unsure, but I knew I knew it. I could not forget it. I turned slowly to face the voice that was so near, and there she was in all her glory. A fur coat and dripping in gold. She looked the same, but even more beautiful than I remember, and she was wearing a wedding ring. I could not believe it. She stood there smiling at me. I stood there staring, my eyes hard as nails fixed on her face. "Kamila," I said in a hard, emotionless tone.

"Ayala, I thought that was you. How are you? It has been a long time."

I could not speak. *How dare you talk to me as if I have been on holiday for the last six years,* I said to myself.

"Are you OK?" she asked.

I felt the anger burning up inside of me. "Am I all right?" I spluttered. I was shocked beyond words. "Am I all right?" She looked at me regretting having asked such a question. "Do I look all right to you?" I answered calmly, but with sarcasm. She was taken back by the remark. "Do I look like I have been to the seaside?"

"Err, well, I know you have been through a rough time, but that is over now, and I was just wondering how you are. Maybe when you have settled in again we could go out some time, like we used to; catch up on a few things. What do you say?"

I was utterly shocked. I could not believe the nerve and idiocy of the girl; surely she must know what we have all been through. Did she not remember the last time we spoke, when she shut the door in my face for being Jewish? Surely to God she cannot be serious. I wanted to scream in her face. I wanted to tell her that Marek was dead, and that I no longer had parents all because of people like her voting for Hitler, knowing full well of his intentions towards the Jews. Did she not read the papers? And who was she to assume that I was just going to come back to my old house after everything and start from where we had left off. And she wanted to go out some time like we used to. How dare she.

I so much wanted to tell her how much I hated her, but I didn't. I just stared hard in disbelief at her denial of the six million victims of her beloved

Hitler and said, "Kamila, you are Polish and I am a Jew. We cannot be friends; not now, not ever. Goodbye." I did not look back. I crossed the road and walked away.

Chapter 29

SEEING KAMILA AGAIN WAS A SHOCK surprise and one I had not expected. It was ironic to see her looking so good in her fur coat and jewels. While Jews were dying in squalor and filth, she and others like her were getting rich off our misery and lost possessions. *I should have ripped that fur from her back. I should have taken the jewellery; it was probably mine somewhere down the line anyway*, I thought as I walked further down the street. It felt good that at last it was the Jew who had the last word. I hoped after today I would never see her again. She reminded me of everything I wanted to forget.

On my way to our house I did a detour just to satisfy my curiously. I had to see if Isaac was really dead. I walked up to his front gate and stopped. It looked like there was someone in. For a moment I thought that maybe he was there. *Should I knock?* I asked myself. I stayed there for a moment or two contemplating on knocking on the door. *What if they are Germans?* I decided not to knock just in case. I mean, just because the war was over, the hatred for the Jews was still as strong as it ever was, and I did not want to shout off at the doorstep of some Jew hater and attract attention to myself.

Just as I was about to walk away the door opened. "Can I help you?"

asked the friendly voice.

At least they are friendly and not German, I thought relieved. The man was about fifty years old, with a dark completion, he had a very kind looking face, and he resembled Isaac. *Must be a relation*, I thought.

"I am sorry, but I was just looking for somebody that's all, but I don't think he is here anymore."

"Who were you looking for, my child?" answered the man, stepping off the doorstep and coming closer.

I moved back a little, as I did not like being so close to men I did not know.

"I was looking for Isaac; he used to live here, but I don't think he is here anymore."

The man's smile faded. "I am sorry, my child, but no Isaac is not here anymore."

"Did you know him then?" I asked now curious as to who he was.

"Yes, I did. I am his uncle. And you are?"

"My name is Ayala. We used to be sweethearts before the war. I came here one day and he had gone, that was five years ago."

The man looked at me with pity. His kind eyes now sad and distant. "I am sorry, my child, then I shall be the bearer of such bad news."

"It is OK," I interrupted. "I know he is dead. I have always known, but I just needed to be sure before I move on with my life."

"I am very sorry," replied the kind man. "May God bless you from now on."

"Thank you," I replied. "Just one more thing if you don't mind."

"Of course not."

"When and where did Isaac die?" I asked.

The man looked at me and sighed. "When the war broke out, Isaac and his father were one of the first to be rounded up and taken to a labour camp. After about five months Isaac fell quite sick and died of typhus, or so the documents tell us. His father was sent to Treblinka in the summer of 1942 and died in the gas chambers. His mother and sister have not yet been found."

I cried as I stood there and thought of my wonderful Isaac so sick, it hurt to think of him in such a place and being so ill.

"Thank you," I said emotionally. "At least now I know what became of him."

"You are most welcome, my child."

I turned to go.

"Young lady," he called again.

"Yes," I answered.

"Wherever you go in the world, whomever you meet. Tell them. Tell them what happened to us. Tell them what they did. Do not let the world forget."

I looked at him silent for a while and smiled. "I won't," I said. "I won't."

I walked off, and carried on with my journey. I felt strange inside. I felt heartbroken at the knowledge of Isaac's death, yet relieved as well. It was as if a small piece of the puzzle was now put back into place. I could now start my grieving process and move on. I strolled along in deep thought, thinking about Isaac and wondering what his last thoughts were. I hoped he didn't suffer too much, but knowing the Nazis' reputation, that was very unlikely.

Before I knew it I was only a few feet from my house. As it came into view I stopped dead and took a deep breath. It looked exactly the same. The same deep brown front door; the tree-lined front garden with its cobbled drive. Even the curtains were the same, save for the blackout blinds underneath them. My heart was racing. I took a deep breath as I walked up to the door. It's strange but I felt nervous of going into the same house I once lived and grew up in. I knew once I entered the house, the tears would flow and I would be swamped in memories of the past, and of the people I would never see again. I was confused. My head was telling me to walk away, but my heart was telling me to go in. *You can do it*, I kept telling myself. *You can do it.*

At the last minute I lost my nerve and turned to go. *Go back*, said the voice inside my head. *Go back.* I stood there at the top of the drive confused. *Am I ready to face the past?* I asked myself. After all I had been through, this should have been a walk in the park. *Oh, what should I do?* I agonised with myself. Finally after a time standing there arguing with my emotions, I decided to do it. I walked up the path, put my hand through the letterbox and opened the door, just as I had done when I was a child. There I was in the hallway, looking straight through to the kitchen. Straightaway the lump came in my throat as I stood in the cold passage. The kitchen looked exactly the same, apart from the mess that had been left. It looked like nobody had cleaned the place in years. There were cups and plates all over the place, and filthy grim all over the walls.

Slowly I walked up the hallway and through to kitchen that had once been my mother's pride and joy. It was a complete mess. I cried at the state of the place. It was heartbreaking. I could see my parents sitting at the table, and Marek messing about with his food. Sobs thumped in my throat. It was all too much.

I came out of the kitchen and walked into the sitting room. Again the mess was beyond repair. There were beer bottles and ashtrays everywhere. My parents' beautiful floral settee now had a hundred and one cigarette burns in it. The curtains were stained yellow from the smoke. *Only a Nazi would leave a place in such a state. Animals would have more respect*, I cried to myself.

I decided to go upstairs, part of me was now curious to see what sort of disgusting mess they had made up there. Once up I stood outside my old room. The door was left ajar, and I could see from an angle that the mess was no better in there than it had been downstairs. I went in and closed the door behind. I leaned back on the door and looked around at my once private and feminine room. It was now plastered with posters of Hitler all over the walls. My pink curtains had been ripped down and had been replaced by thick blackout blinds. This had obviously been a boy's room as there were boy's toys and clothes scattered around the all over the floor. Whoever had lived here had left in a hurry, as nobody would leave all their possessions behind if not.

"I hope they're shaking in their murdering Nazi boots," I sobbed out loud. This was not the room I had once shared all my secrets with Kamila in. Or the same room I used to listen to my music and dream about Isaac. I went over to the wardrobe and opened the door. I gasped in shock as I looked down and there on the floor were all my clothes. Even the green dress that Kamila had given me for the school dance was on the floor of the wardrobe all ripped and torn as it was on that last night in my house. I remembered asking my mother for scissors to tear it with. For five years my clothes had lain on the floor like that. I bent down and went through the pile. There were jumpers and skirts, which my parents had bought me, and coats that would no longer fit. I had not expected to open the door and come face to face with the past so soon. The anger welled up inside me as I remembered the happy days I had spent in this house.

I walked out and closed the door behind me. I went to Marek's room. This I had been dreading ever since I had made up my mind to come back. I knew whatever I saw inside would instantly make me cry, but I had to do it. I owed it to him, and I had come this far. Again I took in a deep breath and went in. Again there were pictures of Hitler all over the walls, and also posters in support of the Nazi Youth Movement. *How insulting to the memory of my brother*, I thought. *How ironic, to have a picture of the man who caused his death plastered all over his walls.* I felt so angry; I wanted to scream out loud. How I hated them. I would go to my grave hating them for everything they had done. I looked around the room some more. Again this must have been a boy's room for all the clothes and toys everywhere. This seemed to make it even more hard to take, knowing that a young boy had been sleeping in my little brother's bed in the warm, enjoying his toys and home comforts, when all the time my little Marek was scared and dying. I felt the anger once more, I felt it rise from the pit of my stomach all the way up to my throat, and suddenly I let out an almighty scream. I screamed so hard my throat was contracting. I coughed and spluttered; the tears were coming fast and furious, as I grieved for the brother I had lost.

Suddenly I lost all control as my attention turned to the vile pictures on the wall. I ran over and tore down every last one, ripping them to shreds in my anger, tearing away the wallpaper as I did. Not happy at just ripping them from the wall I then began to jump up and down hard on Hitler's face as it sat on the floor looking up at me. I could see his beady evil little eye looking right through me from the torn paper. I was still screaming and crying and saying words that I never thought my own lips would say.

Suddenly I stopped dead in my tracks. I spotted something that took my attention away from the pictures on the floor. There on the floor all broken and discarded was Marek's train set. I bent down and picked up a piece, a small carriage that had been broken away from the rest of the train. Crying fresh tears I held it in my hand, I pictured my beautiful brother sitting on the floor playing with his most favourite toy. He loved his train set. I remembered when my parents had bought it for him, and how happy and pleased he was with it. I remembered how everyone who came to visit had to come up and see his favourite toy. Now here it was all broken and torn. It was like his memory had been violated, like his life and all that mattered to him was nothing.

I sat on the floor and sobbed out my heart for the little innocent boy who did not deserve to die. I cried for all the children that died so needlessly, just to satisfy one man's evil ideals. Would I ever be free from the pain? Would I always be reminded of the evilness? Would the destruction of those monsters follow me wherever I went? I asked myself a thousand questions. The answer to all of them was most probably yes. The question was: did I want to live it?

I was still sitting in Marek's room sometime later. It had felt good to let out some anger and frustration that had been pent up in me for years. I knew I still had a lot more to come out yet. I most probably would never let it all out, there was just too much in there, but I did feel a little better for some release. *I can start to grieve now.* I told myself. *Now I can finally grieve for the people I have lost, without the interruption of the Nazis and their guns.* I looked around the room some more. I could still see Marek in there, in his own little room.

It was now late in the afternoon. I did not want to be travelling back in the dark, and I had been here for most of the day. Just as I was about to take my leave, I heard a noise downstairs. I stood stiff on the spot not breathing trying to make out where the noise was coming from. I heard it again. I was terrified, convinced that the Germans had come back again. I heard it again. This time it was getting closer. I crept behind the door of Marek's room, my breathing fast, and my heart pounding. I heard footsteps coming up the stairs, creeping almost. *Oh God, please go way*, I prayed in my head.

Closer and closer it came. Now I was crying, willing whoever it was to go away. I was utterly convinced that some Nazi had returned. I heard the footsteps creep into my parents' bedroom, and then they came out again and went into my bedroom. *Oh God, here it comes*, I cried in my head, as the door to Marek's room opened wider. I leaned back against the wall as if to hide myself further. I closed my eyes. I heard the figure come in. I held my breath, and slowly opened my eyes. When I finally did I could not believe what my eyes were seeing. I thought I was seeing things. *All these years of torture and abuse has finally caught up with me*, I thought. I closed my eyes again, hoping that the figure would go away. Slowly again I opened them after what seemed like minutes, but was in fact seconds. I was not seeing things; the figure was still there right in front of me like a dream come true, my beautiful mother.

Chapter 30

I STOOD STIFF TO THE FLOOR; my eyes transfixed to the ghostly image in front of me. *It cannot be true,* I said to myself. *I am dreaming; this just cannot be true.* The figure of my mother was standing with her back to me; as yet she had not seen me standing there. I wanted to reach out and touch my mother's image, but was so afraid that if I touched it, it would disappear forever. The tears were falling hard down my face as I desperately tried to hold in the sobs that were threatening the silence. *Can this really be my mother?* I asked. *Please God, let it be so,* I prayed. Suddenly the figure started to turn round; she was crying and looking around at my little brother's room. Just as she was about to find me there I found my voice.

"Mama," I whispered.

She stopped dead in her tracks. I could hear her breathing; it was hard and shallow. Slowly she turned to face me. Her eyes staring wide in disbelief. We stood there staring at each other for what seemed an age. Finally she spoke.

"Ayala," she said breathlessly, shocked at what her eyes were seeing.

"MAMA!" I screamed. "MAMA, OH, MAMA!" I was crying out her name as I ran towards her and fell into her arms. She too was crying as she threw her arms around me and held me tight. We were sobbing hard, scared to let each other go for fear of losing each other again.

She was sobbing, her face buried in my neck saying my name over and over. "Ayala, Ayala. God has answered my prayers."

"Oh, Mama, I thought you were dead. This cannot be true," I sobbed.

"It is true, my darling. It is true. I am here."

I could not take it in. "Any minute now I will wake up and it will all be a dream," I said through my sobs.

"It is no dream, Ayala. I am here, and I am not going away ever again."

Again we cried and held onto each other, our faces buried in each other shoulders. We must have been there for an hour or more just looking at each other, not believing what we were seeing. Eventually after we managed to stop the intense crying, we managed to tell each other where we had been and what had become of us. It was hard to talk, as we were both too excited and emotional to get our words out, the euphoric feelings that we felt were just too strong to describe, but eventually we did talk. I told Mama all that had happened to me, about Auschwitz and Barak and his poor family, and of the night I was raped.

"Beasts," Mama cried. "The beasts. Oh my, Ayala. I am so sorry I let you down. I am so sorry for not being there."

"Mama, do not blame yourself, it was not your fault. The Nazis are the ones to blame," I cried. "Nobody could have defended themselves against those animals."

"But I am your mother. I should have been there for you."

"Mama, please don't blame yourself, please. You are here now and that is all that matters."

"Yes, I am here, Ayala, and no hell or high water will ever part us again."

"I love you, Mama."

"I love you too, my Ayala. I love you too."

We sat there most of the night talking. I still could not believe that Mama was alive. I keep thinking that all this was a dream, but of course it wasn't, Mama was here with me, and that is where she was going to stay. Mama told me about how on that fateful day in the ghetto, she had got lost in the frantic crowd, and how they bundled her on one of the first trains. Tears welled up in her eyes as she told me of her horrific journey. How many had died and how she ended up in Auschwitz.

I was shocked to hear that she was there. I told her how I had searched for her everywhere, but she informed me that not long after she arrived at Auschwitz they transported her to another concentration camp called Majdanek. Her story was much the same as mine, with the same degree of atrocities. Mama cried pitifully as she told me of all the horrors she had seen, all the deaths and the roll calls every morning. After liberation she was sent to a misplaced persons' camp, and that is where she has stayed for the last ten months, and then decided to come back here and sell the house.

I told Mama of my intentions to sell the house and that I truly believed she was dead. Mama's opinion of me was quite different. "Ayala, I knew all along you were alive. Didn't I tell you, you were a survivor?"

"Mama, there were times when I wanted to give up and die."

"Me too, Ayala. But after I lost you, I knew I had to survive, because I knew you would need me."

I told Mama of my intentions to kill myself after she had gone missing.

"It was Barak who stopped me, Mama," I told her. "He saved my life."

"Poor Barak, now I will never be able to repay him for what he did. May God bless his soul. He was such a kind man."

I sat there watching Mama talk. She was so thin and her hair no longer long and luscious; having been shaved at Majdanek it was growing back just as dark, but with grey streaks all the way through it. She had lines etched in her face, making her look much older than she really was and her hands were old, she looked like a little old lady, but I didn't care, she was my mother and I didn't care how she looked as long as she was here with me. I told her about Isaac and how I finally knew what became of him.

"Ayala, I am so sorry," she said sympathetically. "At least now you can move on."

"I know, Mama. I always knew he was dead; I just needed confirmation of that. Now I have it and I can put some of the pieces back together."

"You are a brave girl, Ayala. I have always said that."

"Mama, did you find anything out about Papa?" I had wanted to ask that question ever since she had got here, but was afraid to ask for fear of the answer.

Mama looked at me, and then dropped her eyes to the floor.

"It's all right, Mama, I know Papa is dead. But like Isaac, I just need confirmation, so I can start my grieving and move on."

"You are a sensible girl."

"Well, Mama?" I asked again gently.

"Yes, Ayala, your father is dead. I got confirmation of this some months back. He was transported from Belzec in 1942 and sent straight to the gas chambers at Treblinka. I traced his whereabouts the moment I got out of Majdanek. It was the first thing I did."

"Oh, Mama," I cried. "It is so unfair. Poor Papa; he never hurt anyone. I never even got to say goodbye." I sobbed my heart out for my poor father.

I knew all along he was dead, but just hearing it and knowing for sure was still a shock. I cried for hours for my father, for my brother, for the whole Jewish population. It felt good to finally be able to grieve for our lost loved ones. We talked all the way through the night. Mama cried desperately for Marek. She missed him terribly, but like me felt good to be able to grieve at last.

It was now the early hours of the morning. We had been sitting in Marek's bedroom all through the night. In a couple of hours, it would be dawn and the sun would start to rise. During the night, we had decided to tidy up Marek's room. We took away all the ripped posters of Hitler and his youth, took down the blinds and threw out all the clothes. Mama needed to do this; like me she could not leave the house with Marek's room left the way it was, an insult to his memory.

Mama told me her intentions on selling the house. "I cannot stay here now, Ayala."

"I understand, Mama. There are too many memories here. I certainly don't want to stay here now. Apart from the house, what does this town have to offer us anyway?"

"Absolutely nothing. I could never forgive people for what they have done to us," Mama answered. "And if I did stay in this house, I would be haunted by visions of Marek and Papa in every room I went. So I think it is best to move on," Mama said. Her eyes were distant, as if she was in another world.

It was now dawn and we had sat up all night talking and reminiscing. We had no sleep at all, and we weren't even tired. We were running on adrenaline. We sat and watched the sun come up. It was a new day, a new beginning.

I looked over at Mama, and still could not believe God had answered my prayers. "So, Mama, where do we go from here?" I asked.

"Well, I have arranged to go to Auntie Agnes, that is your father's cousin. She was in hiding for last two years, so thankfully she was one of the few from the family that has survived. So I shall stay with her until the sale of the house goes through. I never expected to have a companion though, but I'm quite sure she won't mind," Mama laughed.

"And where to from there?" I asked again.

Mama sighed and looked up at the sky through the window where we had sat and watched the sun come up. "I do not know, Ayala. I do not know. It is just you and I now. Let us see where the road takes us."

I went over and gave Mama a hug. It felt so good to be able to do that again.

"Mama, I love you."

"And I love you, Ayala."

"Come on let's go," I said.

Mama looked one more time around her son's room. With tears in her eyes she whispered, "I love you, Marek, my baby boy. I will never forget you."

With that she closed the door. I put my arm around her and held her tight. "Come on," I said. Just as we were leaving I turned round and ran back up the stairs. "Hold on, Mama. Just one more thing."

I ran back into Marek's room. Down on the floor were his little trains to his train set. I picked two of them up and gently put them in my pocket. "Goodbye, darling," I whispered up into the air.

I came back downstairs and gave Mama one of his trains. "Now we will always have a part of him," I said. With that we walked out and shut the door. With one glance back at the place that had once been our happy home, we walked off hand in hand to face our future together!

The End